FOREVER WILD

A PARANORMAL SHIFTER ROMANCE FOREVER LOVED BOOK ONE

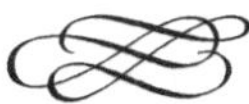

L. J. HAWKE

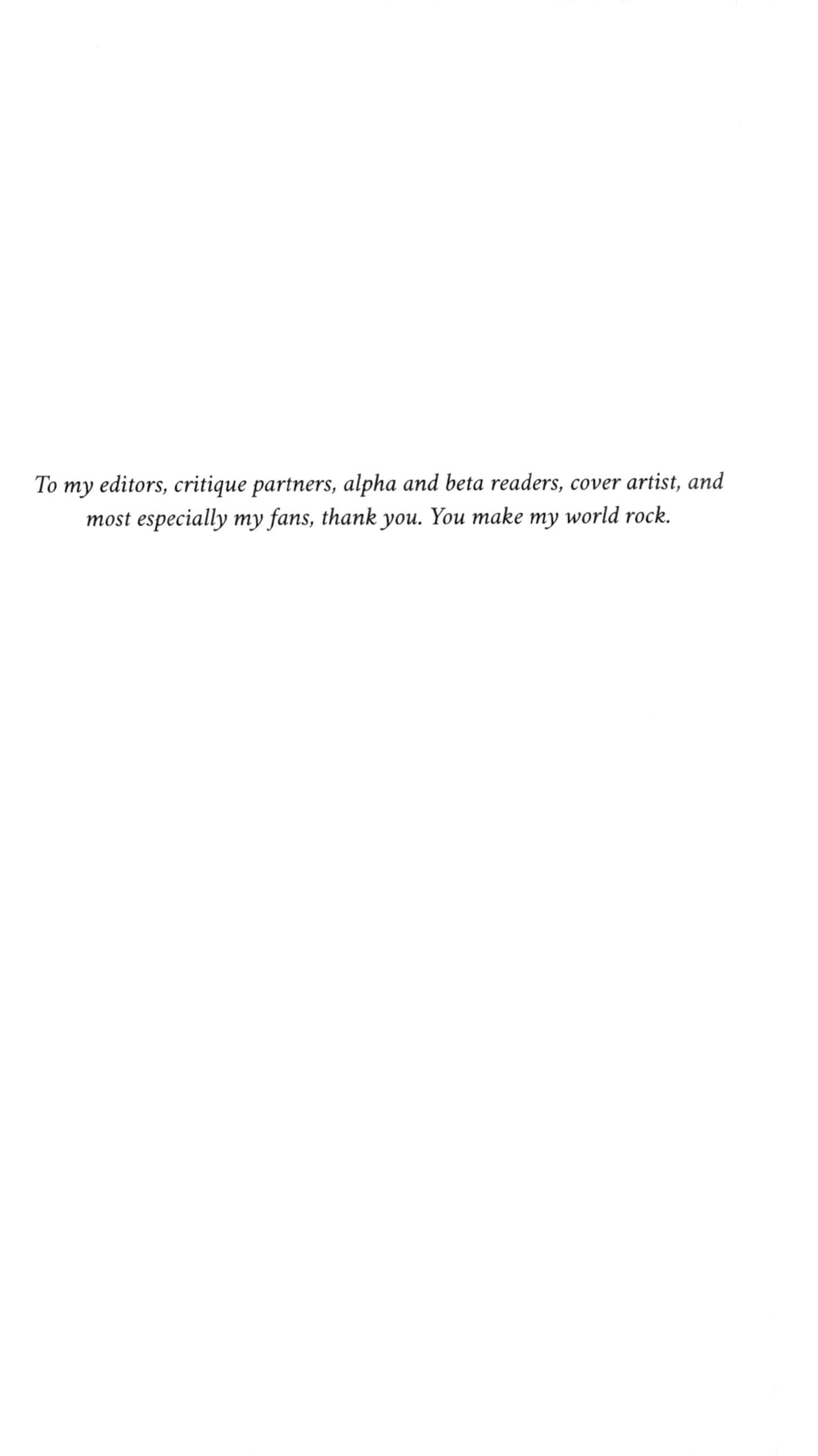

To my editors, critique partners, alpha and beta readers, cover artist, and most especially my fans, thank you. You make my world rock.

CLIMB

Six months into her sobriety journey, when everyone else joined a crew and jumped out of airplanes, her sponsor, Tori, bugged Kandace about her lack of focus. Tori was absolutely relentless about it, expounding while waving around an e-cigarette and stopping to take a drag from time to time, her makeup crinkling from the wrinkles of a hard life. "I get that pearls are not your thing," Tori said, referring to the other on-campus contingent of sobriety, rich kids who got sober to please somebody—parents, the school administration, objects of dating that Tori called "hostages." They got sober long enough to open up the money gates again, make the parents happy, get the significant other back, only to start the cycle all over again. Some got sober, but they were the scared ones, the ones that hid their fear under brittle shells of perfection. Even in the Program, those girls wouldn't give Kandace and her torso tattoo—she tended to wear crop tops in the summer—a glass of water if she were on fire.

So, the focus. Kandace got a bright blue flame on one half of her stomach when she hit thirty days sober, the Program burning away Old Kandace. The angry child, living in a house with no heat save a woodstove, an actual outhouse, and things growing literally everywhere. Her father, Frank, died when a tree fell on him while he was clear cutting and drinking beers with Jeb and Dave, his best friends. Kandace was two.

When she got older, Kandace grew her own food with her granny and her ma. They had headed back a hundred years in time when Grandpa's cancer ate away his lungs, then his mind, leaving them dead broke. Then, Ma lost her series of nothing jobs when she slipped on mud and fell into a hole in a storm, hit her head, and broke her leg in three places. She got pins everywhere and a metal plate in her head, walked with a cane, and got headaches that made her go blind and puke for days at a time. Her recovery, if it could be called that, lasted for two years. Kandace, allergic to something in green plants, wore gloves to pick the crops, except the delicate strawberries. They sold strawberry jam that Ma and then Kandace made by slaving over canning jars in the sticky heat. They sold bushel baskets of zucchini and five kinds of tomatoes. They made pickles, too, both dill and sweet. They made their own vinegar and oils infused with herbs. The stand made a pitiful amount of money, but it was just enough to pay their bills. Certainly not enough for an education for Kandace.

It was Mrs. Yates at the library, the tiny one in Delco, who showed Kandace the world of books, getting her books about her pioneer ancestors. The librarian looked like a dark blonde refugee from the 1950s, her hair curled and pulled back, bright red lipstick, big blue eyes that seemed to know everything. Mrs. Yates liked to wear soft sweaters and swirling skirts, but she had a steel will hidden underneath all the softness. At Mrs. Yates' suggestion, Kandace read all the Laura Ingalls Wilder books. Like Laura, Kandace also wanted to make her life better. The pioneers did. Couldn't she?

Kandace found out that a bicycle could charge a battery that ran a generator, so they didn't have to use kerosene. Ma convinced Granny to let her construct it and set it up, a bike with bent rims and brakes that didn't work thrown away by the side of the road, a car battery, a small generator. Kandace was only twelve when she approached the shop teacher at the high school and MacGyvered it into working, after trying to shock herself to death. Then, they had lights at night.

Kandace did her homework while pedaling a bike that ran the kitchen light that let her see her books. Mrs. Yates got her an ancient computer and a battered printer, and Kandace put the monitor on a rickety table and the keyboard on the bike handles. She got her homework done faster, even if she wasn't hooked up to the Internet yet. She did the Internet thing at the library until Mrs. Yates gave her an encyclopedia and a dictionary on a disc, then a USB. The computer let her use her research to complete her homework. Her grades slid upward.

Getting all the jobs took forever. She began cleaning houses, babysitting all over town once Mrs. Yates hooked her up with the donation bin at the church. Kandace could dress like the other kids in clothes without patches and stitches holding them together. By the time she was fifteen, she had expanded her cleaning and babysitting business by three holler girls that she had trained in how to talk to richer folk and hooked them up with the donation bin. They took on any dirty, nasty job, from cleaning out garages to the hoarder, Mrs. Tyler, who had things she didn't need and couldn't even see stacked to the ceiling in her house. The family that hired them let them keep whatever they didn't need or couldn't sell, like the piles of newspapers. The Historical Society got a lot of it, and the library got books and magazines, many of them very old. Kandace got some clothes that weren't moth-eaten, a few pieces of costume jewelry, and some odds and ends she could sell for a little money. Kandace made Ms. Tyler, the hoarder's daughter, give her a receipt so Granny wouldn't beat her for stealing.

Mrs. Yates made Kandace take courses online, advanced placement courses that her tiny high school didn't offer. Then, the librarian drove all the way down to the holler to confront Ma and Granny. "This girl won't get out of here, stuck like a fly in amber. Do you really want that life for her?" Ma's vapid blue and Grandma's sharp brown eyes looked at her flatly, as if Mrs. Yates were a bug. "I will personally pay for Internet service for two years," said Mrs. Yates. "This girl is one of the few that can get out of here." She pointed up at the electric lights. "I know damn well this girl has gotten electricity for this house for the last three years. She's paid the bills for two. I know you want her to stay, but the day she turns eighteen, she's gone. The two of you can either rot, or step aside as she gets the best education she can to help you down the road."

"Girl's nothin' but trouble," said Granny. "Don't want her here, nohow." Ma just shrugged, her chapped hands folded on her lap. She seemed so tired that indifference had enveloped her.

So, Kandace learned focus. Kandace got out of her holler, then she decided to study computer modeling and engineering at a tiny university hiding in the mountains. Software, too. She found holler friends, her new roommates, and they stuck together like glue. Tania's hair was a lighter red than Kandace's, and despite her childhood in a richer home, had lived on a holler farm, like Kandace. Corinne had long black hair, and was fierce. They would go toe-to-toe with anyone. Tania and Corinne joined Free Code Camp to learn how to code and build websites, so she had to do it too.

Then, Kandace tried to throw it all away by developing her father's illness, drinking until she puked or passed out. Tania and Corinne staged two full interventions, tears and anger warring on their faces, but she didn't go into the Program until after she'd disassembled and reassembled the physics professor's Jeep inside his own lab. Tania came after her with that tongue of hers. "Let's list the consequences, shall we? The professor may be an ass, but he isn't flat stupid. You could get a huge fine you can't pay. You got the money? Not me. You can lose all your scholarships. You got the money to pay for that? Then you can get expelled, even go to jail."

"I want to slap you silly," Corinne said. "He may have deserved it, what with being a self-righteous, misogynistic butthole, but I don't want to lose you. Oh, and one more thing. I'm disappointed in you."

Past her pounding head and bloody eyes, Kandace finally got the picture. Holler girls went into jail and slid into a spiral they couldn't escape, and Kandace didn't want that for herself. She was lucky; she didn't get caught. Kofi, who had helped her, didn't get caught either. It would have been worse for him, losing his track and field and two academic merit scholarships. Guilt burned her insides. She reached out and wrested away the fat blue book Tania held over her head like she was going to brain Kandace with it. Then, Kandace began to read.

Kandace got sober, and the focus of the old days where she sold blown glass she'd scavenged from a hoarder's house to keep the lights on moved aside. She wasn't the same girl anymore. The old rage faded away in the urge to just get through the next minute. That was her focus. Plus, school. Plus, Corinne needed reassurance and Tania needed to quit looking backwards.

Kandace began hiking, because the sitting meditation thing didn't work. She tended to fall asleep, or jitter her way through it, toes and fingers or her leg always moving. So Tori, the sponsor, suggested walking. "Bring a backpack with water, snack food, a trash bag so you don't litter, sunblock, insect repellent, earphones, and your cell phone with you. Download speaker shares and walk. Somewhere, anywhere. Don't count on your phone's GPS. So bring a map. You know with your background that some hollers don't have any bars on cell phones. Just go. Buy some damn hiking boots. Hell, you can probably find some used ones at the used clothing store. Just. Go."

Kandace remembered her promise to say "yes" to all of Tori's madness. So, she found some brand-new hiking shoes at a discount store. Someone from the Society for Creative Anachronism sold her a walking stick with a dragon carved on the side. She began to hike the area surrounding the university. She woke up at an impossibly early hour and said her prayers and listened to speaker shares under the moonlight, passing sleeping cows. She came back, attended class, built models of bridges, avoided the ROTC guy who wanted her to join the Army Corps of Engineers. She worked in the lab, whichever ones she had that semester, for work-study credit.

She ate ramen for lunch and dinner, did her reading every waking minute she wasn't in class or at work. She began walking to her nasty jobs, the cleaning jobs nobody wanted. She specialized in hoarders, garage cleaning, cleaning out old folk's homes when they died or moved into nursing homes. She got really good at finding out what had worth and what didn't, and got a percentage off the top. It kept her in ramen and e-textbooks.

In the spare minutes she didn't have school or a cleaning job, Kandace hiked and listened to speaker shares, workshops, and fifteen-minute walking meditations that made her focus on the world around her. The astonishing shades of green during spring and summer, the crimson foliage and crisp air of autumn. The winters, though, were a problem. She learned snowshoeing and cross-country skiing, but that bored her after a while. Tori gave her a new directive; climb. So, she found an off-campus indoor climbing range, and with her addictive obsessiveness, learned to climb, first on ropes, then freehand. She learned about chalked hands and soft shoes, and how to find her next handhold. Tori's constant admonition to stay in the present moment rang through her mind on the walls. It was all about the next reach, the next breath. Kandace did every course until she could almost literally do them in the dark, in exchange for getting her certification and working at the range. She also got meals there at the salad-and-juice bar. It paid better than the cleaning, but she did those too. Every dollar helped.

Kandace developed ropy arms, strong legs, a thin frame wound with muscle. She ate better, had more control over her schedule, and attended classes during school breaks. Tania and Corinne decided to go for graduate school, and, to her shock, Kandace got in easily and won some scholarships. She built robots and entered them into golf-ball-sucking and climbing contests. She started working on projects online in teams and only did the cleaning for special projects that paid well. She still climbed, of course.

Kandace did enough projects to be successful, enough to start paying off her loans. But, she was in Corinne's boat. None of them could stop their madcap trajectory to graduate with a master's degree in five years long enough to take more than brief internships in order to kiss corporate butt. None of them were corporate people. A cubicle would kill Kandace, and she knew it. She adjusted her classes, sculpted herself into a person who could work online without ever having to go onsite anywhere. She got certified in cloud computing, and did some projects that were truly amazing, like mapping out a proposed hyperloop tunnel for her graduation project she had begun working on as an intern doing baby code.

Tori was dumbfounded. "Wait a minute. The company you work for is gonna dig a hole in the ground, a tunnel, for capsules to go under the ground faster than trains?"

Kandace nodded. "Absolutely. No stoplights. No wind resistance."

"Damn. So what will you do after you graduate?" Tori sucked on her e-cigarette, let out the cinnamon vapor. Her necklace was blue plastic to match her eyeshadow. She used makeup that made her look like a refugee from the 80s. Kandace couldn't talk her out of it. Her jeans were torn, her sweatshirt had its sleeves torn off. Tori was Kandace's kind of person. She just didn't care what anyone else thought of her.

"I need my hookup, get on the Internet. I need to go through my Steps again, get clear before I climb my life."

Tori nodded. "The climb never stops, Kandace. Baby steps, falling down, even falling off the cliff onto a ledge below and having to climb back up a completely different way." She held out a hand, mimed holding out a lamp. "Higher Power lighting the way, but only one step ahead."

Kandace nodded. "This is the hardest climb, getting my ass out of debt, keeping close to Program, not falling off due to temptation. Climbing out of the pit sucks, hurts like hell, breaks me in places. Like stained glass I can't put back together." She thought about the glass panel she'd cut out of a dead woman's house and sold to feed her family for one more winter, so many years before. She stared out into nothingness. "They're both still alive. My money kept them going this far."

"You don't owe them a thing." It was an old disagreement. Her grandma was quick with a nasty word, a slap, a belt. Her mom was fading away, like old wallpaper or yellowed newspapers losing their print.

Kandace nodded. "They won't move from there. They're dug in. I can't just let them die. They don't really need that much of a percentage of my income to survive."

Tori shrugged. "I already sent you to DA. Can't get you farther than that." DA, Debtors Anonymous, had taught Kandace the tools to get her degree and simultaneously send money home and start to pay off her debts. "Not my program." Tori shot her green-eyed laser stare at Kandace. "What are you doing to do in three weeks when you graduate?"

Kandace shrugged again. "I'm going to go through saying thank you and goodbye to everyone. Which will feel like going naked into a sandstorm. Then, to the cabin. Already rented, and the property management company swears they have the Internet hooked up there. And then, I'm going to climb."

"Sounds like a plan. What did I tell you about that?" Tori pointed her e-cig at Kandace.

Kandace grinned. "That when you make a plan, God is laughing hysterically, all the angels, too, their halos all tilted 'cause you had an expectation 'bout results." She bowed her head. "I swear, just lookin' to survive, sober."

Tori nodded. "Good. Now go study for finals." Kandace groaned and headed for the library.

PARTY

Kandace prepared herself for the night of parties. It was going to suck.

Shucking out of her gown, she stood in an interminable line to return the rented cap and gown at the long table. Freshmen and sophomores were there to congratulate her. "Graduate student, huh?" asked a girl with choppy red hair and bright green eyes. She looked about twelve. "Graduate student?" she repeated. "And with honors! Cool!"

Kandace struggled not to slap the girl down. She was just being enthusiastic. It wasn't her fault that Kandace, at three years sober, wanted to slit her wrists rather than par-tay. "Thanks," she said, without snarling. She signed on the dotted line. She gave a silly wave, hating herself for it, but the girl seemed to need it to close the inane conversation they were having. The redhead cheerfully waved back.

Kandace had only two outfits laid out. One was her tomorrow-wear of jeans, a T-shirt that said "Climbers Hook Up" with a stylized carabiner in silver on black, black motorcycle boots with rolled socks peeking out from one of them just under the bed. The other was a floaty silver-and-blue top to go on over her black shorts. Kandace shucked her black tee with an atom on it, rolled it up, and put it in her backpack. She had on a black camisole underneath.

She put on the silvery thing after a quick trip to the bathroom to rinse off the sweat from sitting in the sun listening to Dean Horovitz drone on and on about their shining futures, while everyone else knew the truth about the real world. She added another layer of antiperspirant, which almost didn't work in the moist heat. Kandace also added sunblock and mosquito repellent that smelled like oranges, which made her golden skin look a bit dewy. She expertly applied more drugstore makeup, glad her girlfriends hadn't let her down there. She took the blue frozen packs out of the minuscule freezer, and put them into the bottom of her insulated backpack. She then took out the single juice she had in there and sipped it.

Kandace unplugged the tiny refrigerator, checked over her one box of bedding and winter clothes, put on her backpack, and hauled her box to her ancient black truck. She slid the box onto the passenger side seat and threw the backpack on top of it, went back up to get the refrigerator, wiped it out, and hauled it down. She put it in the truck in the passenger side footwell.

She double-checked herself in the truck's mirror and hauled off to the convenience store. She had to slide around the football players buying cases of beer to get to her drinks—strawberry and cherry lemonades, virgin mojitos—just lime juice, mint, and syrup, sugar replacing her old buzz. She selected various energy drinks and sodas. She paid for it all and jigsawed them into her cooler backpack. She'd brought drinks to many an event, but this was the first time she was planning for an entire night where everyone around her would be getting shitfaced.

The meeting only had three people; Daphne, the lanky, round-faced drama major sophomore, Blue, a red-faced junior with blue spiky hair and a death wish, and Kandace herself. She didn't have time to get across town to another meeting. "They are going to be, like, drinking everywhere," said Daphne. She shared how she planned to go to the Society for Creative Anachronism dressed as a wench, taking money for costumes. Blue droned on and on about his need to avoid all the dealers on campus. He decided, after his fourth rambling share, to go to a movie marathon instead.

Kandace nodded and kept her shares short. "I'm leaving school, my friends, and my life to head out to...nothing. I've applied everywhere. I've been working and taking classes over the summers. I only did one internship and they didn't hire me. Dead silence on my applications. So, I don't have a physical job to go to." The other two kept talking about the evening ahead, so Kandace talked about that. "I have nonalcoholic drinks for the whole night, and I'm going to be with my two best friends." She finally gave up, let the others ramble. No one was really listening. She did the final reading about how the Program comes true in peoples' lives over time. The line about economic insecurity leaving her made her snort internally. There was nothing but that ahead of her. Her school loans would crush her if she didn't work like a dog. But then, that had been her entire life. Why change now?

They finished with the Serenity Prayer, and Kandace wondered how Daphne got the word "like" in there twice. Kandace locked up and handed the keys to Daphne. Instead of passing it on, it felt like running away.

Kandace hiked over to the first party. Tania met her outside with a hug. She looked like a jewel, her hair up in tiny butterfly pins that shone with bling in her deep red hair, much darker than Kandace's strawberry blonde. She had on a teal, fluttery, baby-doll tunic over boy shorts. She looked like sexual candy, something Tania was completely oblivious about. Corinne rushed over in jean shorts and a red top. Her hair was in a French braid. Corinne ran into them both, drawing them into a hug that was nearly violent in its intensity. "We've got a huge list," Corinne said, in a singsong voice. "Let's get to it."

The point of the party-visiting wasn't fun, although Kandace desperately hoped that fun actually happened. The point was to say goodbye to their friends and all those who had helped them. All three of them had stuck together, three backwoods country girls surrounded by people with money. They had all decided to go to graduate school and do it all in five years. Corinne could code rings around others, but her two job offers were from companies in super-expensive northern California. Corinne was going to work online somewhere. Tania was going to fly away to South Korea to teach. No one wanted online marketing/online education majors in a soft economy, and few school districts were hiring. And Kandace...She shut off her line of personal introspection. This was her last night with her friends, and Kandace was determined to be mentally present the entire time. Even if it felt like she was being roasted alive over a spit.

Kandace passed a bottle of strawberry lemonade to Tania, while Corinne snagged a sangria in a plastic bottle from the table full of alcoholic goodness at Sigma Epsilon. They had to go out on the balcony, and Kandace said goodbye to Ricky, who had helped her pass chemistry without committing homicide or suicide. Ricky waved her off. "No biggie," he said. He gave her a sweaty hug, then leapt over the railing into the deep end of the pool.

Delta Gamma was soul-crushing for Kandace in a way that she couldn't talk about to anyone except her sponsor. Kofi, solid and gentle, was trying to prevent his roommate, a skinny, sweaty Billy who was knocking back drinks from getting in a fight, driving drunk, or jumping off a balcony with no pool underneath. Billy had tried getting sober with each arrest, each spin-dry. At this point, Billy's parents had spent more money getting him sober than they had on his five years of education; Billy hadn't yet gotten a bachelor's degree. Kandace knew why Billy was drinking, other than this being the natural state of an alcoholic. He was "celebrating" not graduating with any of his friends. Tania and Corinne went to give their goodbyes, and Kandace hugged Kofi. "I am so sorry," she said.

"He doesn't know it, but after tonight, it's over. I graduated, he didn't. He has absolutely destroyed our relationship." Kofi's melted-chocolate eyes were glimmering with tears. Kofi had graduated with honors; he would be heading to Hawthorne, California to work on a new space vehicle initiative. Billy had been kicked out of two programs and was working on getting enough credits to graduate in six months if he stayed sober. Tonight, Billy was most definitely not sober.

"I'm sorry," said Kandace. "For all of it." Words were so inadequate. She waved to Billy, who raised a beer to her and drank it with a glint of rage in his eyes. Kandace finished off her lemonade, hugged Kofi goodbye, and got the hell out of there.

Out on the lawn, Drama Club members worked with the Audio/Video and Film Clubs to shoot live YouTube videos of performances. Kandace suspected they would have increasingly poor performances as the night went on when she saw the cooler of beer on the lawn next to their tripods. She climbed under the puppeteer stage to say goodbye to Tran, who helped her get through both Drama and Asian Art. "Y'all keep doing what you're doing," she said, as Tran moved a Thai dancer across the stage using sticks.

"Stay frosty," said Tran. Kandace touched his shoulder in lieu of a hug and climbed back out.

They somehow ended up getting mani-pedis at Sigma Delta Gamma. Kandace got her makeup refreshed first, then moaned as her feet soaked in nearly-hot water. She gave a virgin mojito to Tania. Corinne was drinking something with peaches floating in it that smelled strongly of peach schnapps. Kandace tried to ignore the smell, and welcomed the sharp scent of acetone as Shan removed her nail polish from her fingers and toes. Kandace decided on shimmering burgundy nail polish. Shan picked out a slightly lighter one. Kandace knew the woman had taste, so she nodded as Shan dried her feet and put on toe separators.

Kandace sipped hard on her virgin mojito, remembering The Incident. Professor Stanton had decided to call on Kandace multiple times in every class, trying to trip her up. Kandace had taken both calculus and astrophysics before her physics class, so she actually knew more than the professor, who thought pretty girls were stupid. She had studied how to take apart his brand of Jeep for two weeks, and hired Danny and Hector from the local shop to help her, and Kofi as a lookout. They took it apart and put it back together inside the lab. Best money she'd ever spent.

She realized Corinne was talking and withdrew from her happy memory twisted in with guilt over how she had put Kofi at risk. "Tania wants to kick some medieval ass."

Kandace grinned. "Some women like to swing a sword."

Tania threw back her head and laughed. "My reach may be shorter, but the guys are so busy holding their heavy swords that I have time to pick them off."

Kandace and Corinne both burst out laughing. Corinne had to put down her drink because she was laughing so hard she got the liquid up her nose. Corinne held up her hand, got herself under control. "They do like to swing them around, don't they?"

Kandace sighed. This would be her last time seeing her girl fight. Tania was fierce on the field. Once, Tania bested a guy twice her size in less than ten minutes by rolling under his legs and pretending to stab him in the back. Kandace fought off the pang of memory by draining her virgin lime mojito and pulling out a strawberry one.

~

*T*ania wanted to go swing a sword, so they waited until their fingers and toes were dry and followed her out to the practice yard. Corinne and Kandace whooped and hollered for Tania to win. Her first bout, she won. The second was a draw.

Kandace wondered what would happen next. Everyone was leaving, scattering to the winds. Who wanted to stay in a small Missouri town surrounded by cows? What would happen next is that her girls would make tracks out into nowhere. Head out. See the world.

"At least you've got the rock climbing to distract you," said Corinne, about how much it hurt to say goodbye to Tania.

"Sheer rock faces are distracting." Kandace didn't go with the sober crews out whitewater rafting, bungee jumping, or jumping out of planes. That shit was just crazy. But, indoor climbing had appealed to her, and some girl named Bethany had talked Kandace into going climbing with her. Not a free climb, but one with actual ropes. Kandace had done that, too, even gone free-climbing on a very small cliff that had sand underneath so she wouldn't brain herself to death on rocks if she fell. Kandace felt free on a cliff face. The hyper-focus, not her previous strong suit, fed some need deep within her.

Anything to distract herself from feeling like an alligator was eating her alive, starting with her toes. She whooped for Tania some more.

~

The Avengers movie marathon at the Geek House had popcorn with mini M&Ms shaken in. They drank Mountain Dew, and Kandace and Corinne found all of Tania's bruises they could see from the fight and festooned her with ice packs. They got snarky with the movie commentary and laughed their heads off.

~

They all went together to the airport. Breakfast was like a funeral, with Corinne trying to keep up everyone's spirits. Even the super-crispy bacon couldn't make up for the suffocating feeling of loss. Kandace kicked herself mentally. She was still present, and she hadn't lost them yet.

At the airport, saying goodbye to Tania, Kandace found herself promising to stay sober, something she didn't normally do. The disease could kick in at any time and kill her, like a cancer that snuck out to attack again. But, it would probably be years before she saw Tania again, and she hugged her friend and said words she might someday regret.

Then, Tania had to say, "Don't throw yourself off a water tower." The words hit her like a punch to the gut, and she turned her head away so she didn't punch her best friend in the mouth while Corinne told Tania she was being too harsh. Kandace clenched her jaw, pissed at Tania for bringing up Marti. Marti, beautiful butterfly Marti, who had climbed a water tower drunk during high winds and fallen. It had taken Marti four agonizing days to die. Not agonizing for Marti; she was in a coma and never regained consciousness. For her baffled parents and weeping brother, a year before full of high hopes to send their kid off to college, now back to turn off the machines and put her in the ground.

Kandace breathed in, out, then held her friend close after she realized no one wanted another Marti. Kandace told Tania to come back. "Rock and rule it. If I've learned anything, it's that life is too damn short. Enjoy every single minute." They hugged it out one more time, and Tania walked away. Kandace was still stinging about Marti, and now Tania was gone.

Kandace dragged her other best friend out when Corinne wanted to stand there and watch Tania go through the line. "She don't need no heifer making moon eyes at her when all she's trying to do is get the hell out of here." Kandace dragged Corinne out to the truck and said, "Get the hell in. We've got to drive all the way back, get our stuff in our vehicles, and get the hell out of here too."

"I am so sorry she said that shit about Marti." Kandace waved off the apology; Tania would apologize in a few days. "I wish we were staying together. But you've got to go hide out in a cabin again, and I understand why. I really do. But at some point, when you're ready to rejoin the world, I'll be here."

"I know. That's why I can go do my hiding like that. But I need to do the Twelve Steps again. You know the quiet writing is when I do the best with it. You know I need to change. I've still got a porcupine under my skin. I'm not like you. I hate people. I can't listen to them blather on and hug them and tell them that they're going to be okay, unless they're another alcoholic."

"Don't go wanting to be me," mourned Corrine. "I ain't got a job, and you and Tania are the only two who know that I only got two offers and turned them both down. I ain't built for no rat race. I'm a country girl. I'm going to have to live and die based on that."

Kandace said, "I did the damn math with you, and you were right. You wouldn't have made enough to make any dent into your loans, and you would have had to find a roommate situation with six other people just to afford a roof over your head." Corinne was blessedly quiet when Kandace told her to look up every ad for a roommate in a small town anywhere in the state. She had her beast to stuff down inside again. Anger killed alcoholics as dead as car accidents and gunfire, because the former caused the latter.

$$\sim$$

Kandace helped Corinne move out of the dorm. None of them had much. They played Tetris with Corinne's tiny hatchback. Kandace jogged to the resident assistant with the clipboard and turned in the key, jogged back and hugged it out with Corinne. She handed Corinne two sodas, all she had left. Kandace got in her truck and waited until she was outside town before letting the tears flow.

FREE FALL

Tabitha was perky. Blonde, her hair pulled back in an ultra-tight French braid. Blue eyes sharp with knowledge and precision. An optimistic, positive attitude that drove Kandace, with her Goth perspectives, insane. Tabitha was one of the best free climbers in the state, and had decided to take Kandace under her wing. They had a piton, carabiner, and rope climb. Tabitha considered Kandace a neophyte and was determined to break and remold Kandace into the second-best free climber in the state.

Kandace had scored excellent contract work and was coming down after the high of participating in mapping out the Phoenix-to-Los Angeles underground route. In two weeks, she would work on the Phoenix-to-St. Louis route. On her break, Kandace was determined to finish Step Four, writing about her resentments, fears, and sex inventory. Tori was still her sponsor; they connected by phone and Skype. Kandace was on her resentments. The family-of-origin thing kept tripping her up. She'd get over something, only to have another memory hit her in the face with a mailed fist. Kandace wanted to climb a cliff face, then come back, stretch out, and finish off the damn list. Resentments were the last part, the fears and sexual inventories already completed.

They were standing in the doorway of Kandace's rented cabin, surrounded by woods and state parks. It had a galley kitchen, a wooden table, and two chairs separated from the main room by a door, a black screen hanging on a wall, a small desk and rolling chair, and a loft bed up a ladder. The floors and walls were knotty pine, and the front and back walls both had beautiful wide windows. Kandace got killer Internet because the owner was, apparently, very responsive to the writers and nature photographers who liked to rent out the cabin.

Kandace checked over all her equipment again. Tabitha watched, then Kandace wordlessly handed over her pack. Tabitha checked every damn thing and grinned. "Let's go," she said. They climbed into Tabitha's Jeep, and headed out. Mel and Jam were meeting them at the rock face. Mel was Tabitha's girlfriend, a tiny, dark woman with smokey brown eyes and a shifty smile. Tabitha trusted her; Kandace didn't. Jam had her thick black hair in braids the color of the darkest basalt they would climb that day. She had shiny eyes and glossy skin and had to bind her breasts to climb. She was also one of the most intelligent women Kandace had ever met.

~

They met at the base. Tabitha checked over their gear too. Mel rolled her eyes when Tabitha was focused on their packs. Jam took it with better grace. "I go first. Kandace, you mirror my every move. Mel, then Jam. We've got a newbie, so look sharp, people." Kandace let the "newbie" comment slide. They put their harnesses on, checked them. They checked and double-checked all their gear. They then started the climb. Kandace let her focus sharpen, let the rest of the world go; the cabin, the fourth-step writing, her past and future. There was only breath and wind, movement, line, pitons, carabiners, more movement. Reaching up, pulling up, standing on toes, doing it again. Finding cracks and protuberances where there didn't seem to be any.

They were about two-thirds of the way up when Tabitha slipped.

Kandace held on, and Tabitha reached up. A stone fell, clattering, at exactly the wrong moment. Kandace literally couldn't move that hand; two-thirds of her weight was there. She tried to move, but she wasn't in time. Kandace heard the stone smack into her hand, felt it go numb, felt herself slip. She swung out, trying to hold on with a hand that wouldn't work, and she fell. She felt herself smack into the cliff face, and her world went dark.

A male voice shouted. She heard it clearly, wondered about it. A male voice, when she had started the day surrounded by women. Kandace felt something hook onto her harness. Kandace heard Tabitha's normally cheery voice turn sharp and hard, telling the voice what happened, and giving Kandace's name. The male voice was calm, reasoned. Secure in what it was. She focused on the voice. "I'm Camber. Vic Camber. Kandace, can you hear me?"

Kandace felt her bowed back move upward by a small increment. "Mmm," she said, forcing her voice through bloody lips. She felt the blood move down her chin. Her chin hit someone's back. She moved her head to the side, slowly, as if she were moving in molasses. She felt lines. She then slid back and down, into the darkness.

She felt movement. She was on somebody's back. She felt her blood soak into someone's shirt. The shirt was black. She realized her eyes were cracked open. The male voice kept up a steady patter. "Jean, get that backboard together." Someone made noises to her left. "I think her entire right side is dented."

Shaken, not stirred, thought Kandace. Then she felt angry with herself because martinis were not things she should think about. Ever. Olives were fine. But not the martinis they went in. Then, hands, all small, touched her, and she felt something hard on her back. The pain hit, a wash of crimson, and she looked for the black and slipped in again.

There was wailing. It sounded like the loudest baby ever. Maybe six babies screaming at once. She cracked an eye. She shut it again when white light stabbed into her eyes. "She's conscious. Jean, hit her again with the morphine. No one should be awake for this." Kandace felt a sharp fear. Getting sober after this— whatever it was—would suck. Then, the fuzzy goodness of narcotics embraced her, and she slid out again.

~

Kandace woke up again and cracked her eyes. She immediately closed them as white lights stabbed her eyes. Someone physically opened her right eye, and she screamed as she tried to move the wrong arm, and felt her other fist smash into someone's face.

Immediately, that male voice was there again. "I think she's sensitive to light."

"No shit, Sherlock," said a sharp female voice. Sharp like scalpels. "My patient damn near broke my nose. Camber, hand me a...thanks."

Kandace slit her eyes and cracked them open. The light was much dimmer. "Tank oo," she tried to say. The pain from the arm she couldn't move came in sickening waves. She tried not to vomit.

"Your jaw isn't broken, but it is bruised," said the male voice. Camber. "Your face is swollen, you have two black eyes. The right side of your body is a mess. Your leg is badly bruised but not broken. You have three cracked ribs, and you've just been through surgery to add pins and screws to your right arm, which is broken in three places. And your right hand has two broken fingers and a cracked knuckle. I suggest not moving as something you need to embrace. Probably for the next two months. Maybe three."

"Fuh," said Kandace.

"I know, it's shitty," said Camber. "Just so you know, you did everything right, and so did the women you were climbing with. I just happened to be at the top. Belayed down and got you, hauled you up."

"Fuh," said Kandace again.

"I'll say it for you. Fuck fuck fuckkity fuck. That sum it up?"

"Yeah," breathed out Kandace through swollen lips. "Joh."

"No job for at least a month. Between the drugs and the pain, you won't think straight anyway."

"Way to scare my patient," said the woman. "I'm Doctor Evelyn Sunder. I assisted on your surgery. Davis, Camber here's brother, he's the best orthopedic surgeon in the state. No, you're not seeing double, they kind of look alike with the brother thing and all. He'll check on you in the mornings. I've got evenings. I'm going to give you something to help you sleep. Essentially, you need to sleep for the next three days."

"Kay," breathed Kandace. "Ah dic."

Camber breathed close to her face. "We know. We found the key tag on your keys. Three years. But there is no way, I mean none, for you to go through this without narcotics. But my brother has worked with people with your illness before. He has a plan. Trust. Trust in the plan."

"I'm pushing now," said Doctor Sunder. The world went black again.

~

*T*he next three days were days where the meds didn't touch the pain. Doctor Evelyn found out, and told Doctor Davis Camber. Davis upped her dosage. "Idiot woman," he said. "I already gave you a higher dose. I predicted your liver would filter more quickly. You should have told me."

Davis was taller than his brother. Camber had been back to visit her and said, "My first name is Victor, or Vic. Everyone calls me Camber, Cam, or Vic." Call-me-Camber was ropy, strong, with the triangle upper body of a swimmer. His brother, Doctor Davis Camber, looked like a basketball player, long and lean, with very long fingers. His white lab coat seemed to go on forever. Both men had brown hair, Vic's shaggier, Davis' close-cropped, and startling poolsof-black eyes. Davis' eyes were more coal-dark, Vic's more like onyx with glimpses of white gold.

Each step-up in pain was different. Everything needed to heal—bones, muscles, tendons, bruised and abraded skin. Vic brought her ointments that instantly cooled her, icy, like she stuck a body part into a freezer. He also stole her cell phone while she was sleeping, loaded it with speaker videos and a ton of music and books in every genre, and left it with earphones under her hand. It pissed her off, because everything from the song about a beaver—which could certainly be interpreted differently—and an audiobook about a woman and her sneaky, teleporting, crime-solving cats made her laugh. And broken ribs meant it hurt—stabbing herself in the stomach hurt—to laugh. She borrowed Vic's phone to text her work team about the accident. He brought in a printout of their responses, some of which made her laugh. Again.

She ignored the doctor, and at two weeks paid a gopher to have her gaming-ready laptop and gaming headset delivered to the hospital and started coding again. She did it by voice and typing with her left hand, and set up her keyboard for one-hand use. She could use two fingers on her right hand. Kandace praised the universe that she was left-handed, her right side a mass of immovable pain. She hooked up a tablet as a keyboard so she didn't hurt her fingers as she typed. She ran the software, helped her team. She explained about her accident and worked in bursts. The team was fantastic. Piers and Doss from the team split their shifts to overlap hers to take up the slack.

～

*A*t two and a half weeks, Kandace took a taxi back to the cabin. Her things had been left alone, and it had been cleaned top to bottom. She was stunned to find a brand-new recliner there, wide and deep, covered by black satin sheets. "Rubber underneath," said the home health aide that helped move her into the chair. He had the same black hair and dark eyes the color of bitter chocolate as his brothers, but his skin was more golden and his eyes had a slight tilt. "The bathroom is only a meter that way."

Kandace stared at the man. "Is everyone in the medical profession around here related?"

The man laughed. "I'm Len Camber. Yes, that's a mouthful. Before you ask, yes, I have a doctor brother and EMT and climbing squad brother. I'm a home health aide, which is a stupid title. I call myself a health god. My job is to keep you going along, do some physical therapy when the cast goes off." Kandace looked down at the neon-blue cast on her arm. "Which will suck, I agree. I am also a licensed physician's assistant. I can keep you medicated properly. And, yes, I know from your medical file you need to not ingest more narcotics. We have a plan, my brother the doctor, and I."

"I warn you, pain makes me vicious and I have no filters to begin with." Kandace settled into the chair. "This is awesome." She sighed. "Help me up, I have to get my setup together."

Len shook his head. "Pretend I'm a programmable robot. Tell me what to do."

Kandace laughed, then groaned. "Laughing hurts," she said. "I'm already mad at your brother...brother or cousin? I'm referring to Vic. Mad about him putting funny stuff on my phone."

"We're brothers. Technically half-brothers. My bio-dad was Asian, Lim Hyun Ji. He died in a car crash. Last of his family. My twin brother was five. He thought he was invincible. Fell off the damn house. Dad crashed the car driving him to the hospital. Anyway, I went to live with Dad Two because eventually Mom married him. We hike and climb together."

"Talk about no filter," said Kandace. "I'm sorry about your family." She pointed to a box on the floor, actually two boxes pushed together. "I have two lap trays in that box. Then, you get to hook up an awesome gaming setup and put the tray with the keyboard in my lap. I get to code by one hand aided by two-finger typing." He brought over the tray and moved its legs until it tilted just right in her lap. He set up the surge protector, the laptop, and the tablet computer. He then used an HDMI cable and hooked up the flat-screen TV that nearly took up an entire wall. "You are a setup god."

Len bowed. "Now, I will send a menu to your tablet. I ordered a chef too. Meri is our sister. She will cook enough food for three days and refrigerate them into small meals either one of us can reheat in the microwave." He pointed to her small refrigerator and microwave that had been moved out of the kitchen onto a stand to her left. "Four minutes to eat. You can do it yourself when I'm not here."

Kandace sighed. "So, I need to earn more money to pay you and Meri."

"Good idea," said Len. He handed her two white pills and a glass of water. "Take these, then I'll leave you to it."

FIRST DAYS

*L*en Camber really did become her robot, her Jeeves. Len's chef sister, Meri, had black hair pulled back, deep brown eyes, and Len's shade of skin, without the tilted eyes. She sent an exhaustive list of foods with like-hate-neutral radio buttons to Kandace's tablet. "Good god, you're normal," said Meri. "You hate broccoli. Wait until you try my pizza. Don't worry, the green will be the olives."

Kandace laughed, then groaned. "Ribs not healed, woman. Quit making me laugh."

"I'll make you a peanut butter chocolate shake that will make you cry."

Kandace looked over at Len. "She's worth every hour I work."

Len made a face. "And me? The health god?"

Kandace glared at him. "And you. Went without saying. You had to fish it out. Bet you feel stupid now."

Len barked out a laugh. "Vicious. Have to get you a vicious animal. Like you, it will scare everyone."

"I am a vicious animal," Kandace said. "Now, go do things. I can't be your only job." She knew damn well she wasn't. Len circulated, coming back after four hours. He never said a word about other clients, but she sometimes smelled old-woman lavender-and-baby-powder scent on him. Kandace liked to sleep in and work in the afternoon, and she ate yogurt for breakfast, so he arrived after one in the afternoon.

"Stop snarling at me. I'm scared." Len pranced to the door, and Kandace gasped in laughter mingled with sharp pain.

The blender silenced, and Meri came out with a heavy plastic cup with a straw integrated into the lid. "Got lots of protein powder and vitamins in it. Drink it."

"Lie to me. Tell me everything I'm eating is unhealthy." Kandace stopped setting up long enough to take a sip of her chocolate peanut butter shake. She shuddered, then stopped the movement, even though it came from absolute joy. "This is the nectar of the gods."

"Damn straight," said Meri, coming in with blue cold packs. "Now, work. You need to pay me, woman. Or no more shakes."

"On it."

Meri made her small meals. Pad thai, baby pizzas with a crunchy, cheesy crust, roasted chicken nachos on salty chips that didn't taste of grease. Veggie wraps with the roasted chicken. Breakfast burritos with cheesy eggs and crispy bacon. Each meat was used three times—chicken, shrimp, catfish, grilled pork, bacon, sausage, bacon. Kandace had been off the beef for years. She had seen too many cows on her walks. She was working on getting off the pig next, but bacon was one of her remaining addictions, along with chocolate. "I have a secret," said Meri.

"I guess that the pizza crust is something healthy, and the same with the chips." Kandace sighed.

"Almond flour crust. Veggie chips. Are you interested in going vegetarian when you get better? You need tons of protein and calcium now."

"Mostly vegetarian."

"Oh, fun." Meri made a happy dance.

Kandace growled at her. "Woman, I have to work." She went back to coding the paths of holes and tunnels in the ground.

ic showed up a week later with a mess of rainbow trout, already cleaned and filleted. "Stocked pond. So many fish you can reach in and grab one." Kandace growled at the interruption to her workday. Meri grinned and cooked it into more food.

The fresh trout was amazing. Kandace had it in tacos for lunch, stuffed with crab meat for dinner, and then baked with a crispy breading and cornmeal hush puppies for the next day's lunch. "Please apologize to your cousin Vic for me," said Kandace to Meri.

Meri glared at Kandace. "Idiot. Apologies are face-to-face and real or they don't matter."

Kandace narrowed her eyes. "You in the Program?"

"One of them. Put Vic's number in your phone, not just your doctor and Len. And call Vic and apologize."

Kandace put down her fork and looked at her baked trout longingly. "Yes, I will." She put the number in her phone and called after lunch.

Vic laughed as she blurted her apology. "I expect you to growl. You're healing from broken bones. Walking takes a long time. You have work to do online that is real work, important work. I know they'll build those underground tubes eventually. Hook us up from Chicago to Houston, Los Angeles to New York."

Kandace stared at her phone. "How did you know I was mapping Chicago next?"

Vic laughed again. "Woman, do you think you've cornered the market on logic?"

Kandace grimaced. "No. Well, probably not. Maybe."

Vic grunted laughter. "So, have you heard from your former climbing partners?"

"After the initial hospital visit, not a thing. I think they don't want to be reminded of that day. It could happen to them too."

"And I haven't cornered the market on perceptiveness," said Vic.

Kandace snorted. "Are you always carrying women around on your back?"

"Search and rescue, rarely. Mostly just a garden-variety EMT. My objective is to get people from their initial site to the hospital, alive, until they can get further treatment."

"Ex-military."

Vic sighed. "Perceptive. Yes. Davis and I, not Len. We told him to stay put and keep an eye on Meri."

"Anonymity is a thing."

"She told you something."

"A whiff."

"She is one of the most honest and best women I know." They were silent for a minute. "I take it you don't work seven days a week?"

Kandace snorted. "They only let me work four days a week and only six hours a day."

"Movie night. Your next day off?"

"Tomorrow night."

"See you at three, no, four, I'll need a shower first. I don't want to offend you."

Kandace snorted. "I might offend *you*."

Vic laughed. "See you." He hung up.

～

Somehow, Meri and Len were invited, and they brought their own camp chairs with little holes in the armrests for their drinks. Len helped Meri create amazing snacks—crab wontons, shrimp puffs, almond flour bread, salad with herbed tomatoes, mushroom caps stuffed with Italian sausage. She staggered the items so no one went hungry. Davis showed up, smelling faintly of the soap he used to wash his hands, and he fell on the food as if he'd never eaten before. They watched the space dragon movie, then one about a spy family with ten siblings. Meri created popcorn—butter, salted caramel with tiny chocolate chips, and an amazing one with tiny peanut butter chips. They switched to the movie about telekinesis-powered people colonizing the solar system and greatly enjoyed the overlapping love storylines.

Len and Meri went home first, then Davis. Vic stayed, and they ended with a post-elven-invasion movie and peppermint popcorn. "That was hilarious," said Vic.

"Only because of my snarky commentary. The elven princess with the blue hair was the female in heels in a horror movie."

"Don't go upstairs!" Vic said, a line from the horror movie. Kandace snorted, then held her side. He grinned, stood up, and put their glasses in the miniature dishwasher. He came back, his eyes sleepy. "Do you need anything?"

"Nope. I can even shower myself now. I have a special sack for the arm." Kandace stretched a little, grunted. "All our technology, and we can't create a hydrophobic cast?"

Vic laughed. "Bang on my brother for that one."

"Which one?"

Vic laughed again. "I swear, there's only three boys. Meri and Libby are our sister-entities. Libby does the baking thing in an actual shop."

Kandace raised an eyebrow. "Sister-entities? Are they secretly aliens?"

Vic's face got serious. "Sort of," he said. He smiled, slid his camp chair into a sack, and slung it over his back.

"Leave that here. You might want to come back."

Vic grinned, then carefully put the chair in a corner. "Sleep well, Kandace," he said.

"Later, dude." He snorted and left.

Kandace couldn't sleep after Vic left. Pain, too much caffeine, whatever. She needed something. An itch that couldn't be scratched. Like the thin wire she used to scratch her arm underneath her cast. She had great food, new friends, a job doing something amazing. Tania and Corinne were still her cheerleaders, but they had their own busy lives, and she kind of hadn't told them the whole truth about her fall. They would have been on the next plane or driving cross-country, and she wanted them to succeed. So she broke her rigorous honesty pledge and kept them in the dark about the extent of her injuries.

Kandace was also making more money than ever, despite her

shortened hours. There was both private money and a government contract involved. And both corporate and governmental entities in China and the EU wanted in on the technology. So she sent a small percentage to her mother and grandmother and paid off her debts as if she would crumble to dust like a staked vampire if she didn't. She called up another movie, this one about an astronaut who went to Jupiter and met a gasbag alien, and watched the screen until dawn.

~

Kandace awoke to a mad scrambling at her door. There was also some thunking. She stumbled up, dawn light on her face from the floor-to-ceiling windows. She lurched to the door and opened it. A bundle of fur came streaking in, covered with mud. It dashed behind her recliner and huddled. A black bear was across the clearing, sitting down, staring off into nothingness. It rose and ambled off into the woods. Kandace shut the door and said to the thing, "It's not chasing you. It went away." The thing stuck its head out from behind the door, and it was huge, bigger than a Pomeranian or even a boxer. It had triangular ears and whiskers, and had long variegated hair in black, white, cream, smoke gray, and white on its chin. It had bright, highly intelligent yellow eyes. It came out, sat, and began licking itself. The thing resolved itself into a cat. A freaking huge one.

"Water and...do we have any tuna in a can?" Kandace asked herself. She took five limping steps to the galley kitchen and found a plastic butter dish in the recycling. She washed it and filled it with water. She then washed a plastic lid and found chicken in the refrigerator. She diced it and put that on the floor next to the water. She stumbled back to the recliner and slipped back into sleep.

~

Len gave a very unmanly scream when he came in. The cat was on the hearth, licking its paws. "What in the Universe is that?" asked Len.

"Len." Kandace opened one eye. "What did I say about visiting me before noon?"

"It's nearly two."

"Omigod." Kandace levered herself up, lurched to the bathroom, then came back to boot up. She was in the middle of, quite literally, a digger program. She typed madly with one hand, then grunted and groaned her way through Len torturing her. He handed her a glass of water with a non-narcotic pain reliever, and then reheated some crab puffs and stuffed mushrooms for breakfast.

Len sighed. "Maine coon cat. That thing will eat more than you ever could. Is this cat male or female?" Kandace shrugged her good shoulder. Len approached the cat, who let him arrive, then head-butted Len's hand. "Girl. No collar, and her fur is matted. She needs a good combing and a vet. I'll call Teensy."

"Teensy? Yet another relative?"

Len laughed. The cat purred like a Mustang when Len petted her head. "Teensy is sixteen and a veterinary assistant and groomer at the community college. She'll be using Skype with her trainer the whole time," he promised.

"Call her," said Kandace, with a wave of her hand. "Coding here."

"What's her name?"

Kandace snorted. "Sam. Her name is Sam." Sam had lived in the holler too. A childhood friend who had up and disappeared one day, moved away. This Sam was just as disheveled and in need of a good cleaning, and had a feistiness like the first one. Kandace would not turn any Sam away. It was not in her nature.

~

Teensy wasn't a little person, but she was barely larger than one. "Bone disease," she said, at Kandace's flat stare. "Better treatment now." She approached Sam, and Sam butted her head on Teensy's hand. "Female Maine coon." She weighed the cat. "Underweight. Probably been scrounging. Seven kilos."

Len stared at Teensy. "Seven kilos is over fourteen pounds. That's underweight?"

"For a Maine coon, it's within the weight chart. But that's not why I said that. She has loose skin from weighing more and suddenly losing the weight. Poor kitty." Teensy petted Sam's head, and Sam again rumbled like a sports car. "Let's get your fur all pretty, shall we?"

Kandace typed while Teensy ministered to the cat. "Len will bring in the cat food," Teensy said.

"I will?" said Len. Teensy glared at him, so Len brought in two huge bags of cat chow, a huge tufted cat bed, a harness and leash in cherry red, a blinged-out pink collar, and six cat toys. He went back out and came in with a tall cat tower in a box. Len and Teensy put it together. It had wide shelves and a sling big enough for a Maine coon cat. The thing screwed together with bolts and nuts.

Teensy called someone on the phone. "Doctor Malcha, can I administer the shots?" The doctor said something, and Teensy hung up. The cat got two shots, which she seemed to ignore entirely, and a kitty treat that was really heart medicine. "She's healthy and happy now," said Teensy. "I'll text you the bill."

"Excellent. Thanks." Kandace kept typing as Len helped Teensy with getting everything situated for the cat. They released a well-groomed Sam, who then leapt onto the back of the recliner. Kandace grinned and reached up with her good hand, and the cat purred. Kandace laughed and designed a tunnel with a cat rumbling with joy above her head.

FALL

Kandace went past exhausted into red-zone territory. She'd done calculations in her head and transformed them into her code. She'd gotten into even more detail about the Chicago to Houston route and was setting things up well. The Laredo-San Antonio-Austin route split into a Y to go to Dallas and Houston, and that would be a bear to get done. But she wanted it, and so she had to do an amazing job on this one to continue onto that team. The Boston-Fall River-Providence J was being done by another team. Another team was on the Cheyenne, Wyoming to Houston, Texas route. There were teams in Europe, India, and one working on the Japan-South Korea-Hong Kong route which ran underwater. The Cape Town, South Africa to Alexandria, Egypt team was being formed. The Dakar, Senegal to Mogadishu, Somalia route was being hotly debated, but the team would probably form within weeks.

Kandace stood, stretched the half of her body that worked. She felt the pain from the other side and gasped. She wiggled her fingers, grabbed her cell phone, put on an audiobook, shoved the phone in her pocket, and listened as she stepped forward towards the kitchen. There was a thud, and Sam went shooting across the floor. Kandace stepped forward at the wrong moment and collided with the cat.

Kandace tried to reach behind her, but she was too far from the recliner or the table with the computers and the tray on it. She tried to catch herself and found herself falling. The cat kept running. Kandace tried for a push-up, but couldn't quite get her hand up in time. She landed mostly on her left side and screamed. She lay there, trying not to scream again, but she did. She got her hand under her and reached her phone.

She had several choices: The EMT, Vic, Davis the doctor, or the health god Len. She didn't think anything was broken or broken again. But she was in massive amounts of pain. She decided an actual EMT should get involved, so she called Vic. Vic answered the phone. "Camber. Kandace?"

Kandace breathed, wheezed, and tried not to cry. She finally got out, "Fell. Over cat."

Vic said, "I'm hanging up to call 911. I'm also on my way. Don't worry, call Len. He's got a golden voice."

Len did have a golden voice, and so Kandace called him. "Kandace?" he asked in a sleepy voice.

"Fell. Called 911. Vic. Is coming."

"Idiot woman. Let me guess. You tripped over your monstrosity of a cat?"

"Did," said Kandace. She gasped, hitched her breath.

"In, out, in, out. I'm talking about your breathing, not sex."

Kandace huffed out a laugh through clenched teeth. "Ow. No. Laugh."

"Okay. Listen to the sound of my voice. Your breath is a wave. Flowing up on the shore, back into the sea. Back. Forth. Back. Forth. Be the softness of the wave. In. Out."

There was a pounding at the door and a scrabbling. The door unlocked, and the EMTs came in. They flipped her over. She moaned, but concentrated on Len's voice. She hollered as they put her on the gurney.

Vic came flying in. "How's our patient?" he said. The EMTs had a conversation about blood pressure and a lack of blood or even surface bruising, with teasing thrown in about Vic coming back into work in the middle of the night. "You are okay," said Vic. "There'll be scans to be sure you didn't break anything else, or again, but it's looking good so far."

"I. Need. Morphine. Now," said Kandace.

"Davis is driving to the hospital now. I texted him. They're putting in a line and calling him in a minute."

"Good," said Kandace.

"Hanging up now," said Len. He clicked off in her ear.

Kandace felt the prick of the needle, then the icy grip of morphine running up her arm. She relaxed a bit, then a bit more. Vic said, "Let go, Kandace. You're doing fine." He stroked her arm, and she calmed down. Vic shut the door, and slid in with her in the ambulance. He talked about coming home and having a picnic with her, fried chicken, biscuits with honey and butter, and potato and macaroni salads. "Stop it, Camber, you're making me hungry," said whoever was driving.

❧

*V*ic went in with her through the X-rays and ultrasounds. Davis looked wide awake, despite it being past two in the morning. "You are fine, nothing broken, not even hairline cracks. You are in massive amounts of pain, so we'll treat with narcotics, which we'll decrease over the next twenty-four hours to over-the-counter pain relievers. I'll drive you both home, and Vic or Len will stay with you tonight."

"Thanks, Davis." Kandace looked over at Vic. "Thanks, Vic."

Vic grinned. "I'll stay."

"You do know her cabin has only her recliner and a few hard chairs," Davis complained.

"I've got a camp cot in my truck," said Vic.

"Girl needs more furniture, I'm just saying. We had to bring camp chairs to her own damn party."

"I'll get on that," said Kandace dryly. "I doubt I can get anything delivered at two in the damn morning."

"And the snark is back," said Vic.

"I'll get on the release paperwork," said Davis. "Everyone go the hell home and quit falling over cats."

"The thing is bigger than a Pomeranian. How the hell did you not see that?" asked Vic.

"Something fell. Scared cat. Bad timing. I was walking forward."

"I knew you could speak in complete sentences if you tried," said Vic.

Davis snorted out a laugh. "And Vic's snark is back too. I'm glad you're alright, Kandace."

"Thank you for coming in," said Kandace. Davis inclined his head and then left.

"You're stuck with me," said Vic.

"When I'm not flipping out with pain, you owe me a fried chicken dinner."

"You remember that?" asked Vic.

"In massive pain, not deaf."

"Let's get you out of here." Vic got her dressed; she had been put in a hospital top. He got her in a wheelchair and zipped her over to sign the paperwork.

"I love my insurance. The other coders and I all got extra insurance in case of injury. Super-happy I did. It pays for Len and a little of Meri."

"Great. Paid for me, too, I bet." Vic brought his red truck around, and Davis got Kandace in the vehicle while Vic returned the wheelchair. Vic slid in front, and they were on their way. Kandace tried to sleep, but kept getting jarred awake. Backwoods roads were not smooth. The wall of trees made her dizzy, so she kept her eyes closed. Vic helped her out, and walked her to the bathroom, then to the chair. He then got his cot and a sleeping bag out of the back of his truck, then locked the door behind him.

"How did the EMTs get in?" asked Kandace.

Vic said, "I know where you hide the key." Kandace glared at him, put the sheet over herself, and laughed as the cat slunk over, leapt onto the back of the recliner, and lay on Kandace's head. Kandace grinned and slipped into sleep.

Kandace was lucky enough to have the next day off. Len came in and took over for Vic. "I'll be back to sleep here," said Vic. "I've got to go home. And that blow-up pillow sucks. I'm bringing a gel one."

"Double recliner couch, black or red?" asked Kandace, her voice muzzy with pain, narcotics, and exhaustion.

"Black, duh," said Vic. "See you later."

"Later, dude." Kandace ordered the couch on her cell phone, then slid back into sleep.

~

Kandace woke up to the most delicious smells. Herbs, yeast, and chicken smells. She opened one eye, then the other. There were fried chicken legs, three of them. There were two biscuits, cut in half and slathered with honey and butter. There were little cups of a multicolored pasta salad with pesto dressing, studded with multicolored bell peppers. There was also a baked potato, diced, in a sour cream herb sauce on a tray next to Kandace's recliner. "Good god." Meri stood there, a tray in each hand. There was a three-person couch with three television trays to her right that had not been there before. Meri slid a tray on each stand and grinned at Len on one side and Vic on the other. She strode back to the kitchen on long golden-brown legs, and came back with a fourth tray for herself.

Kandace found two pills near her glass of pink lemonade. She popped the pills first. Then she attacked her chicken. Vic put on a movie about a blue-haired fairy princess that ran several universes, and they laughed at the dialogue. Kandace hummed in her chest despite her lingering soreness as she ate.

"My mama's recipe," said Meri, when Kandace thanked her, post-inhaling the food. "Herbs in the breading, and in the biscuits."

"Jealous of you. My mama couldn't heat her own coffee in the microwave, like, ever."

Len barked out a laugh. "Mine makes pad thai that would make you cry."

"Next movie night," said Kandace.

Vic grinned. "Awesome. Len here does things with shrimp that should be illegal. Also makes an orange chicken that we demand he makes for parties."

Meri put a finger to her lips. "Shh. She's about to go all homicidal on her second-in-command, Fenetherial." The fairy princess raised her sword, and they all went quiet.

The next movie was about the theft of a flying car and the consequences for both the thief and the flying car company. It was very weird, with flying cars everywhere zipping around. "Won't happen," said Vic when the movie was over. He stood to clean up, and Len stood up with him. "Flying cars are much too loud."

"Even electric ones?" asked Len. They each took two trays.

"Wind. Vehicles going at a high rate of speed through the atmosphere are very loud." They carried the trays into the kitchen and filled up the dishwasher. The cat followed to try to cadge chicken scraps.

"What should we see next?" asked Meri.

Kandace looked through the listings on her cell phone. "There's that space rift one. The rift causes magic to come back."

"Omigod. Awesome!"

They waited until the end of the magic space movie to eat Meri's peach cobbler with caramel ice cream on top. Kandace sighed. "I. Am. Dying. This is better than sex."

Vic and Len both gasped. "Nothing, not even peach cobbler, is better than sex," said Vic.

"Sex is so tantric. It brings you to higher levels," said Len.

"Good god," said Meri. "Len's waxing philosophical. It's bonobos. Releasing tension. Soothing and smoothing out problems."

"Bonobos? Monkeys?" asked Kandace.

"They don't have war. They have sex," said Meri.

Kandace laughed then groaned and held her side. "Can you imagine our world leaders having sex to resolve problems?"

Len, Meri, and Vic all doubled over laughing. They threw out some very interesting pairings.

"Armies." Vic gasped with laughter. "Sent to have sex with each other to avoid fighting."

Kandace groaned with mingled laughter and pain. "My pain pills are working overtime."

"Have sex instead of fighting. Join the army, go to new places, and screw people," said Meri, and she doubled over with laughter. The cat snuck up under her, and licked the ice cream she dropped while waving around her spoon.

"Everyone would sign up," said Victor.

Len grinned. "Except for those who hate sex. Some people just don't like sex. Not into it."

"True, human sexuality is a spectrum," said Meri. "Bonobos also have group sex."

"I think I like bonobos," said Kandace.

"I second that," said Victor.

"All in favor?" asked Len. The ayes had it.

STEP WORK

Kandace had another round of don't-move from Davis, her doctor. She was tired of online meetings. They were great, and she got to hear from alcoholics and addicts—she attended both fellowships—from all over the world. Their stories ranged from funny to despairing to hair-raising.

Vern was the alcoholic Central Office sent for a face-to-face meeting; the other program was few and far between in their neck of the woods. Len let him in. Vern arrived just past lunch when Kandace hurt the most. She had to wait for her meds to kick in. He was tall and gangly, with big ears and a quiet smile. He wore a T-shirt, jeans, and cowboy boots. "Sorry I'm not female."

Kandace pretended to be stunned. "You're not?"

Vern laughed and plopped down on the new couch with the double recliners. "You got your Big Book with ya?"

Kandace held up her cell phone. "Right here."

Vern took his battered blue book out of his ancient navy backpack. "Did you relapse because of your..." He pointed at her cast.

"Nope. I was terrified of it, but the drugs made me sick to my stomach. So, no, I still have three years."

"So, we don't need to start with the 'Doctor's Opinion.'"

"Nope, I believe my addictions—drugs and alcohol—have their roots in my genetics. I can't change my genes. I was born this way." Kandace pointed at herself.

"Okay, let's start with 'How it Works.'"

"If you don't mind, I'd like to get to Step Five. Are you up for one today?"

Vern said, "I don't have to be anywhere for about six hours. So lay it on me. You sure you don't need a woman?"

Kandace laughed. "My last Fifth Step was about nine months ago. So no." She opened her laptop and turned on the giant screen. "Can you see that?"

Vern looked up at the screen. "They can see that on Mars. You want that feller to take some time off?"

Len came out and waved at Kandace. "I'm off to see my other clients. I would say don't move, but I don't think you will."

"Too sore," agreed Kandace.

Sam strode into the room and chirruped at Len. Len bent down to pet Sam's head, and she chirruped again.

"Lordy," said Vern. "That a cat or a dog?"

"It's a rare cat-dog," said Kandace. Len and Vern both laughed. "That's a Maine coon cat. They grow much larger than regular ones."

"Our girl here tripped over Sam when Sam got spooked. Kandace had a relapse when she fell. Of the pain kind, not the addictive kind." He stood, waved, and left. Sam stood by the door, stunned at being abandoned, and turned towards Kandace in a huff. She walked to the side of the recliner and stared up at Kandace.

"You know I have only one hand, Sam," said Kandace. "Hop on. Oof," she said as Sam leapt onto the arm of the chair and gently patted Kandace's stomach with one paw. Kandace petted the cat, making her rumble. "Vern, there's sodas and a pitcher of water and I think one of lemonade in the fridge. You have to make your own coffee. I don't drink it."

"Reckon I'll get me some soda," said Vern. He stood, walked into the kitchen, and came back with a can of cola. He sat down again, popped the top. "Let's get started, girl. I ain't getting any younger."

Kandace talked about her resentment toward her fellow climbers who didn't visit her much after the first week. "I know all of them live around here, but I haven't heard from even one of them."

"I recognize those names. I suspect that their parents would be incensed to hear about their behavior. You are a stranger here and should have been treated better."

"Thank you. I rarely think about it, but I don't want to feel angry when I think of any of them. Wastes my time, and anger is exhausting."

"Good point. Annoying emotion."

"I do the pinprick method. Learned it from my meditation program. You see a thought or emotion come up like a balloon, and if it doesn't float off, gently touch it with a pin. It pops, and another one rises up." Kandace grinned. "I have to keep from mentally stabbing them."

Vern laughed. "Been wanting to get rid of some of my obsessions. Drives me nuts that those suckers are part of my disease. I'll try that technique."

They zipped through the resentments. One of them made Vern laugh outright. "You're resentful towards the cliff face that broke your bones? Good luck getting it to apologize to you."

Kandace laughed too. "Wish I could. But rock probably thinks so slow that we'd be there a week just trying to get it to say a single word." They laughed again.

There wasn't much on the fears list except rock climbing. "Considering how damaged you are right now, think you'd better leave that to others. That sounds like a reasonable thing to not want to do. So, use a mental trick, like pushing the thought of climbing far away, to change it from a fear to just something you don't wanna do."

"Good one, Vern."

The sexual inventory was a short one. "The first year, I did my Fifth Step, and I stopped the stuff I did while drinking and using. Turns out people look like a much better idea while you're drunk or high."

Vern laughed. "Round here, we call those 'beer glasses'. Makes the craziest idiot look like someone you want to get into a relationship with."

"Have a few of those. Hell, a lot of those back when I was drinking and sometimes using. My friends and I merged a bachelor's degree and graduate school, did a speedy-thing through. Graduated with a master's degree in five years. Didn't have time to date after the first year, when you're supposed to not date, concentrate on yourself. A few people here and there, one-night to two-week things. Nothing between the last Fifth Step and now. Too damn busy, especially since I was trying to earn money to pay back the loans. I knew we would be required to make payments as soon as we graduated."

Vern gustily sighed with relief. "Dodged a bullet on that one."

Kandace laughed. "See, not so bad." She looked at the clock and was astonished at the time. "I didn't have my snack, and I need one. I've got chocolate peanut butter bars. You want one?"

Vern held up a hand. "Prayer first, then I'm heading out." They prayed, and then Vern stood. "You take your hour of quiet time, young lady. Want a meeting tomorrow? We can read Step Six."

"I have to work tomorrow after lunch. Can you come at eleven in the morning?"

"Great time for me."

"You're awesome. Are you going to a face-to-face meeting tonight?"

"Six-thirty Easy Does It," said Vern proudly. "Meeting a newcomer there."

Kandace handed him a five-dollar bill. "Please put this in the basket. I can't donate for the online ones."

"You willing to be a sponsor?"

"Yes." Kandace handed over several of her "anonymous" cards with her first name and cell phone number.

"Great. I've got your digits from the hotline. You said your sponsor left the state?"

"Tori got a job offer in Houston. Said I should find someone here, boots on the ground. Said I put it off for too long. I agree with her, but falling over the cat set me back."

Vern stood up. The cat hopped off Kandace's chair. She walked up to Vern, sat, and chirruped up at him. Vern bent down and patted the cat on the head. "Best cat-dog ever."

"She is," said Kandace. She took out her peanut butter bar snack from a pouch on the side of the recliner and tore it open. The cat heard the sound of the paper, ran to the recliner, and leapt up onto the arm. She chirruped at Kandace. "No, Sam. Chocolate kills cats."

Vern laughed when the cat literally turned her back on Kandace. "That's an alcoholic cat. Doesn't want to take 'no' for an answer." Vern left, shutting the door behind him.

~

Kandace went to work a few hours late, but she was way ahead on her schedule. She slammed out tasks for others on the project management chart, freeing them up for other tasks. She finally caught up to where she could be useful again for things under her own name.

Meri came bustling in. "Why did you leave the door unlocked?"

"My new temporary sponsor did. I was really sore and didn't feel like getting up."

"You can't run away if someone nasty shows up." Meri locked the door behind her.

"I'll loft the cat at such a terrible person," said Kandace.

Meri laughed. "You have only one hand. And that cat is huge. But, come to think of it, the thought of that cat flying at me would make me turn tail and run." She looked down at Sam who turned pathetic eyes on her. "All right, cat, let's go. Dinner doesn't make itself." The cat followed her to the kitchen and waited patiently until she got fed.

After feeding the cat, Meri fed Kandace shrimp-stuffed fish, corn-bread with honey butter, a small salad, and iced tea. Kandace patted her stomach. "Amazing as ever."

"Glad you love it. I've got individual pizzas in the freezer for you, along with tandoori chicken and naan bread for lunch and dinner tomorrow." She grinned. "I've got to go to bed early tomorrow; have a hike in the morning. Hiking is good for me."

"I'll be happy when I can do that again."

Meri nodded. "Flat, level, non-rocky hikes for a long time, I would guess. Did you do your torture device?" she asked, pointing to the straps hanging over the closet door.

"Yes, and I haven't recovered today."

"Your pills!" said Meri. She brought two out, and Kandace swallowed them.

"Thank goodness I'm ahead. I'll be in slow-mo mode tonight."

"Get 'er done," said Meri. She took the empty plate and silverware back. "I'll fill up your tea before I leave."

"Love you," said Kandace.

"Love you back," said Meri. She finished cleaning up, filled up the carafe of tea, and kissed Kandace on the cheek. "I'm off to feed more people."

"Have fun," said Kandace. Meri laughed.

~

Kandace banged out her work, and was surprised when Davis showed up just when she was logging off. Sam ran up to greet him. Davis knelt to pet the cat after he shut the door and locked it behind him. "House calls? Really?" asked Kandace.

Davis laughed. "I had way too much coffee, I'm wide awake, and I heard from Len and Meri that you had a tough day." He grinned. "We can watch terrible reality TV and yell at the people."

Kandace snorted. "We could. The family with twelve wives and three husbands, the people on an island trying to build a raft to get off, or the ones racing across continents with solar cars?"

Davis went to the kitchen, grabbed a decaffeinated cherry cola, and popped the top. "Can I fill you up?"

"Same thing."

Davis handed her his soda, and got another one for himself. "Want some popcorn?"

"Absolutely." They ate popcorn and started with the twelve wives, then switched to the solar car race. The cars had some trouble getting over the Alps due to a sudden storm, but everyone made it through okay.

Davis gave Kandace the last pain pills of the night. "Take it easy on yourself, woman."

Kandace looked up at him. "Your whole family is full of overprotective people." She looked into his eyes and found herself falling into them.

He kissed her on the cheek, gently, his lips a whisper on her skin. "We love you. We watch out for people we love." The cat walked him to the door, and Davis locked the door behind him. Meri, Len, Davis, and Vic all had keys so they could check on Kandace. Kandace turned off the lights with her clicker and lay there in the dark feeling the touch of his lips on her skin.

BEAR

Kandace was sick of her four walls. She had no idea that there were that many shades of wood. The ceiling was vaulted in some sort of yellow wood that seemed to glow from the inside. The interior walls were blonde, brown, and even a nearly black wood. The little separate galley kitchen had wood stained red, with the little table in a cheery red and the chairs in a gold stain. It was small and beautiful. The windows showed trees everywhere surrounding the property and the road across the street. There were at least three trails she could see out of the floor-to-ceiling back windows.

Kandace decided she wanted to see the world outside her windows. She wasn't stupid, however. She put on both sunblock and bug repellent. She stretched and found the cat harness. She didn't want Sam getting out and not being able to find her way home. Sam warbled with the joy of being able to go out. Kandace slipped on low boots with side zippers over her socks, delighted she wouldn't have to tie up shoelaces with one hand. She wore shorts and a loose cobalt top she could get over her cast. "Wait a minute," she said to the cat, and grabbed some shades. She stepped out into the blinding sunlight, and felt like a prisoner escaping a cage. Sam kept pace with her halting steps, and Kandace shut the door behind her. She stood there for a long time, just smelling something other than the cat, food, medicine, and the strawberry-coconut cleanser she used on her body.

Kandace stepped completely out of the doorway, turned, and put her hand on the door, then closed it. The front door was a black wood with beautifully carved panels in it of bears, one sitting in front of a pot of honey with a paw inside, one sitting up under a tree, one walking in a forest, and one climbing a tree. It was weird and wonderful. She gently stroked the wood, and smiled at the whimsy, as she had the first day she'd moved in. She turned, stepped forward, and made her first shaky steps onto the porch. She very carefully went down the porch stairs one at a time. There were only two, but it seemed the most dangerous situation in the world to her. In moments, she stood on the ground, actual rocks under her feet. Kandace looked down at Sam who warbled encouragingly. "Left or right?" Kandace asked the cat. Sam turned her head to the left. "Left it is." Kandace slowly turned and walked to the left, her steps hesitant. She felt like a person locked in a cage who is suddenly released into the wide world. She made it around the corner and realized the porch was wrapped around the house. "We'll do that part next," Kandace told Sam. Sam sniffed and walked at Kandace's slow pace.

The woods beckoned. "I'm not that stupid," Kandace said to the cat. "No trail walking today." Sam chirruped. Kandace made it to the corner and turned. The trail led back, and from what she'd read before her sudden fall and slam into a cliff, Kandace knew it led to a lake. "Different day," Kandace informed herself and the cat. Sam chirruped again and sniffed a bush. The trees nearly touched over the top of the trail, creating an inviting bower of green.

Kandace made it around the back corner and loved the barbecue pit and the L-shaped outdoor couch. She said, "Let's finish the house perambulation, then the porch, then bring out drinks and a snack." Sam chirruped happily. They went over to inspect the furniture, and it was neither dusty nor covered with pollen because it had rained three days before. She went around the next corner and saw another trail. She sighed, resisting the urge. She swung around the front and climbed up the two stairs very slowly. She walked around the wrap-around porch, and even did a few lunges and warrior moves. She put her good hand on her knee, and said, "This is your home for....well, if I get enough money, maybe I'll even buy the place. Are you going to stick around if I drop the leash?"

Sam stepped forward and put a paw on Kandace's knee. She put her face in Kandace's and kissed her nose. "Lovely girl," Kandace said. Sam kissed her again. Kandace reached down and unsnapped the leash, leaving on the harness. Kandace hung the leash around her own neck.

Sam stayed at Kandace's left foot while Kandace did her slow warrior moves around the porch. It was lovely with a nice railing, Adirondack chairs, and even a porch swing. Kandace shuddered at the thought of being on something that she might fall out of, so she resisted the siren call of drinking sweet tea and rocking back and forth in the swing in the gorgeous sunshine that caressed the porch. Kandace walked entirely around the house, avoiding the water tank and the air/heating system on the side. There were solar panels on the roof, providing low energy costs.

Kandace turned the corner again, opened the door, and went back into the house. Sam followed her with another chirp. Kandace took the harness off the cat, hooked the leash back on it, and hung it up on the nail just inside the door. She also locked the front door. She went into the kitchen and grabbed something Meri had labeled "snack box". She put it into a canvas bag and also put in her tablet computer, head-phones, carafe of pink lemonade, a citronella candle and a matchbook, the small bottle of mosquito repellent, a small bowl and a bottle of water for the cat, and a can of soda. Kandace slowly walked out the back French doors, the cat still on her left, and set herself up on the couch with the cat on her hip, outdoor pillows under her legs. She arranged the food and drinks on the little round table next to her good arm, lay back, rested her arm on the arm of the couch, put in an audiobook, and relaxed. Sam sniffed bushes, but came right back to rest on the end of the couch, paws tucked under, head on her tail, and dozed in the summer sun.

Lunch was bread, cheese, sliced apples dusted with cinnamon, almonds, and roasted chicken. Sam asked politely for a little cheese and chicken, with a paw laid gently on Kandace's arm. Kandace grinned and obliged. Her audiobook finished, so she switched between reading a book and an article on how to recover from broken bones as quickly as possible without overstraining oneself.

Sam sat up straight, and Kandace looked out into the forest. A black bear came out of the forest and sat. It held up a paw in a wave, and Kandace waved back. It put its snout in the air, sniffing, and waved again. Kandace waved back. It had huge black eyes and a long snout. It had a round body with glossy bristling ebony fur and was obviously well fed. It pointed its paw at a bush with bright red raspberries. "Go for it, bear," said Kandace. She stroked the cat to keep her calm. "Don't worry, Sam," she told the cat. "I don't like raspberries." The bear lumbered over to the bush and used its mobile lips to pull the berries into its mouth. Kandace watched, smiling. She didn't feel fear. The bear seemed to be very polite and seemed to be far more involved in eating berries than people. Kandace alternated reading and watching the bear eat, listened to its—his, she saw—happy grunts.

The bear sat down and pointed towards the cat's water bowl. Sam sat regally and seemed to nod. "It's okay with the cat, so it's okay with me." The bear moved very slowly and stuck a tongue in the water. He slurped as he drank, making Kandace smile. Sam didn't seem perturbed as her water went into the bear instead of herself.

The bear backed away, turned toward the bush, and lumbered back. Kandace stroked Sam, who rumbled like a muscle car. The bear ate its fill from the bush, leaving some raspberries for later. The bear sat again and nodded at Kandace. It raised a paw. Kandace raised her hand. "You're a really nice bear. Come by anytime." The bear nodded, stood, turned, went back down on all fours, and lumbered down the path towards the lake.

Vic's truck rumbled up. Kandace waited until she heard the door slam. "Around back," she hollered.

Vic came around the side of the house, a bucket of chicken in one hand, a second bag of sides hanging from his wrist, and a tray of sodas in the other hand. "Girl, nice to see you up and about, but aren't you getting eaten up by the mosquitoes?"

"Nope," said Kandace, pointing at the still-burning, insect-repelling, citronella candle. "Citronella and mosquito repellent, a girl's best friends."

Vic unloaded onto the round table. "Got any repellent for me?"

Kandace handed him the bottle, and he smoothed it on. Kandace noticed his muscular arms while he did it. She fished out wet wipes for them to clean up, pulled out the sides, and slathered butter and honey on the biscuits. The cat meowed, and Kandace kicked the now-empty water bowl closer to her and un-breaded and tore up a chicken breast for the cat. Sam jumped down and began to eat.

Vic wiped off his hands, then opened a water bottle and poured it into the cat dish once the cat's chicken was gone, screwed the lid back on, sat down, and took out the potato salad and two sporks. "I hate sporks. Half-spoon, half-forks are just totally stupid."

Kandace laughed. "I agree." She grabbed a chicken leg. "How was your day?"

Vic sighed. "The usual. Pick up people who need help. Transport them to the hospital. I also rescued a little boy from climbing way too high in a tree, with the fire department. The boy knew me, so I climbed up the ladder and got him down. Jimmy Vacher. Lives in the next town over, Dichart. Named for Emmanuel Dichart, a forest baron. He died, the sawmill closed, and so did the button factory."

Kandace quit inhaling her chicken leg, and put the bones in the sack. She said, "Sad. What do people do around here?"

"We've got hiking, climbing, bungee-jumping for the crazy, back-packing, nature-watching, leaf-peeping in the fall, that sort of thing. My friend, Aunette Roundstone, refurbishes cabins all over these hills. She did this one, actually. People now have something they can rent out, make some money."

"Who owns this property? I pay some holding company." Kandace attacked the potato salad.

"My family's business. We put themselves as the layer between the people, most of them not trained in how to refurbish property, finance, and rent out the properties. So we refurbish and rent them out, and pay them the money after we take our cut. There's families all over this valley. People with falling-down cabins, shacks, and old stills now have a way to rent out the edges of their properties, so to speak. There's families that have been selling off for decades, and that's reversed. They're actually buying back their family land, not just paying the bills."

"Ah, and people like me rent out the refurbished cabins."

"Yes, and tiny houses too. There are leaf-peepers, birdwatchers, authors who want to get away from the world. Kayakers, hikers, insane-sport enthusiasts. We've got skateboarding, motocross, and X-game training in the summer. Lots of snowshoeing, snowboarding, cross-country and downhill skiing, and tobogganing in winter. The people around here make money from nature, so they are a lot more educated about environmental issues than most holler folk. They have a reason not to have a hog farm or chemical plant around here. The cows are grass-fed, the chickens in coops with yards. Gardens every-where. Orchards that actually produce fruit that is picked by real people."

Kandace pushed the potato salad away; she had eaten exactly half. "Like the raspberry bush over there." Kandace pointed. "The black bear really liked it."

Vic stopped, a chicken wing halfway to his mouth. "Black bear?"

"A very polite one." Kandace bit into her biscuit. She slowly, in between eating the biscuit and licking her fingers, told Vic the story of the bear.

He nodded and made noises other than biting chicken off the bone, little humming noises that let her know he was listening. When she finished he said, "Sounds like a real nice bear. I wonder which one it was?"

"Which one?"

"There are three around here. All roughly the same size. Those ones won't hurt you. Like you saw, they're more interested in berries than people. There are other ones, wild ones, but you can say the same about them, except for females and their young. All three of the local ones are male. So, no protect-the-cub issues."

Kandace grinned. "No lady bear yet."

"Not yet." Vic grinned.

NOOK

ovement made her sore as hell then, as she grew stronger and used abused muscles and joints, Kandace felt better and better. She still had a few weeks before getting the cast off, but she wanted to get out of the house.

Len had the perfect solution. "This is Romy," said Len, bringing her around the house to the back where Kandace had her breakfast. Romy was a teen with bright blue hair in pigtails, coffee-colored eyes and skin, and crimson lips. She had on platform black sandals, black cutoff shorts, and a *Morbid Angel* T-shirt. She had on eyeliner and black-and-silver makeup. She looked like a cast member of a goth movie.

"Hello," said Kandace.

Romy ignored Kandace and strode over to Sam. "You are a Maine coon. A little small for a coon. I will give you snacks, healthy ones." She held out her hand for Sam to sniff.

"That's Sam," said Kandace.

"Hello, Sam," said Romy. She stood and looked at Kandace. She held out a fist, and Kandace bumped fists with her. "I have a Jeep. I have been instructed to drive slowly to town. I work at a coffee shop, and will take you there three times a week. The owner loves cats, and it is not a problem to bring the cat." She looked down at Sam. "Sam, you will have your own pillows. A green one and a blue one."

"Price for this service?" asked Kandace.

"I get money for e-textbook rental and tuition for my online school," said Romy, her eyes on the cat.

"May I ask an extremely rude question?"

"Asperger's. I'm on the autism scale. I don't like eye contact or to be touched."

"You have to be who you really are. First step to awesomeness. I'm hiring you to drive, not get lovey-dovey."

Romy nodded. "Want to go now?"

"You may also have to carry stuff." Kandace pointed to her cast.

"Part of the deal," said Romy.

"Let's get packed." Len carried in the dishes and filled up the dishwasher while Kandace and Romy filled up the computer bag. Len brought her an empty cold-drink carafe, water bottle, and plastic bowl for the cat, and Kandace packed them. He also packed two of Kandace's pills. "So this is why you wanted to do the workout before breakfast," Kandace said to Len.

He grinned. "Baby has to get out sometime." Kandace laughed and pretended to take a swing at him. Len stepped away, laughing. Sam was very eager to step into her harness and chirruped, ready to go.

The jeep was a battered blue two-seater. The cat jumped onto the floor of the jeep, then Kandace got in. The cat hopped on her lap with a chirrup after politely waiting for Kandace to click her seat belt. Len shut the door. "Have fun! Vic will be by to pick you up after work."

"Thank you." Len kissed Kandace on the forehead and shut the door.

As promised, Romy took her slowly down the mountain. The coffee shop was actually only halfway down, weathered blue and gray wood with cedar shingles. There were lots of green plants all around the outside, and herbs in pots. There were fat, soft chairs outside on the verandah with pretty little carved tables. Romy went over and unlocked the door. There was a long bar in front of the window with bar stools covered in black tufted cloth, fat chairs around low tables, and a long coffee bar with interesting drinks including a wide variety of teas, Mexican hot chocolate, and many iced fruit, coffee, and chocolate drinks written in brightly-colored chalk with illustrations of tall glasses of teas and fat mugs of coffee. The side window looked out over a ravine with a stream at the bottom.

Once inside, Romy pointed to the far corner where there were low, fat, soft chairs similar to bean bag chairs, low tables, and fat floor cushions. Kandace realized that it was her own private nook. She slowly made her way over, dropped the cat's leash, and slid the over-stuffed computer case off her arm. She slid into the seat and reached for Sam. She got the cat's leash unhooked and put water from a water bottle in the dish for the cat. Sam sat on the green cushion and grinned a cat grin. Kandace petted Sam's head, and the cat chirruped.

Kandace pulled over a table and was surprised to find that it fit over her lap and tilted. "A computer desk!" she cried out. She set everything up and even found an outlet strip. She got everything plugged in, opened the laptop, and started work. Romy came, silently took her empty bottle, and filled it up. Kandace sipped and was pleasantly surprised to sip strawberry-watermelon juice. She put on her headphones and pounded out her work.

The coffee shop that seemed to be in the middle of nowhere next to a ravine was surprisingly busy. There were hikers, bikers, and locals in for lunches of sandwiches, salads, quiches, and fruits. Sam was a hit, visiting people, getting petted, and cadging bits of chicken or cheese.

Romy kept up with the orders, and a tall teen who actually spoke to customers showed up to help with the lunch rush. Romy came over just after the rush and said, "What do you want? I'm going on break, then I leave in an hour."

"Can I see a menu?" Romy sighed. "Wait, I'll go up." Kandace leveraged herself up and walked to the bar.

"Out of quiche," said Romy.

"Romy, remember, you must say something positive when you say something negative. Balances the equation." The tall girl smiled. She had auburn corkscrew hair, green eyes, and a ready smile. "I'm Colleen."

"Kandace."

"Our paninis are excellent," said Romy. "Other end of the equation."

Kandace grinned. "Can I have the brie and apple panini, salad with herbs with balsamic dressing, and a mint Mexican chocolate, iced?" She handed over her credit card.

Romy took the card and ran it through. "I'll drop it off."

Sam hopped up on the counter, sat, and stared, golden-eyed, at Romy. "I promised you treats," said Romy. "These are organic cat treats." She took two out and dropped them on the floor. The cat chirruped, then jumped down to eat the snacks. Romy cleaned the counter with disinfectant. "No cats on the counter," Romy informed Sam. Sam chirruped.

Kandace sat down, then bashed out more work after lunch. The cat perambulated, making friends with the afternoon crowd. She got a second order of the super-delicious Mexican mint chocolate and finished off a whole different segment of work.

Kandace was stunned when Davis came into the coffee shop. "What are you doing here?"

Davis pretended to be hurt. "I'll leave if you want."

Kandace laughed. "I thought you worked all the time during the day!" He bent down to kiss her cheek.

"I had some late shifts, so I'm off for a few days," Davis sat and gusted out a sigh. "Love the Ravine Coffee Nook." He put his refillable carafe down on a side table. "How's my favorite patient?"

"Len got me out of the house, and it's great. I let the cat out on my own bathroom break, and she was ready to come back in when I was finished." Kandace closed her notebook, unplugged it, and put it away.

"Smart cat." Sam came over and rubbed against him. He held out his hand, and the cat sniffed then demanded to be petted. Davis laughed and complied. "How was it with Romy?"

"Interesting girl."

Davis laughed. "She grows on you. Bright girl. She wants to be a neurobiologist."

Kandace grinned. "Woman makes a mean mint Mexican chocolate."

"Wow!" said Davis. "I should have ordered that. I just got a regular iced mocha." They both sipped their iced chocolate drinks. "I hear you saw a very polite bear?"

Kandace told him the story. "I hear there are three male bears that live in the area. No hunters?"

Davis cringed. "No, the people around here hunt deer only. In defense of the hunters, the deer are overpopulated with few natural predators. They starve if they aren't culled a bit. They aren't hunted on this mountain, but the surrounding ones. Nowhere near here, and the licenses are very specific." He sipped his coffee. "There are two female bears, but they don't go to your part of the woods. Hear your bear likes raspberries. Have to plant more bushes."

"I like the bear, and Sam didn't react as you would think. She was very calm and didn't need much reassurance." Kandace sipped more chocolate, and put away her headset and cords.

"Do you have to work more?"

"No, I want to take some time off. Getting out of the house seems to have hyper-focused me. Plus the awesome drinks and food."

"That's one of Meri's other jobs. She designed the menu here, delivers everything, and Libby, our other sister, bakes the panini bread, muffins, and croissants. Meri also, as you know, delivers food and creates meals for people too."

"She said some are injured, like me. Some are elderly, and some are just super-busy."

"One of them is a family with three sets of twins."

Kandace's jaw dropped as she was slipping the computer into its case. "Three?"

"Twins run in these mountains. Makes my job very interesting. Kids tend to fall out of treehouses, decide to go down hills on skateboards, that sort of thing. And, sometimes twins egg each other on."

"Kids. Have to super-love them, but if they weren't so cute, sometimes you'd want to kill them."

Davis laughed. "True. You want kids someday?"

"Absolutely, but not yet. I have to pay off every debt first. And I have some giant ones. I've already paid off the two smallest, and working on the third smallest now. I am doing this as fast as I can. All the injuries set me back. I am really happy that I paid for my own insurance with an accident rider. The deductible wasn't as high as it could have been, because I wasn't terminally stupid." Davis laughed. "I paid off all the medical stuff first. I just have to get this stupid cast off."

"Two and a half more weeks. Then freedom."

"Can't wait." Kandace held up her arm.

"How do you feel about a steakhouse?"

Kandace grimaced. "I'd feel like a child. Someone will have to cut up my bacon-wrapped chicken."

"I know the chef. It will come out that way, and your baked potato with everything?" Kandace nodded. "That will be cut up too. Do you like grilled mushrooms and red bell pepper?"

"Super love. Do they have desserts?" Kandace made sure the entire computer was in the bag, including all the peripherals and the cord.

"They have apple pie with cinnamon ice cream and caramel sauce."

"Let's go!" Kandace stood.

Davis laughed, stood, and took Kandace's computer bag. "They're not quite open yet. And we need to drop off Miss Fantastic too." Sam meowed and glared.

Kandace laughed. "Do they have outside seating?"

"Yes, actually, they do." He sighed. "Looks like kitty is getting chicken too." Sam chirruped at him, and he laughed. "I suggest a park first. A short walk to stretch your legs. The steakhouse is on the other end."

"Excellent," said Kandace. She stood, poured out the kitty water into a potted plant, and packed the bowl.

Davis led the cat and woman out to the truck, the computer bag slung over his shoulder. He helped Kandace up, and then lifted up the cat. "Oof!" he said as Sam curled up in Kandace's lap. "Have you been feeding her rocks?"

Kandace laughed. "No, just chicken." Sam chirruped, and they both laughed.

~

*D*avis parked in the middle of the street in front of a hardware store. The park was on the other end. The cat walked to the park, and Sam seemed to love it. She walked a half step before Kandace on the left, once again keeping to her slow pace.

Davis was full of stories about the town. "The hardware store is still owned by Reginald Eggars. His family dates back to one of the black regiments in the Civil War. His son Shawn went to college, and now he's the school principal. Eggars Junior, Skyler, is female, and already taking business courses in high school. Junior wants to take over the store."

"You're dug in."

"In these valleys, yes. There are three of them to choose from. There's a lot going on around here. Lots to see and do. Lakes to fish in, if that's your thing, water skiing if it isn't. Swimming. We've got the best swimming holes in the state."

"I like it because there are so many nice paths." Kandace grimaced. "Which I can't hike yet."

Davis grinned. "One day at a time."

"That's my line." They both laughed.

The steakhouse was a low brick building surrounded by ironwork. The patio was off to the side. The hostess opened the door, looked down, and smiled. "Hello, lovely," she said to the cat. Sam chirruped at her.

"That's Sam, and I'm Kandace." Kandace smiled.

"Very nice to meet you both. I'm Dannica. Davis, hello." Davis kissed her cheek. Dannica was lovely, with curly espresso hair with matching bright eyes, caramel skin, and slightly tilted eyes. She wore a white button-down shirt, black pants, shiny black shoes, and a black apron. Dannica looked down at the cat and said, "One moment." She took two steps back, grabbed two menus, and walked them around the building to the patio. The cat chirruped, obviously happy, and walked through the little gate. The cat approved of the two-top and went underneath the table. Davis pulled out the chair for Kandace. Kandace sat. "May I order?" Davis asked.

"I'll look at the menu first," said Kandace. "I might get tempted by something else."

Davis laughed. "By all means."

Dannica nodded, "I will send out your server. Water? Tea? Coffee?"

"Cola," said Kandace.

"Same," said Davis.

Kandace did find an appetizer she wanted. "I love bacon-wrapped shrimp," she said.

"That's a no-brainer," said Davis. Their server came out. "Jack!" said Davis. He stood, and the men hugged. Jack was huge, a bear of a man, with olive skin, a square jaw, and short black hair.

"Davis, nice to see you again! Miss..."

"Kandace," said Kandace.

Jack knelt and looked under the table. "Aren't you a lovely one," he said. Sam chirruped at him.

"That's Sam," said Kandace. "She'll be wanting some diced chicken, and she likes diced raw green beans."

"Of course," said Jack, standing again. He moved smoothly for a man his size. "Do you both like steaks?"

Davis nodded. "We would like to start with the bacon-wrapped shrimp, then one bacon-wrapped filet mignon, one chicken, loaded baked potatoes, and your roasted red peppers and mushrooms."

"Would you like clam or corn crab chowder with that?" asked Jack.

"Crab," said Kandace. "A cup, not a bowl."

"Clam chowder," said Davis. "A bowl."

"Excellent," said Jack. "Would you like a small Caesar salad?"

"That would be perfect with the shrimp." Kandace grinned. "I am ravenous today."

"I will be right back with your drinks," said Jack.

"Thank you," said Davis.

Jack left, and Kandace asked, "How do you know Jack?"

"He's the owner and a family friend. He wanted to offer us a tasting table in the kitchen, but milady here needed her outdoor space." Davis peered under the table and put his hand down. Sam rubbed her head on his hand and gave a low rumbling purr.

The dinner was exquisite. The cat got some chicken, green beans, and shrimp under the table. The dinner came with rosemary cheese bread with herb butter. They ate their fill and relaxed. They talked about the town, nature, the layout of the valleys that intersected on a watershed, the gorgeous summer weather. They kept it light, and Kandace felt herself completely relax.

~

Davis walked Kandace to the truck, a hand on her back. He helped maneuver her up, then handed in the very contented cat. Davis drove, and they listened to country music on the way back, both tired and logy after the huge meal. Davis walked them in, waited until both cat and human had used the restroom, and made sure Kandace was back in her recliner bed. He kissed her cheek. "You're exhausted."

"Am not." Kandace's voice was sleepy.

"Let me get you some pills." He got her a glass of water to go with her medications.

She took them, grimaced. "Want to watch a movie?"

"Of course." Davis kicked off his shoes, and took the couch after he made sure Kandace had a light sheet over her. The cat leapt up. They watched a science fiction Western about a colony world under siege. Kandace barely made it to the closing credits before falling asleep. Davis tiptoed out, found the key, and locked the door behind him.

REVELATION

*L*en arrived early. Kandace was already on her exercises. Len sighed. "Methinks you don't need me anymore. Your cast is coming off soon, and you know what to do and how to do it. You really can't level up until you get your cast off. I'll come back then, get you on the slow path to full use of the arm."

Kandace puffed on the exercise mat. She was doing very slow crunches, her arm tied to her body. "So, go away. Come back for lunch or dinner until the...unh...cast goes off." She carefully rolled to do leg lifts far enough over so her weight wasn't on her arm.

"Heard you went out with my brother."

Kandace's face went red with exertion—or embarrassment. "He asked me to eat dinner. I was hungry. We went."

Len grinned. "Good. Heard you saw a bear. A black bear."

Kandace grunted, and carefully rolled onto her other side. "Everyone wants to know about the bear."

"I hear Davis wants to plant raspberry bushes for the bear. Everybody likes berries." He narrowed her eyes. "You're dewy. I hear women don't sweat."

Kandace grunted and sweated as Len teased her. She finally went into her final stretches on her yoga mat. "Stop busting my chops and find out what Meri left me for breakfast." Meri was now delivering food that could be reheated, now that Kandace was more mobile.

"Get your own damn breakfast box, and I insist on a movie night."

"Hey, rude, dude," said Kandace. She finished her final stretch and rolled up the mat one-handed. "The movie night is good, but you have to make me my damn breakfast while I get cleaned up or no movie and popcorn for you."

"Fine. One breakfast coming up."

Len found some strawberry yogurt, cut up fruit, and poured orange juice into a sealed cup. He fed the cat, and Kandace came out of the bathroom, dressed, with wet hair. Len sighed and said, "Sit, eat, and I will braid your hair. It's getting long."

Kandace brought out a comb, brush, and hair tie. She handed them over and sat and ate and relaxed into Len's clever hands and hummed deep inside. Kandace loved getting her hair done, for anyone to touch her hair or her scalp. She'd been doing her own hair since she was seven. Kandace dropped a hair tie, and Sam had a wonderful time chasing it. "Kitty crack cocaine," said Kandace, and Len laughed. Len made a complex braid of her auburn hair, streaked with gold. "You should get paid for this."

"Who says I don't?" Len found a red hair tie for the braid, then stood and took the dishes back to the kitchen. Kandace followed him and he filled up her drink bottle while she rinsed the dishes and put them away in the dishwasher.

Kandace washed up, grabbed her bottle, kissed Len on the cheek, and said, "Tomorrow night, six o'clock." He grinned, and she followed him to the door and locked up behind him.

～

*L*en came alone to movie night when the sun was still in the sky, and they watched one about the first human to invent antigravity boots. They had fun making jokes about what people would do with the technology. They ate garlic naan bread with tandoori chicken, and the cat got tuna. Sam went from person to person, chirruping, demanding more love throughout the movie.

The final credits came up. Len kissed Kandace's cheek, and she kissed him back on his smooth, golden skin. "You know, Vic wants to spend time with you too."

"What the hell? Are you passing me around like candy?"

Len laughed. "Nope, just being fair. You're one of the most extraordinary people we've ever met, and we want you to get to know us, and we want to get to know you. You'll have fired all three of us permanently in a few weeks. Then...we'll see." He grinned, helped her clean up, and said, "I'll come back in two days. We can go for hikes. Very short ones." Len locked the door behind him.

Kandace's head spun. Getting to know her? Being fair? What the hell did all that mean? Was she a party favor or a person to them? She was exhausted, but decided to throw down a little bit of work. She did two of the things on her list then decided to crash. She wondered why all three brothers seemed to like spending time with her before she slipped into sleep.

~

The next day, Romy picked up Kandace and Sam after breakfast. Sam the cat was overjoyed, for she got love from the residents, hikers, and nature enthusiasts, and gave loud rumbles, chirps, and head butts in return. Kandace was able to compress her work into high-intensity work blocks, fueled by Mexican iced chocolate and paninis. Romy found that Kandace was willing to listen to her college dreams and help her choose the best classes to take to get rid of the "baby classes" of the first two years of college. She was true-Goth, with a slightly depressive outlook and an appreciation for death metal music. "Death is a part of life," Romy told Kandace.

"Have you ever been to *Dia de los Muertos* in Mexico?" asked Kandace, referring to Mexico's Day of the Dead.

"No, but I want to go."

"What's your plan to go?"

"My plan?"

"Well, if you have something you want to do, write it down. Then make a list of what needs to be done for that to happen. Then break what you want to do into small chunks, and do a little every day, week, or month until you get it done."

"I will do that," said Romy. A customer came up to the coffee bar, and Romy said, "I must go."

~

*V*ic came to pick up Kandace and Sam, dropped off the cat and computer at the cabin, and drove Kandace to the town park for a walk and some conversation. "I love what I do. Keeping people alive until a doctor can get to them." He bought Kandace some ice cream from a little shop. "What about you?"

"I love what I do. I get pay increases with each contract, and I am being sought out for side jobs. I'm bashing out the next school loan. Living here is so much cheaper than lots of other places." She licked her chocolate mint ice cream cone. Vic gave Kandace a strawberry ice cream smile. "You look like you suddenly chose to wear lipstick."

"Are you criticizing my fashion choices?" asked Vic and licked his lips.

"Never."

"Good. Can't have that." They turned around the corner, walked past an antique store, and Kandace stopped at the bakery. The smells drew Kandace in. A beautiful black-haired woman with tilted brown eyes and skin like steeped tea wearing a pale blue apron was behind the counter. She looked a lot like Meri.

Kandace walked up to the counter. "Quick. Warm brownie before the ice cream melts."

The woman laughed and said, "Pecan?"

"Absolutely." The woman plated a brownie and popped it in the microwave. Kandace paid for it, and then the woman handed her the plate and a small spoon. "We'll chat post-brownie goodness."

Kandace grinned. She then put her cone on the plate next to the brownie, sat down, and began to eat. Vic grinned and finished his strawberry cone. "Thanks, Libby. Chocolate emergency, apparently." He accepted a wet napkin from his sister.

"Women have those, Vic," said Libby, with a huge smile. "Get with the program."

"Yes, ma'am."

Kandace took in the byplay while moaning with pleasure. She finished and said, "Pecan with sea salt caramel? Why didn't I hear about you before?"

"You mean Len never told you about Libby?" Vic asked, shocked.

Libby narrowed her eyes. "That no-good, dirty, low-down son of a...He's courting you, and he doesn't mention his sister?"

"Wait a minute. Len took me on short hikes. Really short, with lots of sunblock, and insect repellent. I thought it was part of my physical therapy. Vic, you took me for ice cream, and Davis took me out for dinner. You're all...dating me!"

Libby went over to the door and flipped the sign to Closed. She then locked the door. "We were going to close in fifteen minutes anyway, I've been up since four." She then walked very deliberately over to Kandace, and held out her hand. "Hello. My name is Liberty Ann Camber. Please call me Libby."

Kandace shook her hand. "Nice to meet you."

"I know all about you, but you apparently know little to nothing about our family, or how we...date," said Libby.

"Libby, the woman doesn't have her cast off until next week, and she could club us to death."

"I could, once I know what the hell is going on. Quick, get it out while I'm high on chocolate, pecans, caramel, mint, and sugar."

Libby snorted. "Good point. Anyway, Len probably told you we have the same father, different mothers. And that his brother died when they were young."

"Yes," said Kandace.

"Our family tends to date...siblings. Or the siblings tend to date one person everyone falls in love with." Libby grimaced at the stunned look on Kandace's face. "Put aside the fact that both Len and Davis have medical, and by that I mean business, relationships with you, and didn't wait until you were healed and not seeing them for medical reasons. That's skeevy, and I'm pissed at them both. Vic here is the only one legitimately courting you."

"Okay, skeevy. Less skeevy than three men trying to do...what, date me at once?"

Vic held up a hand. "Getting to know you. Pre-dating, so to speak. Please don't hurt my brothers. Or me."

"Pre-dating and dating are the same damn thing," said Libby. "I know, it has a no-sex rule, but so does courting."

"Courting?" asked Kandace. "Are you in some weird sort of cult? Or dating with some sort of religious strictures?"

"Both and neither," said Vic.

"That's clear as mud," Kandace snapped. "Speak truth."

Vic sighed. "We're a family that believes in Nature. Most creatures in nature are polygamous. They date more than one partner, and may have family groups consisting of multiple children from multiple partners." Vic's voice was low but clear, raspy with emotion.

"And yes, most animals have gay couples too. And bisexual ones. But Len, Vic, and Davis are all straight, and they are all attracted to you," said Libby. "I'm the bi one of the family. Makes sense with the number of kids Dad had. Percentages and all."

Vic grunted, and turned to Kandace. "You are extraordinary. You are so small but strong. Highly intelligent. Wise beyond your years. You love the natural world, and adopted a cat. We all think you are amazing. You also smell..."

"Like candy to my brothers. Pheromones that they scent. You do diddly and squat for me, but my brothers are all highly attracted to you." She glared at Vic. "They are supposed to claim their courting intentions, and explain what's going on to you at the beginning."

"Cast not off yet," said Vic, through clenched teeth.

"So, your mothers..." Kandace tried to pick her jaw up off the floor.

"One dad," said Libby. "Two moms, and they all live together." Kandace sat there, frozen. Libby reached out and touched her hand. "My brothers are all such exceptional people. This is weird, I know, in more ways than one." Vic glared at her, but Libby shot daggers at him with her eyes. Libby turned back to Kandace. "It means that you will be loved, nearly worshiped. You will have whatever you want or need. Love, companionship, help with kids."

"Kids?"

"Do you want them?"

"I do. Later. I need to pay off..."

"Your school loans. I get that. Pay them off yourself, or ask the family for help. With so many people working and paying into the coffers, we can draw enough to live on if we want. But, none of us want that. We want to work and pay into the coffers, for our children, for our mothers and fathers for when they get old, for the insurance and money to start businesses or university tuition for everyone." Libby sat down and kept her eyes firmly on Kandace's face.

"The holding company," said Kandace slowly. "You're the ones revitalizing the area."

"Trying to," said Vic. "It's slow progress. We can't just reopen the button factory. Not a cost-effective business. We have other businesses. For instance, Libby's bakery. She has two students working here and a single mom."

"You all work in the medical field," said Kandace, focusing on Vic. The hurt in her eyes made Vic quail.

"We do. We should have gone into things where we could hire people. It took a long time to donate to the hospital and open the clinics."

Kandace stared at him. "You're millionaires?" she squeaked.

"Not exactly," said Libby. "Keeping this town and the ones around here going is expensive. We kind of...goose things a little."

Kandace stood. "I must go home. Vic, tell Len his services are no longer needed. Neither are yours. I'll have to find another doctor to get this cast off. None of you come over or near me." She looked over at Libby. "Did Meri know they were courting me?"

Libby said, "I can't speak for her, but I doubt it. That they were interested, probably." She said quietly, "Please sit."

To her own surprise, Kandace sat. "What is it?"

"Might as well rip the bandage completely off," said Libby. "This is a secret, more so than the fact we've been trying to revitalize the area. You can't tell anyone about either one."

Kandace slowly nodded. "Are you raising bears?" she said, flashing back to her raspberry-loving visitor. "An animal sanctuary?"

Vic choked, and Libby snorted. "No," said Libby. "We don't raise the bears. We are the bears." She stepped back, and Kandace was stunned when Libby went over, closed the blinds at the front of the store, then stripped naked. In a flash, a glow of light, she was a bear, small, black, and dark-eyed. She sat and held up a paw.

Kandace saw intelligence in those dark brown eyes, the same as with the bear that sat so politely in her backyard. "Len's my raspberry thief," said Kandace woodenly. She knelt, and when Libby raised her paw, she touched the paw. Kandace stood, nodded, and said, "You are beautiful." She stumbled towards the door. "Do not, under any circumstances, call or try to contact me in any way, none of you. I'll call an Uber." She choked. "Or walk." She unlocked the door and stumbled out, carefully shutting the door behind her so that no one could see the...

The bear.

LION HEART

Kandace woke up late. She felt exhausted, gritty, and angry. Hurt. She stumbled to the bathroom and found Sam staring at her when she got out. "Food, I get it." She had perfected opening the cans of cat food one-handed using a butter knife. She mixed half a can of wet cat food with kitty crunchies and carefully lowered the plastic cat bowl to the floor. Kandace checked the water which was strangely chilly next to the tile floor. She screwed off the top of the tank and put in some ice cubes from the freezer. She screwed the top back on, and refilled the ice tray.

Breakfast was orange juice, a banana nut muffin, butter, and a small bowl of strawberries. Kandace stumbled to the bathroom, slipped on the plastic sleeve that encased her arm, and took a shower. The shower was small, so she kept her arm out of the water. She got out, dried off, put on lotion, and was glad she'd left in the complicated braid. She had work to do, other things to do with her fingers. She managed to get her blue running shorts and big red New Orleans T-shirt with the jazz trumpeter on the front in gold on over her head.

Kandace tried to focus, but she wanted to throw things rather than work. She did some work, stood up, walked around, grabbed a soda, and tried to re-focus. It didn't work. She stood back up, which forced the cat to move. Sam glared at her. Kandace did her stretches, and was surprised at how much range of motion she had. She tried not to cry. Her brain was whirring so fast it sounded like a blender to her. She had to get out of the house.

Kandace put on sunblock and insect repellent. Sam chirruped, ready to go. Kandace grabbed her walking stick, went out, the cat at her side, and looked back and forth. She chose the path on the right. She walked absurdly slowly, pushing sticks and small rocks out of the way with her staff. Tripping would hurt and may re-injure her arm and ribs. Her ribs still twinged. The cat stepped forward, enjoying the dappled sunlight coming down from in between the bower of trees. There were mushrooms under the trees, ferns, vines twining. Kandace also spotted poison ivy, and marked the spot by punching three holes in the ground with the stick. She would have it removed later. Or wait until she felt better and take it out while wearing a hazmat suit.

She walked out, listening to the enormously loud drone of the insects. Suddenly, the droning hitched and stopped. The cat lifted her head, sniffed, then turned and pushed on Kandace's leg. "Hey!" said Kandace. There was a cough to the right, and Kandace slowly turned.

The mountain lion was tawny, with white, bushy fur in her ears. Her eyes were yellow, and she was crouched on a stump. Sam hunched her back, her fur splayed, and hissed.

"Get the hell out of here," said Kandace. She got into the warrior pose, and held up her staff. "You will not harm my cat."

The mountain lion stood, then sat, just like a dog. It raised a paw in greeting.

"Oh, shit. Fine. But I insist on talking like a human. I'll leave a robe out for you to get dressed." The mountain lion coughed. "Good, that's settled," said Kandace. She turned and began to walk back. "Come on, Sam."

Sam hissed. Kandace knelt, looked Sam in the eye. "I swear, the mountain lion will not hurt us." She called behind her. "I'm sorry about your having to get nude, but my cat will keep trying to protect me."

There was a flash behind her, and a female voice behind her calmly said, "I don't really have a problem with nudity."

"Great," said Kandace. She petted Sam's head and stood. The cat's fur slowly returned to normal.

Kandace slowly turned, and the woman standing there was beautiful, with sharp cheekbones, a flat nose, golden skin, and slightly tilted eyes. She had a Venus de Milo thing going on with her, a fall of blue-black hair covering her small breasts. "I'm Lynette Camber."

"Len's mother. I'm..."

"Kandace and Sam. Sorry for scaring your cat. She's beautiful." Lynette gestured towards the cabin. "Lead on."

Kandace turned and made her slow way back to the house. "Not sorry for scaring me?"

"If I'd shown up in my bear form, you would have thought I was one of the boys," said Lynette, drawing even with Sam. Sam sniffed her leg and ran ahead.

"Shapeshifters can shift into more than one thing?" asked Kandace. "I can't believe I'm having this conversation. Lynette, I'm a holler girl."

"You went to college, all through graduate school."

"But not far. I'm still a holler girl. Still loving that sound," she said, as the loud sound of droning insects started up again.

Lynette grinned. "A holler girl. Well, I'm not. We're originally from the other side of the world, three generations ago. My last name was Choi. The Korean black bears were hunted during the war and after. Not many animals survived. Some deer, squirrels, chipmunks, but nothing bigger. No shapeshifters. My great-grandmother and some other relatives got out before the war, scattered themselves in the wild places. Intermarried, hence the puma genes. Any member of that family that stayed..." Her voice cut off.

"I'm sorry," said Kandace. They made it to the edge of the forest, and stepped out into the sunlight. They crossed the yard more quickly. Kandace let Lynette and Sam in, strode to the living room, and came back with a red silk robe.

"Appropriate. Thank you." Lynette put on the robe.

"Would you like a soda?"

"Coke, if you have it. I'll get it. You sit down." Kandace sat at the kitchen table, and Lynette got two Cokes out of the refrigerator and sat down as well. She moved with catlike grace, like Sam on steroids. Lynette popped both tops and pushed one over to Kandace.

"So, what's with the mountain lion visit? Scoping me out?"

"That, and making sure my boys obeyed. You told them to stay away. The other two will, I think. But Len...He's touched you, gotten your scent in his nose. He loves you absolutely, you know. He won't intend to violate your strictures. But his bear self will come sniffing around, literally."

"So, either I date them, or him, or I move away."

"Far away." Lynette sipped her Coke. "I love all my sons. Just because they weren't born to my body, that sort of thing means nothing to us. Kids are kids. Bumbling, stumbling through life, craving sweet things, fighting, wrestling in the yard."

"I can't tell if you're talking about baby boys or bear cubs."

Lynette laughed. "We start the change at elementary school age, five or six. I really don't see much of a difference between the two. They're smart, strong, intensely loyal."

"And love sweets." Kandace remembered how all of them drank sodas on movie nights, chowed down on the sweets Libby made.

Lynette nodded. "Those are my boys. Now, I know this is a lot to take in. I also know that my young men love you. They—we—trust you with our secrets. We know you are trustworthy."

Kandace sighed. "I am. One, even if I told people, everyone would think I'm nuts about the shapeshifter thing. I have no interest in spending my damn time in a padded room."

Lynette nodded. "Probably would be the end result."

Kandace nodded once, hard. "Two, I'm a holler girl, raised on stories of *haints*—that's ghosts. Never saw one. But I know there's more out there than we know." She rubbed her face. "Absolutely know, at this point."

"So, the choice is yours. You're an adult, more so than most of the females around here. My boys can spread their net wider. Medical work means they meet a lot of people. More so with hiking and rock-climbing. But no one has turned their heads. No one."

"No one? Meaning no prom, no kissing behind the barn, no sweaty times in trucks or hatchbacks or by the lake?"

Lynette doubled over with laughter. She gasped, coughed, righted herself. "Yes, they did. They were normal boys. They had crushes." She took a sip of her Coke. "And sex. With condoms. We are really clear that you don't go dropping shifter babies all over the place. Davis got himself...he's sterile now. He said it can be reversed. Did it when he started medical school. Didn't understand why he would do it, but then someone else in their program said she was pregnant with his baby, tried to get him to marry her, pay all her medical costs. Davis said it wasn't possible, had proof of his vasectomy. She dropped out." Lynette shook her head. "Damn shame. We need more female doctors. But, we do need less liars," she said, with narrowed eyes. "Turns out her sister put her up to it, and that the baby's daddy was a physician's assistant at the same hospital and was in on the whole thing, a shake-down. The man got fired, and last I heard, the woman married the baby's father and moved out of state."

"I'm not a liar. My Program insists upon rigorous honesty." She looked at Lynette. "You got a problem with my being a drug addict and an alcoholic?"

"Nope. My father was in the Program. Got off alcohol before I was born because both his wives threatened to divorce him."

Kandace raised her eyebrows. "Wow. Complex family."

"You have no idea. I'm the forward scout. I like your bluntness and rigorous honesty, as you put it. And we can trust you. And my boys wouldn't make a horrible mistake in picking a woman to love. One might, but all three? No way."

Kandace narrowed her eyes. "They lied. By omission."

"You're recovering from a horrific accident. They jumped the gun. They were counseled to wait to court you, with all of the truth on the line, but you kept inviting them to movie night and things like that. They got impatient to get to know you."

Kandace snorted. "They didn't inform me, clearly, about the idea that all three would date me, and I thought I would eventually..." Her voice trailed off.

"Have to choose among them. Such stupid boys." She reached out, gently took Kandace's good hand in hers. "You don't have to choose. Each one has such different personalities. Vic is the daredevil, but is careful to protect himself and others. Davis is the scientist, analyzes everything to death, but has enormous compassion. And Len, he is the most Zen of them all. If you say you won't date all three, he will handle it better than the others would."

"What is it like, dating more than one person? But you didn't..." Kandace trailed off, confused.

Lynette laughed. "Dating includes the sister wife or wives. Or brother husbands. We need to get to know each other too. No control freaks, no manipulators or liars. Those people kill marriages dead. We need real, honest, genuine people. And sometimes we share a bed, love him together."

Kandace put a hand over one ear. "Too much information."

"Sorry. I'm telling this to you for a reason. They are brothers, and they dated the same woman once. Becky. Flight attendant. But she flew away, and never learned our family secret."

"Well. Okay."

"Your head is spinning. I can see it whirling behind your eyes." Lynette stood. "I will leave you now. Call Meri or Libby if you want to speak to me. This lifestyle is for the rare person who can love without jealousy. Without the games most people play. You will be free to make any decision you so desire, but once you choose, you will be in a web of family and responsibilities, obligations. Wait until you get your cast off. Heal. Take your time. You don't have to jump in with both feet."

"I can court, and then stop if I want to, and no sex until the decision is made?"

"Yes. The sex stricture about courting is because that changes everything, bonds people. You must be sure you want the bond."

Kandace nodded. "I'll talk to all three if I want that."

Lynette nodded. "All right. I'll pass that on." She finished her Coke, rinsed out the can, crushed it easily with one hand, and put it in the recycling under the sink. "So, you want to court my boys?"

"I can't stop thinking about them. All three of them. But they'll have to wait. Dating with a cast is damned inconvenient."

"I'll pass on that message too. I take it you want the cast off. An X-ray, and..." Lynette made a snipping motion with her hands.

"My first shower without a cast." Kandace grinned.

"Next week. Thursday," said Lynette. "Ten o'clock. Mountain Breeze Medical and Urgent Care." Lynette took out a card and laid it on the tiny kitchen table. "Call if you need anything." She stood.

"Thank you," said Kandace. She stood as well.

Lynette smoothly slid off the robe, folded it, and laid it over the back of her chair. She opened the door, and went out, shutting the door behind her. Her lithe body stepped forward, and the light came back. The mountain lion looked back with yellow eyes and lifted a paw. Kandace waved back. The mountain lion bounded forward and ran into the forest.

Kandace shut the door then looked at the cat. Sam stared calmly up at Kandace. "Well, that just happened," said Kandace to the cat. "Three men want to date me, all of them intelligent and sexy, and don't forget rich. They have two mothers, and a web of family ties of people marrying multiple people and having kids. What the hell would Lynette be if this went forward? A mother-in-law, one of two?" She rubbed her face. "Then there's the fact they can turn into animals." Sam chirruped. "No offense," said Kandace. She bent down and petted the cat. "Well, I have work. Let's get to it." The cat chirruped again, and Kandace stretched and padded back to her chair to work.

Not that she got much work done that day, her mind whirring. She looked up data about shifters, and found so much fiction, legend, and conflicting stories that she gave up and tried once more to work on her checklist. She had no idea what she was going to do.

Shifters are real. Holy shit. And three bears want to date me. She looked at her red hair and snorted. *But I'm not Goldilocks, am I?*

CAST OFF

They met at the trailhead, all three shifter brothers in shorts, hiking boots, and short-sleeved shirts, all with small packs on their backs. Davis wore black shorts and a shirt that wicks away sweat that was more expensive, a name brand in black, with the distinctive swoosh. The other two didn't wear name brand attire. Len had yellow stripes running down the side of his neon-red shirt and dark blue shorts, and Vic had a gray top and black shorts. They each took a sip of water and began to hike.

"She got her cast off yesterday," said Vic.

Len sighed. "We know. We can't descend upon her like a Mongol horde."

"Your ancestors, not mine," said Vic.

Davis snorted. "We all love her. We all kept two huge secrets from her. We all feel she is the right, correct, and true mate."

"Right, correct, and true?" Vic stared at his brother. "Have you been reading legal briefs in your spare time?"

"He's not wrong," said Len. "She is the right one for us."

"We know that." Davis shifted his weight, worked to keep up with angry Vic. "How can we convince her of that?"

Len shrugged. "I'm planning on apologizing profusely, then just being myself. It's not as if we need to put on an act with her, one she'll see right through and hate us for later."

"Mongol Man is right," said Vic. "We have to be who we really are."

Davis shook his head from side to side, as if he were in bear form. "She knows we're rich. The cat's out of the bag on that one. But the only thing money means to her is paying off her debts, and she doesn't need us to do it. In fact, if we offered, I think she'd be insulted."

Vic took a peanut butter chocolate crunch bar out of his pack, shouldered the pack, and consumed the bar. His brothers stared at him. "What?" Vic stuffed the wrapper into a bag, then shoved the bag back into his pocket.

"We just ate at Libby's. How many calories do you need?" Bears burned a lot of calories, but Davis was professionally worried at this point.

"Terror eating," said Len.

"I thought that was nervous eating," said Davis.

"Nope, he's terrified she won't choose us, or him. He broke the news to her or was there when Libby did. He's afraid all her backwoods rage will focus on him." Len deliberately slowed, and Davis tried not to groan in relief.

"Quit talking about me as if I'm not right here," said Vic.

"I'm terrified too, and I'm hiking, not stress eating," Davis offered.

"Terror eating," said Len.

"I am not terror eating, whatever that is!" said Vic. He stomped ahead.

"Touchy," said Len.

"Do you think we're too hard on him?" asked Davis. They watched Vic climb some stairs carved out of rock and disappear around the corner.

"Nope. He's got to learn to control emotions like terror or annoyance if he's going to win our girl."

"She won't put up with it. Even after severe injuries, our girl literally came out fighting. Damn near broke another doctor's nose." Davis grinned at the memory.

"She's probably going to be more pissed at you." Len pulled slightly ahead. "You dated her, took her to a swanky restaurant, while you were still technically her doctor. As Libby put it, skeevy."

"I honestly didn't look at it that way. You two got to spend more time with her than I did. And our mothers have told us that each person falls in love at a different rate, in a different way." They began climbing the stairs carved out of rock. "I just wanted to get to know her and wanted to get her out of the house. You're the one that told me she was super-sick of being cooped up in the cabin."

"You could have taken her out for ice cream. Or to Libby's. Or just walked around."

"I could have," said Davis evenly. "But I got just as wrapped up in her as the two of you did. Libby and Meri were right. We should have stuck with movie nights, gotten glimpses of her from time to time, shared information, and worked on the friendship thing first."

They reached the top of the stairs, turned left around the curve. Vic was still up ahead. Len sighed. "We're all equally responsible for screwing up. We've all got to make abject apologies and see how much she'll let us in. We've got to earn her trust."

"Once you lose it, you can't always get it back." Davis wanted to terror eat himself.

They caught up with Vic on the stairs. Vic glared at both of them. "We can't fuck up again. Hurry up, I want to apologize to her after this." Len started to hum the old song "You Can't Hurry Love" as all three men picked up the pace.

~

*K*andace banged out another set, thinking of the shower she'd get. The video was of standing yoga stretches, such as arrow-meets-warrior pose. No bodyweight was allowed on her bad arm. She thought about having a second blessed shower after her workout. She eyed the half-kilo weights, but the urgent care doctor had been clear. No weight, not yet. Libby went to the torture loops hanging over the door, and huffed, puffed, and occasionally screamed her way through some poses. Sam watched, bemused, and licked her ankle.

Kandace took a hot shower and used a sugar scrub with honey to scrub herself. She used a back scrubber to get everywhere. She got out, steamy with smooth skin, lotioned herself up, and was overjoyed at finally being able to use two hands. One was clumsy as hell, as if she'd never used it before, so she put her hair up in a high ponytail. *Have no idea why they want to date me.* She stepped back and looked in the mirror and changed her mind. Her ribs were no longer taped, and she stood tall. She'd lost weight while flat on her back, surprising herself. But the first two weeks she hadn't wanted to eat, and she'd been pushing herself. Far too hard, according to the doctor. Her leg muscles were corded from all the squats and lunges, her belly nearly flat from the reps she'd been able to do once the fire from her broken ribs had faded. Standing abs exercises, but reps, nonetheless. She had taken what Len taught her and pushed it a tad too far. *Story of my life,* she thought.

She dressed in cutoffs, and was able to get a sports bra on for the first time. She grinned. She put on a much-smaller T-shirt from the loose ones she had been wearing and shorts, both blue. She looked up. She could use the loft now, but she didn't feel like pulling herself one-handed up the ladder, and her other arm would be injured if she slipped and used it to break her fall. She looked at her recliner and sighed.

There was a knock on the back door, and Kandace, shocked, rushed to open it. Sam followed, chirruping. Meri came in, and put the canvas bags of groceries on the kitchen table. "Love, if you want to fire me, do it, but you said you hate to cook..."

"Hate, despise, violently oppose." Meri snorted. "Besides, I can afford you." She shut the door. Sam sat and meowed.

"Very well." Meri fished out a can, opened it, and laid three treats on the floor. Sam sniffed them appreciatively then began to gobble them up.

"Now that you're done spoiling my cat, what's for breakfast?"

"You do realize that your breakfast is everybody else's lunch?" said Meri. She shoved over a bag. "Put these away."

"Don't just do something, stand there!" said Kandace. She reached for the food.

Meri laughed. Kandace handed it all over—peanut butter, cat food, cat treats, fruit, vegetables, wonton wrappers, tortillas, hefty cans of soup, medium ones of crabmeat, and tiny cans of green chiles, meats, cream cheese, cheddar-jack shredded cheese in a plastic bag, yogurt in strawberry and peach. "The secret is to marinate," said Meri. She pulled out three plastic bags, and filled each one with different sauces and spices—olive oil with cracked black pepper and five-spice Italian seasoning, honey mustard with lime and fresh sprigs of rosemary, taco seasoning, and the brown sugar and spices needed for a rub. The diced pork went in with the taco seasoning, chicken breasts into the olive oil one, chicken legs and thighs into the honey mustard one, and two racks of ribs got a rub. She refrigerated all of it, and washed her hands.

"I am in awe," said Kandace. "I'm also ravenous."

"Crab rangoons and stir-fried pork. Sort of a mu shu with hoisin sauce, without the pancakes."

"I love you." Kandace grinned sappily.

Meri laughed. "Go work."

Kandace went back to her chair and banged out some work, desperately trying to ignore the fantastic smells coming from the kitchen. "Food!" said Meri. Kandace stopped at the end of a coding line, stood up, and went to the galley kitchen. She washed her hands, and Meri plopped down opposite Kandace. "I'm inviting myself to lunch."

"Duh, anytime. Except if I have a horrible deadline, but that's rare these days. I do try to work ahead, if the code lets me."

"If the code lets you?" asked Meri and poured the lime-honey tea.

"It has a mind of its own."

They ate in companionable silence until both were finished. "I am amazed again. Wow."

Meri stood, brought the dishes one step to the sink, rinsed the dishes, and put them in the dishwasher. "My mama says you've agreed to court my brothers."

"I did. But they're going to have to crawl through broken glass after not telling me what the hell was really going on."

"About the shapeshifting?" asked Meri, drying her hands.

"No, that I get. Are you a bear?"

"Bear, small wolf. So, I've got some mixed genetics, like the boys. But the wolf is really hard, and ranchers around here are afraid wolves will eat their livestock. Bears don't eat chickens, so they're left alone around here." She sat down. "You're avoiding answering the question."

"There are three of them that want to date one of me, and none of them made that clear. Or that the point would be for me to fall in love with and marry all three of them."

Meri nodded. "Are you pissed at me for not telling you?"

Kandace said, "I should be, but no. That was their job, and they didn't do it."

"Fair enough," said Meri.

"Have you...dated?" asked Kandace.

Meri shook her head. "I'm too busy right now. Dating one person is a lot of work and...well, I've talked to Libby. I think we want...one, like our moms. We both love *me time*."

Kandace said, "I have got to stop having my jaw hit the floor. You and Libby want to share a man?"

"Probably. We'll find someone," said Meri. "It takes time. The boys were getting really tired of looking. You're what all of them want, all of them need. Beautiful, funny, smart, don't take shit from anyone. Even damaged, in enormous amounts of pain, you tried to be cheerful, and made it clear why when you were snarly. You work your program, try to be the best you that you can be. You're their unicorn, their special creature that might run away at any time."

Kandace's eyes grew hard. "I don't run. And I'm right pissed that it was nearly six weeks before anyone bothered telling me the truth. And I'm not some sort of unicorn with rainbows coming out my ass, leaping through the meadow. I'm me, and I'm awesome. And probably the only one in three counties strong enough to handle all these damn secrets. Eye-popping, brain-melting secrets. Not one of you Cambers thought to tell me a damn thing. I've changed my mind. Get the fuck out of my house. For now."

Meri stood. "I deserved that. Once. Don't ever talk that way to me again and expect to be friends. It's not just my secret, you heifer. It's family after family, cascading through the valleys around here. If our secret got out, people would come here, poke, prod, kidnap. Steal our people, our children. Destroy our way of life. A lot of us work in the community, have positions of authority, like Davis. He's an amazing doctor. No one would let him treat people if they found out he could turn into a bear. They would be afraid, although each and every one of my brothers would literally die for others. Vic risked his life to save yours. You got one time to poke at them too. Once. One time. You ever bring it up again, I'll put salt in your food and burn everything. You hear me?"

"I do." Kandace put her jaw back in place, stunned.

"I'd better leave before I keep talking. You protect our secret with your entire existence, girlfriend. It's worth ours to us." Meri went out the back door, and it clicked shut behind her.

Sam came out from under the table, stood up, and put a paw on Kandace's leg. Kandace stroked her. "I'm sorry, pretty kitty. Aunt Meri just told me how it was. Shoulda figured it out my own damn self." She put her head in her good hand and sat there for a long time. She stood up, shaking with emotion, stretched, then went back to work. She had apologies on her brain the entire time, Meri's look of fear in those beautiful eyes clear in Kandace's mind. They had a secret that they had to keep that was worth their lives. She began to understand their point of view a little better.

~

*V*ic was the first to arrive the next afternoon. Kandace was in back, pounding out coding. "I come in peace," he said. He walked up to her, sat down. He put two paper sacks down on the table in between them. "Kandace, we kept two enormous truths from you, and if we were going to wait, it should have been absolute until you were fully healed. Or we should have told you when we first realized your character, that we could trust you. We screwed up both ways, and I am so very sorry I acted that way."

Kandace held up a finger, and tapped out her line of code. "Sorry, this is just nasty code here." She closed the laptop, put it aside. "I get that one of your secrets could get you killed, but the other one should have been on the table."

"I know and I'm sorry," said Vic. "I promise to practice what one of our moms calls your 'rigorous honesty'. No more secrets. Unless it's not mine to tell, or will harm someone if revealed. I do ambulance and rescue work and know a bit more about the towns around here than is good for me."

"I get that, but you owe me a huge amends."

"I brought peanut butter shakes and something Libby calls a 'peanut mint chocolate fantasy'. It's a muffin."

"Give," said Kandace, holding out both hands. Vic put the shake into her strong hand, and the muffin into her still-weak one. Kandace sipped the shake, swooned, and bit into the still-warm muffin. She chewed, swallowed, and said, "Forgiven."

Vic laughed. "Thought you'd like it."

Kandace ate two more bites and said, "Peanuts dusted on top, peanut butter, mint and chocolate mini-chips throughout, and a chocolate cake base. Tell her I will buy her out and freeze these things for later."

Vic nodded. "I'll text her. Then I'll suck on my shake and throw out a few date suggestions. We suggest you date us one-two-three, then time off for yourself."

Kandace nodded. "If I need an extra night, I'll say so."

"Group dates after that time off day. We intend to be a family."

"How does that work? Same house or different houses?"

"When we marry?" Kandace snorted, and Vic grinned. "If we marry, it's your choice, obviously. But the same house is preferred. We hope to have kids. Bio, adopted, don't care. You down with that? After you pay off your debts, of course."

"Aha. No attempt to bribe me by paying off my debt?"

"No, but we could buy them out and make it all one loan, to us, five and a half percent interest. That's Davis' idea, and we all back him up on it, even our mamas."

"That could work." Kandace sucked on a peanut butter chip. "This muffin would be good with pecans too."

"I'll tell Libby."

"So, I want pizza tonight, a group date, set some ground rules. Italian sausage, olives, and mushrooms on my pizza. You order whatever the hell you want for yours. We can do it delivery, chow down here, maybe go for a walk later, all three of us. I have three bears and a cat to protect me."

Vic nodded and stood. "You make the rules. Just, please, if you're going to end it, be clear, smash all our hearts at once."

"I will." Kandace tilted her head. "I don't play relationship games. Had tons of that crap when I was drinking. I'm tired enough without exhausting myself with such foolishness."

Vic stood up, kissed her cheek. "Text us an hour out. We'll be here." He looked down into her eyes. "And thanks for going so far out of your comfort zone that it might as well be on another planet."

"We'll mess it up," predicted Kandace. "None of us are perfect, but don't break my trust again." Vic nodded, petted the cat, and left.

⁓

The entire day, the thought of the date made her feel a pop, a frisson of happiness. Kandace kept popping the bubble and refocusing. She also got a ton of housework done, because she worked in bursts and took breaks. On her first one, she stood and did high knees, then cleaned the sink, then went back to work. The next break she did good mornings, her head touching her knees then back up to a flat back, followed by wiping down the kitchen counters. She kept at it until she was two tasks ahead, texted the boys, did standing abs exercises, and finished putting away the dishes. She'd had snacks but no dinner, and she was hungry.

Kandace changed into her favorite black bicycle shorts and her soft Def Leppard "Hysteria" T-shirt, grabbed a soda, put on mosquito repellent and brought out four citronella candles and lit them all. She took Sam for a short around-the-cabin walk, and the cat seemed to enjoy it. She sat down with an e-book on the outdoors couch, propped herself up with pillows, and laughed and cheered her way through the space-alien-lawyer series she liked to read. She closed her eyes a moment and slid into sleep.

She awoke to the smell of pizza. Sam had abandoned her for Vic. Davis was putting the pizza on plates, having obviously raided the kitchen, because they were the blue stoneware from her own cabinets. Len was sitting cross-legged at her feet. She propped herself up, and he scooted closer and began tapping on her feet. "You have forever to stop that," she said.

"It's alive," observed Davis.

"She was so excited to see us that she fell asleep," Vic said dryly.

"She is a patient recovering from a major accident. Plus, the girl works nonstop." Len sighed. "I regret giving her the exercises. She pushed herself too hard."

"Wake up, love." Vic handed Kandace a plate. Her personal Italian sausage, mushroom, and black olive pizza smelled like heaven.

"Pomodoro," said Kandace. She then bit into the pizza and groaned.

"Italian for tomato," said Davis.

"You implemented my solution." Len smiled beatifically, then accepted a plate of pizza.

"Solution to what?" asked Vic. He folded himself up on the end of the couch opposite Len and Kandace.

"The Pomodoro Method," said Davis. He ate his pizza in tiny, elegant bites, pepperoni disappearing little by little into his mouth. "It is a method of working for, generally, twenty-five minutes, then doing something else for five or ten minutes."

"Standing abs exercises?" Len asked Kandace.

Kandace came up for air. "Among others. High knees, that sort of thing. Have to move the cat off the mat a lot though."

"Neck pain, back pain? What do you feel, love?" Len asked.

"Creaky," said Kandace in between bites. She had to inhale sometime. "And this hand feels floppy, like it was newly grown and attached."

Vic slipped Sam some pepperoni. "No onion on any of this. You hate it, and the cat could die."

"Excellent." Len popped the top on a soda and handed it to Kandace, and she drank deeply.

"So, rules?" asked Davis after all of them had three pieces of pizza.

"I have no idea how your kind? People? How you guys date." Kandace let her complete confusion show on her face.

"We court, which means we date, all together and singly. The point is for you to get to know us and for us to get to know you. When you are ready, and feel you want to marry us, we will all choose who will be the legal husband and wife, and we will seek a home large enough for all of us. We raise our children together, and within driving distance of others of our kind, so we can give and receive help in times of need." Davis popped the top on another soda.

"And you'll need to meet our family." Len reached for another slice. "It will take a long damn time, because we're huge and spread out. All our decisions are ours, but there is a huge network of obligations and sets of rules for shapeshifters."

Vic put down his Coke. "Rule number one, our secret can't get out. Ever. To anyone. We're not in Utah where it is a felony to be married to more than one person, which is just stupid. I get why, that some evil people marry young people, elders decide who marries whom, child abuse, secrets. That sort of crap. But if everyone is an adult freely choosing, I don't see the problem."

Len grimaced. "Secrets are the problem. But we wouldn't put up with that idiocy. We are wildly protective of our children. Yes, they grow up with as much responsibility as they can handle at the age at which they can handle it, like bringing your cup to the sink at around age three to be washed, that sort of thing. But they are kids, and no one can harm them without repercussions far more severe than anything the outside world implements."

Vic nodded. "We have reasons for our secrets. People in the back-woods sometimes react with suspicion to plural marriage, and people having, as they put it, too many damn kids, but we all get the right to live as we choose. But our main secret...if even one person finds out, if even one of us is discovered, we are all at terrible risk. We were hunted nearly to extinction from Europe to Africa, from China to here. We chose our way of life to maximize the number of survivors. Even if one group is attacked and wiped out, we can survive else-where. We hide in plain sight."

Kandace nodded. "I have already said I will keep your secrets. Unless you hurt someone in front of me. And if a kid is hurt, you will wish you hadn't, to the point of losing my life."

Len touched her foot. "We all feel the same way. We aren't violent people. We're bears."

Vic grinned. "We're violent to salmon. Remember that trip to Alas-ka?" All the men laughed.

"We are really...protective," said Len.

"We are also not cowards," said Vic.

Kandace sang a little Nightwish, "7 Days To The Wolves". Len smiled his slow sunshine smile. "Great song."

Davis grabbed another Coke. "Okay."

Len snorted. "Our girl likes heavy metal. Keep up."

Davis threw a full can of soda at his head. Len reached up and caught it, almost lazily. He popped the top, and grinned at his brother.

Kandace glared. "No fighting over me. My rule. You'll all get equal time, except if someone needs a lot of extra love. And I think we should have sex separately when we decide to do that, for now."

"I accept," said Len.

"Okay," said Vic.

"I accept," said Davis. "Both rules."

"Since we'll marry at the same time, the anniversary should be celebrated for three days," said Len.

"Jump ahead much?" asked Vic.

Kandace choked. "Four days. And we'd better plan one hell of a honeymoon."

"Shit," said Vic. "I thought this would be harder."

"Why?" shot back Kandace. "Because I had to figure out how to handle having people that switch into other shapes in a burst of light? Because I wouldn't date one person, but three? Because you are putting secrets and family obligations on me that have life-or-death repercussions? Because I have never thought of marrying three people at once? What the hell?"

Vic stood. "I underestimated you. I get that. Are you going to hold that against me forever?"

Kandace carefully put her plate on the table. "This is our first date. Not forever. And yes, you did severely underestimate me. I am strong, despite my getting wounded. You are complex and complicated, and all I wanted was some damn peace. I remember my head smashing into a wall. I remember being slapped for asking what my grandmother wanted with all of her screaming. All her needy insanity. My mother just stood there, let her mother bash me. I. Was. A. Child. I made my way on my own, and I succeeded. I ran myself into serious debt, but I wanted real projects with meat on them, real things done for real people, not just little three-page websites. I hate math, but I learned how to handle algorithms, make them dance. I bashed through every single wall they put in my way, no matter how high. Do you think I'd back down even a little bit because I got into the most complicated relationship on the entire planet?"

Vic's jaw dropped. "Whoa. I didn't know. You don't talk about that much."

"My grandma was insane, still is. Compulsively doing things twenty-four hours a day that don't actually accomplish a single thing. Control, manipulation. I'm not a damn submissive. Never will be."

Len spoke in his most calming voice. "We get that. You have to be strong enough for us. We're wild, and we'll be that way forever. We saw that in you, that strength."

Davis carefully put down his plate. "I am so sorry that happened. Some people get terrible parents. We are open to adoption and want to help get other kids out of their messes. But bio-kids are good too."

"I have to be fully healed, inside and out." She took a deep breath. "I finally cut them off after I got hurt, no more money to my abusers. I also made sure that they have no idea where the hell I am and can't find out from the school. I changed my phone number, my email address. The whole damn thing."

Len carefully put down his plate and soda, stepped forward, and held Kandace. "We are so sorry, baby."

Vic, then Davis, stepped forward. Davis stepped behind her, put an arm around her neck, and stroked her hair with his other hand. Vic went to her uninjured side, and stroked her hair and her arm. They all three held her, and she let go. At first, she was crying so hard she was screaming. Then the tears went silently down her face.

She went into the bathroom, washed her face in the sink, and came back out to see everything cleaned up. There wasn't any leftover pizza. The boxes were in the recycling.

Len walked up, put his arm around her. "Come on. Let's go."

They all piled into Vic's truck, including the cat. Sam hopped up on the floorboards then sat between her and Vic in the back. Vic patted her shoulder. "I'm really sorry."

"No, I had to let it out. Sorry I got...intense." Sam chirruped, and Kandace stroked her head. "Sorry, Sam. I know you are trying to help, and I was busy ignoring you." Sam kissed her cheek and nuzzled her jaw, and Kandace nuzzled back.

They went over a rough road out into a field. They parked on the edge, and Len and Vic handed her up onto the hood. She lay down on the windshield, and Len climbed up behind her. Vic handed up Sam, and he and Davis lay on either side of her on the hood of the truck. Len lay on the roof, and stroked her hair. Sam got on Kandace's stomach and purred mightily. They all looked up at the millions of stars above their heads. Kandace felt her mind and soul both fly free.

FREEDOM

Freed from her cast and now able to drive, Kandace took the jiggling back roads wherever she so desired. She often worked at the coffee shop and ate the delicious paninis while hammering out complex coding problems. Sam was beloved by everyone around, and the cat trilled as she made her rounds and accepted petting and receiving kitty treats as her due.

She went to Libby's a lot too. She went for ice cream, went around the block, and found herself in love with salted caramel pecan brownies with mint chips on top. "Have to start high-intensity interval training to work this off." Kandace sat out on the patio where Sam the cat was allowed.

Libby slipped Sam a kitty treat. "I bake these cat treats myself, salmon and cheese. And you're still recovering. Reinjury is very possible."

Kandace nodded. "True, very true."

"Who's meeting you today?" Libby raised her hands to fend off objections. "I know which brother likes which treat."

"Len."

"Okay then, I'll be right back."

Kandace held her face up to the sun. "Nope, wait about half an hour. Please. I just want to enjoy the sun."

"You got it, girlfriend. Need more tea?"

"Nope. Half a pot left." She pointed to the clear heavy plastic teapot half-filled with blackberry tea.

"Cool. You need something, press the button." There were buttons on the outside tables that rang at the cashier's station.

"Will do." They grinned at each other, the cat trilled, and Libby went back to work.

Kandace stared sadly at her plate. No ice cream, no precious brownie left. She was stuck with only tea. Kandace pulled up a book on her cell phone, and the cat lay down on her chair and flipped on her side, sated. Kandace relaxed, felt the heat of the sun on her face. She stretched, getting the gnarled feeling out of her body. She didn't hunch over the computer anymore with her over-the-hip tray she used, but she still felt like she'd been living in the dark like a mushroom.

Kandace alternated between reading and half-snoozing in the sun. She had her hand on her cell phone when it was snatched out from under her hand. Kandace grabbed, caught the edge, then threw out an elbow, then a foot. A teen with scruffy hair and a blue T-shirt would not let go of the phone. Kandace grabbed the teapot with her bad hand and smashed it against the person's stomach. The thief let go of the phone with a whoosh. Kandace stuck her phone in her pocket and stepped forward. She grabbed the girl by the collar, drew the thief up to her face, and said, "What the hell are you doing?"

The girl smashed her face into Kandace's. Kandace felt her nose break. She didn't let go, though, and she spit and sputtered blood over the girl's shirt.

The door opened, and there was something flying through the air. Kandace ducked, and the girl didn't. The girl's head went back, and Kandace let go before she also fell. The girl landed on her rump. The broom handle went back, and Libby stood there, her face fierce. Kandace knelt, and said, "Stay down. Getting up is dangerous for you." Her voice sounded mushy to her, and Kandace let the tears flow down her face, washing the blood from her face in trickles. Sam came out from under the table and leaned up against Kandace's leg. "I am alive," Kandace told the cat.

"You are," said Libby. She turned and tapped on the glass. "Police will be here in a hot minute," she said, her voice going growly in her anger.

"What the hell?" asked the girl laying on the ground, her hand on her head. "Just wanted a cell phone, and you laid me out? I don't do nothin'."

"You messed with the wrong person," reiterated Kandace.

"I texted..." said Libby.

Len came running around the corner and skidded to a halt. "I see the cat's okay," he said. Sam warbled, and Kandace choked out a laugh. "I already texted Davis. He's on his way."

"I don't need a house call," choked out Kandace.

"I beg to differ," said Libby. "Nat!" she ear-piercingly cried out.

A brown-haired cop with eyes like flint loped around the corner. The cop took in Kandace, Libby's broom, and the teen on the ground, and sighed. "Janna, I told you not to lift people's stuff. I also told you that camp's not on the table anymore, and that you'd eventually run up against the wrong damn person."

"Screw you. These people beat me up."

The cop put the cuffs on Janna, pointed up at the camera that would show the entire altercation. "Clinic, then jail."

Janna stood and spit at the deputy. Nat stepped back. Kandace stepped forward and grabbed the girl's face. "You have no respect," she said. "This cop has a job."

"Scrw you!" Janna howled. "You don't know nothin' about me."

"I know that my phone wasn't yours. Why the hell did you want to take it?"

"It's money," said Janna. "Money you don't need, wasting time in some coffee shop, drinking damn tea."

Libby outright hissed. "This woman broke half her body at the beginning of this summer and has been recovering flat on her back.

And you just broke her damn nose. Your worthless behavior caused harm to others. You proud of yourself now?"

"I didn't do nothin'."

"Yes, you did," said the cop. "Let's go." They left in a cloud of Janna's shouted expletives.

"Sit, please," Len said, and guided Kandace to her chair.

Libby took the damaged teapot from her hand and set it on the table. "I'll bring ice. And some painkillers."

Len sighed. "Davis is better at this than I am. Hell, both of them are, but I can do it really quickly."

Kandace didn't nod; she wasn't that stupid. "Do it," she said thickly. She tilted her head back, and the snap and subsequent jolt of pain as Len reset her nose nearly made her pass out. Len gently scooted her chair back and leaned her against the side of the building and said, "Davis is on his way."

"Screwed up our date night."

Len shook his head. "I don't think you planned to be assaulted."

"No," said Kandace. "Certainly not." The world spun in nausea and pain. Libby brought out a wet cloth and a blue ice pack, and Len cleaned up her face, then Kandace held the ice pack to her nose.

She heard the voice of the cop again. Libby gave her statement, and signed something. Kandace sat quietly, waiting for the world to stop moving. The cop said, "I'm Deputy Nat Sadawan, and I'm an officer for the county. Do you feel up to me asking you a few questions?"

Kandace held up a fist and nodded it up and down. "Not moving my head."

"I get it," said the deputy. "Can you tell me what happened?"

Kandace explained what happened. Len read her statement back to her and helped her sign it. The deputy thanked her and said, "I will be in contact," and left.

Davis showed up, kit in hand. He carefully checked Len's work, and got her nose taped up. "I prescribe ice packs for your face. I can give you anti-inflammatories for the pain and something for your stomach. Len will get it all for you and get you some now. Hang out with my brother, make him rub your feet and feed you delicacies or something."

Len grinned. "Drugs, delicacies, and foot rubs coming right up."

"Okay. Getting my vehicle back?"

Davis sighed. "I will drive it, and Len will drive me back after we get you settled in."

"Thanks." Len brought up his ride, and they got Kandace and Sam inside. Len took it slow, and Davis went ahead with Kandace's ride. He parked, and waited to help Kandace and Sam out. They got her into the bathroom and washed the blood off, helped her change shirts, got her back in the sling and into her recliner. Len and Davis put ice packs on her face, shoulder, and hand, and the cat climbed on to purr. Len took Davis back to his car, and came back.

Len grabbed himself a soda, sat, and told stories to distract Kandace. She accepted a can of soda, and promptly put it on her face as an improvised ice pack. "Dad is a mountain of a man. He got skinny kids. Don't be under the illusion that he runs anything, though. My mom, Lynette, and my other mom, Jen, run everything. We had the upstairs-downstairs house when I was little, then we all refurbished this falling-down ranch, and then every single freaking one of us got our own bedroom, and on the same floor. Got more bathrooms too."

"Downstairs or upstairs?"

"My mom wanted downstairs, so that's what she got," said Len. "Didn't mind it. She called it her "turtle place" and I always felt like I was living in a turtle shell, safe and protected. Took us years to get the bigger house done, and I grew up with a hammer in one hand and a pipe wrench in the other. Weird I didn't go into construction, but I wanted to help people recover. My mom fell off a roof when I was in middle school and had injuries similar to yours. A tile cracked."

"I am so sorry." Kandace touched his hand.

"I learned what to do with ice packs, what stretches to do. I went to school for physical therapy, and got my nursing degree, then the physician's assistant thing last year. I do really well with cardiac patients and keeping old folks at home, and I know people who can redo their houses. Ramps, rails, opening up spaces so people can move around."

"Back to childhood," said Kandace. "Mmpf," she said, as Len dug into the arch of her right foot.

Len shrugged. "I always had someone playing on the floor with me as a kid. My brother died because the idiot went up on the roof as a bear, fell off as a boy. I tried talking him out of it in bear form, slapped his nose, but he took it as a dare." His face grew haunted. "Dad died trying to get him to the hospital. Drunk driver took them both out. Both the ambulances were tied up with car accidents that day."

"That sounds absolutely horrific," said Kandace.

"I suspect it's part of why we all went medical, we boys. We knew each other's family, of course. Struck all of us hard. Then Mom married Dad Two, Charlie, and moved in with all of us together. When I went bear, like my brothers and sisters—Meri and Libby are the youngest—we tumbled in the yard. Bears have babies in pairs, so everyone had someone to play with, and Dad or a mother had to be out with us. That got complicated when I was too young to have good control. I used to piss everyone off to no end. But we had fish in the stream 'cause Mama stocked it. I learned to fish behind the barn, by paw and line, and bow and arrow, and spear. I'm pretty good at it. I can gut and clean a fish in less than a minute, and I learned sushi from my mom. She worked in a sushi restaurant as a teenager. I loved making the rice with vinegar, and learned to buy the best fresh shrimp, crab, and salmon. Got really good at scallops, fried shrimp, corn fritters."

"Good heavens. And you haven't cooked for me."

"Come to think of it, when your stomach isn't roiling, I'd love to make sushi for you. Do you have a bamboo placemat?"

"What? No." Kandace shifted, groaned, and moved over her soda can ice pack.

"Used to roll sushi rolls," Len informed Kandace.

"Okay, you're also a sushi chef. Backup plan if taking care of people like me peters out."

"I never really thought about it."

"You want to make plans, backup plans, and backup plans to backup plans." Kandace gestured to her face, beginning to sport two black eyes because of the broken nose. "I'm the poster child of needing a backup plan. I've worked ahead, already texted that I'd be off for the next few days. I've covered plenty of slack for others; they have no trouble taking up mine. The project will be done, on time, under budget, and done right so they won't have to hire people to come behind us and fix our mistakes."

"That's life, I think." Len moved to his backpack, took some oil out of his pack. "Jasmine almond oil." He rubbed her right foot, and she groaned. "You make mistakes, try to clean up, and move on." He dug in, and she sighed. "Why did you hold onto the phone?"

"I held onto the phone because it held all of your numbers, our texts in it."

Len's hands stilled. "We're just beginning, love." He then kept rubbing her feet as she groaned in happiness.

SKEWERED

Romy came over with iced chocolate in a plastic cup with a glass lid and straw. "Thank you, bless you, thank you." Kandace put the glass against her nose. Her eyes had gone from black to yellow and green, with streaks of crimson.

"I don't usually have people use drinks as ice packs. You may need actual ice. I could bring a bag." Romy spoke in her flat voice. "It will be a canvas bag, not plastic."

"Thank you." Kandace remembered that Romy didn't do subtle, and liked explicit directions. "I would like for you to bring me an ice bag. Charge me a dollar for the ice." Kandace handed over a dollar bill.

"I cannot do that."

"Then put it in the tip jar."

"I can do that."

Kandace was able to bash through the first part of her daily task list. The sunglasses helped. She tied the bag Romy brought to the side of her glasses and froze her left eye first. Kandace sipped her drink and combined typing and dictating her work, switched eyes, took the ice pack off when it melted. The nook was in the back, and the espresso machine was hissing far louder than the sound of her voice.

Kandace took a bathroom break, stretched, and went to get a

cheese bagel with strawberry cream cheese, a new chocolate drink, and more ice. A wide woman in a floral dress with bright blue eye makeup that clashed with her faded green eyes said clearly, "Whore."

"Excuse me?" Kandace looked around, but no one was in line behind her.

"You're datin' them Camber boys," said the woman.

"Why do you care about my dating life?" asked Kandace. "Are you that bored, or do you not have enough problems of your own?"

"What?" said the woman.

"I said, are you so bored that you investigate other people's lives?" Kandace called over to Benny, who had a power washing business, washing houses, sidewalks, that sort of thing. The huge man with the diamond earring came in for coffee and a panini for lunch, and loved Sam the cat. "Benny, you care about other people's dating lives?"

"Naw," said Benny, pushing his hat up on his head. "Too freaking busy." Sam purred against his leg.

"What about you, Romy? Do you feel concerned about other people's dating lives?"

"No," said Romy, handing the woman in front back her change. "I am taking three online classes. I do not have time to think of that." She turned, grabbed a croissant, butter, and a tall glass of juice and handed them to the long-haired woman in front.

"I don't care, either," said the long-haired woman. "I am an accountant, and I guarantee I don't have time for such concerns." She gave a dazzling smile and walked to a table.

"What do you want, Mabel?" asked Romy. "Coffee with two sugars?"

Mabel huffed. "Well, I never!"

"Never what?" asked Kandace, pitching her voice so that it carried, a skill she learned in college. "Called a woman a whore that you don't know while standing in line?"

The room went dead silent. Mabel turned bright red, which made her overdone blush look like two stripes of coral on scarlet. "I..." she said.

"Mabel, what do you want?" repeated Romy, immune to the air

suddenly rushing out of the room.

"I..." said Mabel.

"Black coffee, two sugars," said Colleen. Her eyes were cold. "Two ninety-five, Mabel." Mabel handed over three dollars, and Colleen took five cents out of Romy's drawer, gave it to Mabel, then handed over the coffee. Mabel took the coffee in a to-go cup. "Just so you know, Mabel, you can't call our customers whores and expect to get served again. This is your last coffee from us. Have a nice day now." There was applause—not just a scattering, but nearly everyone in the room. Mabel's face turned apoplectic and she rushed out.

"Busybody," said Benny.

"You can say that again," said Colleen. Sam chirruped at Benny's feet, and everybody laughed.

$$\sim$$

*R*omy had gone home when Len came in, sat down, and burst out laughing when he saw the small ice pack tied to Kandace's sunglasses. "New fashion?" he said, pretending to adjust imaginary glasses.

Kandace snorted. "You try typing with two black eyes. They're no longer swollen as much, at least. But my nose feels like a banana on my face." Len smiled sympathetically. Kandace took off her sunglasses, untied the little bag, then put the glasses on her head and the bag next to her drink. "Have you heard about Janna, the attempted phone thief?"

"No. What?"

"I got a letter of apology. Officer Sandawan had me send pictures of my face. She's never been violent before, and the judge was not happy. The judge did agree to let me pay for her to go to a work camp, a place where people rescue horses. Hope it works on her."

"That's good. Did Mabel ever apologize for calling you a whore?" asked Len.

"No," said Kandace. "She got her ass handed to her though."

"I heard," said Len, his normally kind, gentle voice dark with anger.

Sam unfolded herself from where she was lying on Kandace's outstretched feet, stretched, and went over to Len. She stood on his legs and chirruped. "Hello, lovely girl." Len petted the cat, and she leapt up onto his lap.

"Hey!" said Kandace. "Traitor cat."

"You are lovely with your eyes turning green and crimson." Kandace pretended to throw something at his head. He ducked. "So, Janna isn't going to prison?"

"She's not going to get probation this time. The work camp will go on her permanent record. I really want to help her, but the justice system has to work. And Janna needs to be stone cold sober and make her own decisions."

"You're my kind of insane. I might have forgiven her, but I wouldn't have paid for the camp."

Kandace shrugged. "Girl gets one last shot before she screws up her life permanently." She gave Len a narrow-eyed smile. "So, what do you want to do tonight?" she asked as she finished her last lines of code then shut down her computer.

"What do you want to do? I think you're sore and staring at a screen all day. Would a movie be good or bad?"

"Home or out?" asked Kandace.

"Out. The movie theater in Brana City has a little Mediterranean place that serves steak and shrimp on skewers with mushrooms and bell peppers, and baked potato soup. There's an Italian pizza joint and..."

Kandace held up a hand. "Baked potato soup and skewers. We can see the movie and have popcorn."

"It gets better. They have popcorn balls with salted caramel and pecans."

"I am in love with this idea. What about sodas?"

"Soda bar," said Len.

"Dah-um!" Kandace tucked her portable mouse in the pack, then the laptop. She slung the pack over her back, stood, and stretched. Len had long ago given up trying to carry her computer; she was super-protective of her laptop with its wide screen and neon blue glowing keys, with a matching neon blue mouse. She went to the counter to hand back her improvised cold pack.

"Sorry, pretty girl," Len said to the cat. "Let's get you to your tuna and litter box." Sam chirruped about the tuna, hopped off, and regally accepted having Len put on her leash. They walked out Kandace's truck. Kandace hopped in, and the cat hopped up to her feet, then leapt to sit on the passenger seat.

~

*L*en followed Kandace home. Kandace hopped out at the cabin, let the cat in, put down her computer case, and went into the kitchen to feed the cat. Sam went to her litter box and came shooting out for the tuna. Kandace rushed to get out of the house before the cat began to object.

Len grinned at Kandace. "Let's go. Country, rock, pop?"

Kandace grinned. "Oh, you of the generalizations."

"What?" asked Len.

"Country. Country rock? The crying-in-your-beer songs about a woman or your truck?" Len laughed. "A woman kicking ass and taking names?"

"My favorite kind."

"Then there's rock. Country rock, hair bands, metal with the death and thrash genres, all filled with sexual innuendo and great guitar licks."

"Start me up," said Len, quoting from The Rolling Stones.

Kandace laughed. "Then there's pop. Boy band, girl band, K-pop..."

"I love Korean pop music."

"There's Japanese pop and Thai and what have you," said Kandace. "All different flavors."

"Yes," said Len.

"And there's blues, screaming out your pain and love. And soul, belting out deep emotion from the soul. B.B. King and Lucille."

"He was buried with her. The King and that guitar had a forever love." Len found a station that had covers of blues and soul from new artists. One young man with an enormous voice brought the house down with B.B. King's "The Thrill Is Gone." The guitar playing was perfect. Kandace and Len sang along. Len's voice was growly, different from the cool smoothness of his normal voice. Kandace's voice was a bit mangled from her face being smashed in, giving her a nasal voice.

They got to the little mall with the movie theater, a hamburger joint, the skewer place, and the Italian place. Len made a beeline for the sweet and smoky smell of barbecue on skewers. Kandace didn't even bother looking at the menu. She went straight up to the pit, sat on a barstool, and started pointing. "One shrimp, one chicken, and a bowl of the baked potato soup." She paid, then looked over at the soda bar which had an actual soda jerk ready to mix up cherry, chocolate, and many other flavors of soda. Kandace hopped up, ran over to the soda bar, ordered a chocolate cherry coke, had it mixed, and waited for her soda.

"ADD," Len said to the man with copper skin and black, wavy hair cooking the skewers.

"Figures," said the man. "How ya doin', Len?"

"In love with a hummingbird, obviously."

"That can be tough," said the man, flipping the chicken skewer. He squeezed a lime over the shrimp ones. "The usual, man?"

"Yeah, Ty, but half," said Len. "My woman wants to see the movie."

"Which one?"

"Have no idea. She likes all kinds."

"Hummingbird woman."

"Yeah," said Len. He called behind him. "I'll have what you're having."

"Sure, babe," said Kandace.

"Babe?" mouthed Len. Ty laughed and put on more skewers. He ladled out the soup, and Len got started.

Kandace danced back. "Hate to ask. Len, you been beatin' up on women lately?"

"Ty, Kandace. Kandace, Ty. No, Janna happened."

Ty groaned. "Heard she was back in rehab a few months back. My little brother dated her. Twice. Not a good idea."

Kandace sat down and started on her soup. Her eyes rolled up in her head. "I love this! Len, this is our place now."

"We have a place!" Len's eyes lit up. Ty noticed and grinned.

They finished dinner, bought sweet tea and popcorn balls, and went into the movie. It had lasers and a secret and spaceships. Len didn't care what the hell it was about because Kandace held his hand, dug her nails into his arm during the space battles, and when the secret parentage was revealed, she held onto his arm like a limpet. They stayed through the credits, and Len helped her up. She ran to the ticket booth, and Len jogged after her. "More!" she said. They hit the bathroom and the snack stand, and went back in. The next one was about people that gathered energy from the elements, traversing a world. It was gorgeous and heartbreaking, and definitely needed about six sequels. Kandace was sobbing on his arm at one point, and he held her close.

He took her out and waited while she cleaned up her face in the bathroom. She came out freshly scrubbed, her eyes still glistening with tears. Len touched her face. "Your black eyes are obscene in your beautiful face."

Kandace looked up into his eyes. "I fell for you first." She reached up, stroked his face, and kissed him with all her exuberance laced with bright love that he thought his heart would stop. It probably did, for a single beat. He held her gently, held her face near her ear so he wouldn't hurt her, the other hand on the small of her back.

He looked down at her. "You never let yourself be broken, and you've been smashed three times now."

She laughed ruefully. "I've been broken lots of times. I just don't let it stop me."

Len looked down at her. "My friend called you a hummingbird tonight. So beautiful, fast, full of life, grabbing the best life has to offer." He bent down, gave her a gentle kiss.

She grinned, a flash of joy in her eyes. "I kinda am that way, aren't I?" They shared another scorching, wild kiss, and he walked her back to the truck.

COLD WATER

*V*ic was next in the dating rotation. He took her out to the lake, leaving a very pissed-off Sam behind. "Actually, this is at the end of the trail on the left behind your cabin, but hiking now with your face hurting isn't wise."

"And swimming is?" asked Kandace. She was wearing a shimmery blue swimsuit with boy shorts and a twisted bandeau top. She'd ordered it online, and was stunned when it had fit. She was two sizes smaller than she had been on the day she graduated college.

"It is basically an old quarry. Ice cold."

Kandace touched her nose, her two black eyes turning yellow, blue, and crimson. "A giant ice pack. I get it."

"Surrounded, like being inside an ice cube. Have you heard from Deputy Sandawan?"

"I paid for a work camp for Janna to work with horses. I hope that calms her the hell down."

"Go Kandace." Vic pulled a cooler out of his truck.

"I want to help her, but right now her walls are three feet thick. Like being surrounded in concrete. Juvie will just build up more walls, not break them down."

"So she's...what? You?"

"Me without my friends. They saved my life."

Vic dropped off the basket, went back to the truck. He brought out beach towels, lounge chairs, a bag filled with sunblock, insect repellent, and towels to join the picnic basket. Vic spread out the blanket, then carefully helped Kandace cover herself with sunblock and insect repellent, and they both put on bright blue life jackets. "We jump in, but I don't think that's best for you. We carved toeholds in the rock, so you can walk in, like a ladder. We also have a rope attached to either side, screwed into the rock."

Vic went first, and helped her down. The water was, as promised, ice-cold. They both floated, their life jackets their own individual flotation devices. Kandace used the water as an icepack for her face by rolling to float on each side. She sighed with relief, relaxed, floated. Finally, she realized she was shivering.

"You're turning blue. Let me help you up." Vic helped support her as Kandace used her strong legs and the rope on her good side to climb back up, and they dripped water onto the rocky ground. They dried off, reapplied the sunblock and insect repellent, and draped themselves on the deck chairs. Vic handed her a cherry soda, and they lay back and relaxed. Kandace had on shades and let the sunlight enter her bones.

"I love this place. It's on our land. We used to come down here, jump in as bears, climb out as humans, do it again and again."

Kandace laughed. "An aspect of shapeshifting I have never considered. I doubt I would ever have thought of such a thing."

"I love it. I can't imagine any other life."

Kandace sighed. "You make it sound fun."

"It is fun. Fishing, finding honey. Natural beehives used to be everywhere. Now, we bears own or purchase from a half-dozen honey farms. Clover, mostly. Nice rosemary honey, and dandelion too. We get manuka honey from New Zealand, mesquite from Nevada, buckwheat from Pennsylvania. Lavender from way over there." He pointed. "Sell them to other bear clans. Families, but we call them clans, because they get big. Multiple spouses, children."

"Million-dollar question. Is this recessive or..."

"Three out of four of our kids will be shapeshifters. It's a hell of a dominant trait. And, we do mix. We usually marry other bear shifters. But we've dated around the clans. Not for all of us in particular, it could have gone the other way, one of us dating several of them. But, never worked out. Holly was controlling as hell. Sergia was a lunatic. Melana was...lascivious. Sounds like a teen's wet dream, no? But threw herself at other guys to the point that it was a problem for her family. Finally got her married off as a second wife to a grizzly clan. She's far more well-behaved in front of others now. At home..." He shrugged. "We crossed the country, and things just never...gelled. Clicked. For any of us."

"But you could have dated non-shapeshifters, like me. Sorry, stupid question. I'm a terrible risk, aren't I?"

"The other problem is that all of us are straight males. If any of us had been gay or bi, it would have been easier. There are plenty of men we respect all over the place. That is also the problem. The amazing females pick up the awesome males, or in whatever combination that is, and we somehow got...."

"Left out." Kandace reached for another cola.

"It's kind of generational. We're ten years younger than the crop ahead of us, and the current generation..."

"Is taken or crazy."

Vic popped the top on a Coke. "To put it bluntly, yes."

"Crazy is one of my best characteristics," said Kandace proudly.

Vic laughed. "You aren't our last, only hope. But you are extraordinary, strong, tough, and willing to take on three batty bears."

Kandace laughed. "Help me, Kandace, you're our only hope." Kandace used a Princess Leia voice.

Vic laughed so hard he snorted Coke out of his nose. "I love your sense of humor. Star Wars girl."

"Hungry girl. What did Meri pack?"

Vic opened the basket and took out containers. "Grapes. Brie, French bread, sodas, grape juice. Olives. Slices of...bacon?"

Kandace's face let up. "Pancetta, Italian bacon. Meri packed one of the oldest meals in the world. Bread, grapes, cheese, olives, a little cured meat. This is a five-thousand-year-old meal." She took a slice of bread, cut off a slice of brie with the plastic knife Meri had included, spread it on the bread. She took grapes, pancetta, and a little refillable bottle of grape juice. She took a bite of cheesy bread and grinned.

"I love this," said Vic. "But no honey...wait!" He held up a tiny pot, opened it, smelled it. "Rosemary honey. Dip your bread in it, or drizzle it on."

Kandace poured a tiny bit on her bread, bit in, and groaned. "Omigod. This is the best honey I've ever eaten."

Vic grinned. "I have swayed you to my side. The bear side." Kandace laughed.

They ate, rested, and swam some more. Kandace watched Vic change himself into a bear, leap into the water, then come out human, and laughed. She waited until she was nearly at the bottom of the carved-in handholds, and swung out on the line. She pointed her toes and slid into the water that enclosed her like an ice hug. She came up, spluttered, and lay on each side again. She patted the head of the bear that swam over, one bigger than Len's. Bigger head, bigger paws. The bear swam to the side, there was a flash of golden light, and then a naked man, ass and cock hanging out, climbed out. "Where's your damn shorts?" Kandace called up.

"Bears don't wear shorts." Vic turned himself into a bear again and went over the edge.

She laughed and decided to relax and cool off in the water. Finally, exhausted, she barely made it back up. She dried off and reapplied the sunblock and insect repellent before collapsing into her chair. She watched the bear go over for the last time, and the man climb back up. Kandace raised her eyebrows at the size of his junk. "I need to take you home. You're exhausted." Vic had hard abs, a tight ass, and a very awake dong.

"Get dressed," snapped Kandace. "You're violating the rules."

Vic dried himself off before putting on his shorts and a battered, torn T-shirt. He put on sunblock and insect repellent. "The rules said no sex. Not no nudity. Besides, Len's given you showers. He's seen you naked. We haven't. Although that bathing suit comes close."

Kandace glared at him. "What about no jealousy?"

"I'm an ass. Slap me down. I'm a bear. I need a good slap on the nose sometimes."

"Bad bear," said Kandace, and punched his arm. 'Feed me some ice cream on Libby's brownies, caramel almond crunch ice cream on her sea salt caramel peanut butter brownies, and then take me home."

"Demanding. I like it." Vic smiled slowly. "I hear and obey." Kandace snorted.

~

*V*ic took Kandace for the promised ice cream, and watched her put it on a brownie and attack it as if it would run away from her. "Damn, girl."

Libby came over. "Stand back, Vic. Never come between a woman and her chocolate."

"I can see that," Vic put his cinnamon ice cream on an apple tartlet and dug in. "Now I see why she puts ice cream on your stuff."

"Penny and I are collaborating." Libby pointed to the wall. "I've proposed that we buy the place next door, smash down the wall, and make it an ice cream and soda joint as well. Be an after-school hangout."

"Well, I'd come," said Kandace when she came up for air.

"You two have wet hair. Quarry?"

"Quarry," agreed Vic.

"Cold water is refreshing on the two black eyes. What's the girl who assaulted me's deal?"

"Drunk mother, father beats her when he shows up. State takes her away and gives her back. Girl can't catch a break, but that doesn't mean she can break my customers' noses."

"Hope the horses thing helps," said Kandace.

Libby nodded. "Thank you for paying for that. I hope it gets her straight."

They finished their dessert, then Vic took Kandace for a long drive and laughed to himself when an exhausted Kandace fell asleep.

He drove her home, holding her hand as she slept, head on her towel.

~

Davis got Kandace next and treated her to another lovely dinner, this one primo tacos. She told him about Vic and the quarry. He told her about learning to drive at fourteen...with his feet, which luckily did not involve an accident. He kept her laughing, and then took her for a short walk. "You know I like you. Admire you, think you're amazing."

"You save lives, Davis, and helped me through one of the darkest times of my life. Except getting sober, and when one of my Program friends jumped off the water tower drunk. Those were both horribly ugly."

Davis stared at her, wide-eyed. "I assume your friend didn't make it."

"I'm afraid not." She smiled sadly at him. "It did get me sober in a hurry, hearing about what happened to her. Visiting her in the hospital."

Davis patted her hand, let the serious moment roll by. "So, the doctor thing is good?"

"In the win column. What's in the win column with me? My keeping you employed?"

Davis threw back his head and laughed. "No. You are brutally honest. And you're funny. A great joy to be around."

"I'm not sophisticated," warned Kandace.

Davis sighed. "We're all holler people. I'm ex-military. I like nice things, but not six-thousand-thread-count sheets or that sort of thing. I come here because my friend cooks the best damn steak in the county, and because I want to relax. Being a doctor means you're on your feet. Then there's all the paperwork. Anyway, I need to take a break, relax, and I figured you wanted out of the house."

"You figured right."

"I don't need someone to be drinking with their pinky out." Davis imitated a person drinking a martini with a pinky out, a smarmy grin on his face. Kandace laughed. "I'm just a guy who has a job that pays more than most. It does for a reason. You have to put people back together right the first time. And, with so many uninsured or under-insured patients in the county, I don't make as much money as people think."

Kandace sighed. "I'm not interested in your wallet. I am interested in you."

They took a slow walk around the little town. They had their first slow-burn kiss in front of the ice cream shop, got some cones, their second smooch in front of Libby's on the way out. Kandace felt warm despite the ice cream. Ready to melt.

FISHING

Vic threw the line out, making sure to hit the depths where the fattest fish swam. He let it sink, took his time about reeling it back in. Davis stood with him, looking nothing like his usual self, in cutoffs soon to fall into nothingness, blue faded to white, a ratty muscle shirt with the name of the long-dead Sparkers Gym in fast-fading letters with a frog lifting weights emblazoned on the front, his boat shoes with socks sitting next to Vic's battered tennis shoes at the other end of the dock. Vic's cutoffs were even older, and he wore a muscle shirt with a bear drinking beer on it. The light shimmered on the river, making the flow of clear water hard to see with all the sparkles. The family dock stuck out onto the river that fed the lake. The frogs bellowed, birds chirped, and cicadas droned. The seemingly silent morning was actually very loud.

Vic got nothing for that cast, shrugged his shoulders, and threw back out. Davis was taking his time with his own cast, maneuvering the line through the mud, knowing that he could reel in one of those fat catfish. Sure enough, there was a tug on his line. He set the hook, took his feet out of the water and braced them on the dock, stood, began reeling in the fish. He gave the line play, making sure the line didn't break, because that was a big catfish. Vic finished reeling in his line, recast, and put the fishing pole in its holder. He got the net, knelt, and was ready when Davis finally got the fish up close enough to the dock. The catfish was huge, enough to feed two of them. "Damn, Davis. Trying to outdo us again?" asked Vic. He unhooked the fish, expertly slammed it on the dock, and had it hooked on the line and back in the water with the other fish they caught that morning.

Davis grimaced a little, but he was used to his brother's speed. He would rather have used ice to kill the fish. But, Vic spent more time as a bear than any of them, even though Len was trying to give him a run for his money lately in order to keep track of their girl. Vic was taking his aggressions out on the fish, which Davis understood. Very stupidly, he decided to broach the subject as Vic re-baited his hook with crawfish. "So, our girl has decided that she loves Len."

Vic growled and threw back out. "Shut the hell up," he said in the low tone he reserved for when he thought one of his brothers was being a complete ass.

"You know that with poly, some people fall in love with other people at different rates," Davis pointed out. "And with me, it's glacial, because I keep having to move my nights around. I think I'll have to have two dates in a row at this rate."

Vic growled very, very low, a danger sign. Davis sighed, threw out his line, and dragged slowly in the deepest water. He reeled back in, threw out, sat down, and worked to get at least two more fish for the fish fry. From time to time, he sipped from the carafe of sweet tea at his side. It was too early in the morning for beer. Vic had his back to Davis, a clear sign that he was absolutely pissed. Davis gave up needling his brother, reeled his line back in, cast out, and the pull on the line damn near pulled him in the water. He hooked his foot around the wooden piling on the corner of the dock, leaned back, and carefully stood up from a squat, his foot still on the piling. He was absolutely terrified the line was going to break, so he let it play out, reeled it back, out, in.

Davis grimaced, and his breath came in light chuffs. He was strong, but not the strongest of the brothers. The strongest one came in behind him, net in hand, ready to catch Davis if he was about to take a header off the dock. Out, in, out, in, muscles straining, sweat beginning to pour off of him, the cicadas and frogs deafening in the early-morning light. Vic stood ready, knelt, and managed to get the net under the glistening, slick fish. Both brothers put their backs into it, leaned back, and got the fish up on the dock. They both skittered back, not wanting the fish to flip itself back into the water. Davis got it unhooked, trying not to hook himself, and Vic strained to do his vicious flip. The enormous catfish lay on the dock, dead, and both brothers stood, heaving, getting the breath back in their bodies.

A Jeep pulled into the end of the trail. Vic left a victorious Davis there to catch his breath, and hiked up to help Meri bring down her cutting stump, the plywood she used, and the bucket. Meri followed with her fillet knives, cooler lined with blue cold packs frozen solid, and butcher's paper to wrap the fish. She came down to the dock, looked down and said, "You killed Bubba!"

Vic sighed. "We didn't know it was him until we got him up on the dock."

"You still killed him. You bastards." Meri's eyes shot daggers at both her brothers.

"Davis caught him," said Vic defensively.

"And you killed him," said Meri.

"He had to," said Davis, as he reeled in his brother's line and started to take off the hook. "We only caught four."

"Five," said Vic. "I caught one before you got here." Meri washed her knives and the plywood with antibacterial soap, slowly as to let the antibacterial soap work, then Vic helped her load the huge catfish onto the plywood. The wood groaned under the weight of the fish. Meri sent Vic with a bucket to rinse the fish before she filleted it.

Davis broke down the fishing poles. "You're right, we probably shouldn't have done it. Everyone's going to be mad at us." Meri took pictures of the fish and sent them to the anglers in town. It wasn't boasting; it was the end of an era. People had been after that fish for years. Bubba had been the cause of many long, lazy days out on the lake, drinking beer and talking about nothing.

Vic shook his head. "Our woman, our catch."

"You are such a throwback. Did you really just say, 'Me catch big fish, me big fisherman?' Do you really think Kandace will care?" Meri got the fish rinsed off, then put Bubba on ice. She then put on her Kevlar glove and cleaned the smaller fish, her fillet knife flashing. She filleted the smaller fish in seconds, cutting behind the head, down to the tail, then flipping the fish to get the meat out. She rinsed and wrapped the fillets in paper and put them on ice, then Vic helped her move Bubba onto the board.

Meri took her time, cutting at an angle at the top of the head, expertly turning the knife when she hit bone, and cutting through the ribs. She cut to several fingers' width before the tail, and Vic helped her flip the fish over. She got the fillets off the skin, then did it to the other side. It was messy work, but she got it done as quickly as she could with such a big fish. She got all of the fillets out, wrapped them up, got them into the cooler. Vic helped her with the disgusting job of throwing out the pail of offal, and cleaned the knife, plywood, and stump with antibacterial soap. He also worked with her to get the cooler over the tailgate, tied down, and the back closed up.

The entire time, Meri couldn't stop glaring at Vic. "You're supposed to throw back everything under five and over ten pounds. You know that you're going to have to pay a fine. A hefty one, at that. And you didn't ice him to kill him. Damn right I'm pissed at you, and I'm going to stay that way. You're all freaked out because Kandace is the first girl in years worthy of y'all. She's beautiful, smart, got a ribbon of steel running down her spine like a good Southern woman should. She's everything you've ever wanted. And you've got to take your time, which drives you batshit crazy, Vic. You're all about climbing that wall, saving that victim, doing the next big thing that will catch her. Well, she doesn't work that way. She's a slow burn, and you're pissed off that Len figured it out before you did. He saw her heart, and it's a big one. And you're afraid you just won't measure up. Len's got the whole Zen thing, which for some reason she's attracted to. Davis has the charm and gloss he got at medical school. Throw in the good looks and the hours he spends in the gym when he's not running off his feet taking care of patients, and you think she'll fall for him next. Well, so what? Quit acting like a damn caveman, because she will never in a million years go for that. Be you, take risks, use that slow Southern smile to get her." She poked her filleting knife at his chest, and he stepped back. "But don't, and I mean don't, ever pull this crap again." She finished cleaning up, got back in her Jeep, and drove off in a spray of gravel.

Davis said quietly, "I'll pay the fine."

"No. I killed the damn fish, and I knew I shouldn't have the minute I did it. I was acting like a jealous moron, the one thing that is never allowed in poly. I need to shower and work out." Vic took his fishing rod and tackle box, put them in his truck, and drove off.

Davis let his brother go, stripped down, and dove into the river. He did the bear thing, caught his own damn fish. He knew the fish would fill up both his bear and human body with energy. He got himself up on to a flat rock, turned himself into a human, and dried off. He lay there for a bit, and thought about what Meri had said about his charm. He was damned afraid of coming off like a slick city man, something he'd learned to do in St. Louis. But, that wasn't him, not deep inside. Yeah, he was kind of a button-down guy, hair neat, hands clean. Had to be in his line of work. Nobody likes a sloppy, slovenly doctor. He learned his habits well, turned himself into the kind of man people could trust with their bodies, their enormous physical pain, that he was going to make things better. And, preferably, not turn ordinary people into junkies by prescribing medication he shouldn't, or for too long a time. That's where Len came in. And physical therapy, massages, pain programs.

His girl was a junkie. She now drowned herself in cola, chocolate, treats, like any clean and sober alcoholics and junkies who got high on sugar and caffeine. Some of them turn to adrenaline. From what she told him, Davis knew that Kandace had chosen not to go that route, except with the cliff thing. A close friend's plunge off a water tower cured her of that one. The cliff thing was more of a meditation thing for her. Kandace was so scared of sliding back into addiction sometimes. He could see it in her eyes that she weaned herself off the pain pills far too early. Len could see it too. Vic couldn't see that vulnerability yet, couldn't connect with it, and because of that he probably would continue to be a slower start than the others. Meri was right, as she often was.

Davis stopped woolgathering and swam back to shore. He stood on the dock, drying himself in the hot wind of summer before putting his clothes back on and making his way back to his truck.

~

*V*ic showered at the gym, and belatedly realized he should have washed up in the stream first. His truck would have to be detailed now that he'd gotten into the truck smelling like fish bait. He put on his gym clothes, and sealed the fishy ones in double plastic bags. He did stretches, jumped rope, slammed out what felt like a million sit ups. Then he gloved up and went after the speed, kick-boxing, and heavy bags. He did a lot more work with weights until his muscles refused to continue. He stretched, headed to the showers. He was very happy that he'd had several gym outfits in his locker, because now he had two very stinky sets of clothes. He dropped off the truck to be detailed, ate a sandwich and veggie chips at the diner, and picked the truck back up.

Vic was headed to the store to gather whatever his mother needed for the party when he saw their girl's banged-up truck in front of Cailynn's Climbing Gym. He parked before he realized he had done it, and sat there with his jaw hanging open. He finally put his jaw back where it belonged, got out of the truck, and went in.

Kandace was at the base of a wall, a little one, staring at it. Her black helmet seemed to sink into her hair. Vic paid, and tapped out the belayer, Rick, a high school kid who brought in extra bucks at the climbing place. Rick just nodded and passed over the line and carabiners.

Kandace kept staring at the wall. "You're not going to talk me out of it?"

"I'm belaying you. Put your right hand up, and your left hand on the lowest one. We don't have all damn day."

She snorted at him, then sniffed. "You smell like fish."

"I've had two showers and a workout, and I still smell like fish?" He grinned at her.

"I'll make you a bet the fish is for the catfish fry." Kandace moved to the wall, reached up with her left hand, then her right foot, and stood. She grunted at the pain, but kept going. Len had her doing many stretches, and she was allowed to do bodyweight exercises now. She reached, stood, took her time going up.

A woman with poofy blonde hair walked up next to him. "Are you sure she should be doing that?"

"Tabitha," said Len.

Kandace looked down. "So, Tabitha. You come around after months flat on my back." She reached up, found another handhold, moved her right foot up. "Did you think I was contagious?"

Tabitha stared up at her. "What are you trying to prove, that you're a badass?"

Kandace barked out laughter. "That's something I never have to prove. To quote Popeye, I yam what I yam, badass and all." Kandace deliberately made her way to the underhang, and slowly made her way under and up it, never having all four limbs attached to the wall at the same time. She flexed her feet and made her way over the edge to the top. She rang the bell, and made her way down the flat part at a steady pace. At the bottom, she turned and looked at Tabitha. "Wow, you didn't run away. I thought that was your way."

Tabitha stiffened at Kandace's icy tone. "We couldn't do anything, and it's not like we were real friends."

"You could have been, and now you never will. Your loss." She looked over at Vic. "Another?"

"Absolutely," said Vic. He looked over at Tabitha. She stood there, fists balled, eyes wide open. Vic couldn't tell if it was shock or rage. Tabitha came from one of those families no one ever talked back to for fear of retaliation. But the Cambers had their own power.

Kandace got her feet under her and looked over at Tabitha. "Are you still here?" She turned, looked back at the wall, and started her second climb.

FISH FRY

*L*ynette spied Vic and Kandace together. He had his hand on the small of her back, and she laughed at something he said. Meri had them in a line. Lynette dipped the catfish in the egg wash and cast them into the herbed cornmeal breading, Len flipped the fish over and finished the breading process, and Meri grabbed the fish with tongs and put them into the oil, which popped and hissed. All of them wore aprons over their cutoffs and T-shirts. Davis was hard at work on the hush puppies, forming the balls of cornmeal dough.

Lynette used her chin to point to the happy couple. "Whoa," said Meri.

"Looks like your little counseling session worked," said Lynette.

"But I'm still pissed about Bubba," said Meri.

"We all are." Lynette sighed. "He has always been the most aggressive. But he has found a way to connect with Kandace that pleases her." Len smiled as Vic made Kandace laugh. "I love to see that smile."

Davis dropped the cornmeal balls into the deep fryer with a spoon. He grinned. "It is a sight to see, isn't it?" he said to Len.

"It is," said Len.

"I am happy for your brother," admitted Lynette. "And for all of you." She watched Kandace and Vic work together to open up the legs of the heavy plastic tables and swing them upright. "She's a hard worker, doesn't shirk responsibility."

Vic and Kandace started on the chairs after they got the tables in place. Len nodded. "She is extraordinary. Doesn't give up."

Lynette and Len stopped because they were finally out of strips of fish. They both stretched out their hands, then washed up in the outdoor sink. Lynette grabbed the basket of potatoes and put them into a strainer. Len scrubbed them in the sink, then cut them into chunks for the potato salad. Lynette took out the stone-ground mustard and pickle relish. "So, you two are good?" Lynette asked Len.

"Our first kiss," said Len.

"I am very worried," said Lynette. "Mabel."

Len snorted. "Busybody, judgmental woman."

Lynette nodded. "Her mind is a sealed box. I asked her once to remember the part of the Bible that says, 'Judge not lest you be judged?' I asked her if she forgot that part."

Len gasped. "What did she do?"

"Exactly what she did in front of Libby. Turned beet red and couldn't talk."

"Yeow," said Len.

"Woman couldn't think herself out of a paper bag," said Lynette. Len snorted laugher.

Lynette put the chunked potatoes for the potato salad into a bowl and included stone-ground mustard, pickle relish, dill, and a touch of tartar sauce. "Makes it tangy."

Len grinned. "Family secret. I'll never tell."

Libby came in with a tomato-bread-basil salad and plunked it down. She followed their eyes and saw them looking out the glass wall at Vic and Kandace putting the plastic watermelon-printed table-cloths onto the tables. "What?"

"They bonded over something," said Lynette, pointing to Vic and Kandace with her chin. Lynette rinsed a bunch of fresh basil leaves and two fat tomatoes and handed them to Libby, then took out the buffalo mozzarella. Lynette cut the fat slices of mozzarella while Libby cut the beefsteak tomatoes into slices of the same width, then they assembled the basil-tomato-mozzarella "sandwiches". Len washed his hands, then handed over the balsamic vinegar. Libby drizzled it over the tomatoes, then Len sprinkled on ribbons of basil.

Lynette washed her hands, then took out a machete and a watermelon. Lynette hacked the watermelon in half, then fourths. Len and Libby stood back. Lynette's muscles bunched as she expertly hacked it into slices and slid the slices into a fat plastic bowl. They put away all the spices, washed the knives and cutting boards, and wiped everything down.

They carried the bowls and plates out, and Len grabbed a handful of tongs and serving spoons. They put the food on the table, then went back in for the lemonade, squeezed that morning, and sun tea in a huge glass jar with a tap on the bottom, and glasses.

Jen came out from the office, the one with a door that let her out into the backyard. She had blue-black hair ruthlessly captured in a silver pin at the back of her neck. Her skin was the color of a hazelnut. Her nails were cut short and painted silver. She had a blade face, with obvious Native American ancestry in the nose, the brow. She wore a loose teal blouse and black shorts, and had dangly turquoise and silver earrings, necklaces, and bracelets. She carried herself like a panther, stalking across the yard. She sat, and Lynette brought her some sweet tea. She kissed Lynette on the cheek, and smiled up at her. "Sorry, had to get that stuff done if we were gonna get paid." Her voice was low, husky.

"That's fine," said Lynette. "Just in time." She sat down next to her sister wife, and they clasped hands before letting go.

Kandace stepped forward. "I'm Kandace," she said.

"Jen." Jen waved towards the seat on her other side. "Sit, please." Kandace found herself plopping into the seat without thinking.

Libby sat on her other side. "You've been Jenned."

Jen laughed. "She thinks I could order the sun to stop, and it would." She smiled indulgently at her daughter. She held up her hands, and everyone sat. Jen sang something that Kandace couldn't understand, and then they all started passing around the plates rather than the food. Whomever was in front of the food put it on the plates. Soon, everyone had full plates, and they began to eat.

Kandace was stunned. "Meri, you couldn't have made all this. You're too busy. This is the best damn food I've ever eaten."

Len pointed. "Libby made the bread and caprese salads, and Lynette here did the potato salad and the watermelon."

"Wow. Libby, did you bring a dessert?" Kandace begged with her eyes.

"Woman isn't done with picnic food, and she's trolling for dessert," said Libby with a snort. "Yes, I've got you covered."

"Don't leave me hanging," said Kandace.

"ADD woman," said Meri.

Libby snorted. "Strawberries, whipped cream, shaved dark chocolate."

Kandace moaned. "Stars above, woman, you're killing me."

Jen laughed and changed the subject. "I've got the Little Hollow covered."

"What's the Little Hollow?" asked Kandace.

"A holler that needs cash fast," said Libby. "We're—the family business—in the process of turning the views into cash. It's the only thing we can sell."

Kandace put a very confused look on her face. She couldn't talk with fish in her mouth.

"You're in the holler. You have no work, no job. Your pappy done died, drank his fool self to death. Your brother got out, went to the army. How do you feed your mama and your four little brothers and sisters?" Libby asked Kandace.

Kandace swallowed. "Running or selling drugs. I knew plenty of pot farmers in my day, farms clinging to hillsides."

Libby sucked her breath in through her teeth. "We've got those, next hill over."

"Sell whatever piece of scrap you can get your hand on. Grow, can, raise your own food. Take any shit job that lasts more than a half hour. Pick corn in fall, apples. Whatever the hell. Winter, you're screwed, unless someone pays you to dig them out, or you have enough extra food put aside to sell," said Kandace.

Everyone stared at her. "Holler girl," said Libby. She held up her fist, and Kandace bumped it.

"Which is better than a hollaback girl," said Meri, quoting a Gwen Stefani song. All the women doubled over laughing, while Len, Vic, and Davis looked on, confused.

"What the hell is a hollaback girl, anyway?" asked Libby.

"Learned to spell 'bananas' from that song," said Meri. They all laughed again.

Jen cleared her throat. "So, we're getting some shacks turned into fishing places near the rivers, usually at the edge of their properties. Even got three in a cluster, fill 'em up, turn 'em and burn 'em. New guests every weekend. Fire pit, convenience store nearby so they can stock up on beer. No firearms allowed, drunken assholes can't go running our woods with guns. Hard to assault people with fishing poles. It's usually easy to duck." Vic snorted, and Davis laughed.

"So, money, real cash coming in," said Kandace.

"Even charge renters for firewood, chopped and ready to go for the fire pit," said Jen. "Family kids keep 'em stocked, get paid for running supplies up on their bikes. Thought about writers, artists, leaf peepers, bird watchers until we learned about people like you, into coding or writing. We added some satellite dishes so people have the Internet even in the holler. Got huge vistas. Cabins and tiny houses dotting these hills, bird blinds to watch nesting sites far enough away so the birds aren't bothered by the people."

Kandace grinned. "Put paperbacks in the cabins to read on cold winter nights, wood stoves. Some people like getting snowed in. Get all romantic in winter. Plus, cross-country skiing, snowshoeing, snowboarding, even snowmobiles."

"Shit," said Jen. She looked over at Len, Vic, and Davis clustered at the end of the table, working their way through piles of catfish and hush puppies on their plates. She pointed a fork at them. "This woman has great ideas. Don't screw this up."

"No, ma'am," said Vic.

"Never," said Len.

"Of course not," said Davis.

After dinner Davis, having had little time with Kandace that week, left the others to clean up while he walked her around the property. "Your moms are nice. And terrifying."

Davis laughed. "Jen's the one that got me through med school. I didn't sleep for eight years. I was terrified of letting her down. The military paid for it because we needed to get it paid for, and they would let me specialize. Still treat vets. Go out for two weeks every few months to the VA, work to get them caught up. I see the holler people here. Anyway, she pushed me, harder than a drill sergeant."

"So, she keeps everyone going. Where's your dad?"

Davis sighed. "Tiny house apprenticeship. Learning how to build them. He wants to sprinkle them over these hills. I thought he was nuts until I heard what you said today. He wants to hire people all over these valleys, train them up in something that is a hot business that also involves craftsmanship."

"I love that idea." Kandace held his hand, flipped it over, stroked his palm. "You have great hands, hands that put people back together. Like me."

"When I was looking at your X-rays, I never thought, 'Hey, I hope to date and possibly marry this person.' You were just a skeleton in a lightbox." He kissed her hand. "I have had less time with you. I'm sorry, but I have a lot on my plate."

"I think we have to take two days when you have time, split them up around the other two when you're gone." She reached up, stroked his face. He leaned down for a kiss, a gentle one.

He smiled down at her. "Works for me."

They continued walking. "Jen is worried, and I'm getting there. The people around here, many don't give a shit about poly. They don't care about what people do behind closed doors. But it just takes one religious nut to inflame others to take action. Stupid actions."

"What actions? I can defend myself."

"It only takes one person with a screw loose. Someone to convince a gullible person to do something with a knife, a torch, a baseball bat." Davis looked out over the rolling land in a thousand shades of green. "I've treated a woman whose husband went after her with a baseball bat. She's in a wheelchair, and some redneck lawyer got him off. She's in another state, and he died a few years later in a fall when he was drunk. But not before he beat up both his sister and his new woman. He only got six months in jail, total. My colleagues treated a woman set on fire because she talked back to her husband. He got the needle, both of them dead for two years now. And I've treated people with nicks on bones from knives, broken bones. Male and female. None of this in war zones. All of it was here. Right here, in the valley."

"You're afraid."

"No, I'm not stupid or blind. Some asshole tells another idiot that this kind of violence is okay because the other person is female, or a different skin color, or originally from somewhere else. My mom, Jen, she's from here, thirty thousand years before anyone else. One asshole tried to beat her up, and got thrown through a door when the door was closed. She was sixteen. Smart, fast. Our dad would have been stupid beyond belief not to fall in love with her."

"Lynette is awesome too."

"She is," agreed Davis. "I know you can defend yourself. But I can, I will protect you. Not with Vic's rage under his skin, like a swarm of bees. Not with Len's implacability. But with my brains and technology. I'm going to install cameras and teach you the places to hit with a baseball bat."

"You gonna get me a Louisville Slugger?"

"And take you to baseball games, if you want."

She grinned up at him. "Good. Buy me a ball cap too."

"I can do that." Davis kissed her again.

She stood back, looked up at him. "I think we're ready to start getting intimate. You three buy a vat of condoms, and we'll get started. I can't make a choice without intimacy."

"Have you fallen in love with all three of us?" asked Davis.

"Getting there," she said.

"Get all the way there," he said, and leaned down and kissed her again.

"Tease." Kandace laughed and ran away.

"Is this the chasing part?" Davis jogged after her.

ATTACK HUG

Kandace sat very, very still in the chair, letting the light hit her face. The last heat wave had passed, and the wind was hot but not burning. Kandace no longer had black, green, yellow, or red around her eyes and nose. Her nose was its normal size but had a little dent in it. Libby came out and put the plate down. "Toffee dark chocolate with pecans, two pieces."

Kandace sipped from her tea bottle. "You got a minute?"

"Give me five." Libby went back inside. She came back out with a bottle of water, and sat down.

"You ever heard of Touchstone Haven?" asked Kandace.

"Nope," said Libby.

"Commune. No weird leader, the idea is just to live as you want, preferably while treating the environment well. Sexual freedom. They've got land around the edge, figure we can build a house thing. Not that far away, actually technically closer to the hospital for all three of my men."

"Why?" asked Libby.

"Your mama, Jen, is worried. And so is Davis." Kandace bit into the last chunk of toffee and sighed.

"Ah, torches and pitchforks."

"I get their concerns. I've grown up in hollers all my life. Most people make some sort of sense."

Libby let loose with a deep-throated laugh. "Most of the time."

"But they're right. It just takes one person drinking moonshine and snorting crushed-up pills. Or someone who's been listening to 'Satan is in the valley' nonsense." Kandace sighed.

"Or someone going off on a dare." Libby's voice was flat. "What do you need from me?"

"Can you drive up there with me, look at the land, talk to some people?"

Libby stared at Kandace. "Not one of the boys?"

Kandace shook her head. "I need help, another set of eyes. I need to find out if this makes any sense before bringing it up with the boys. Or even going in too deep with them. What would my life be like with all of them? I just can't see it. This way, I can see it."

"Why can't you just stay here? My parents live here, and no one's messed with them in years."

"We can. Did the kids at school have any idea you had two moms?"

Libby gave her a blank look. "Let's look tomorrow."

∼

They went for a drive just after the lunch rush after one of Meri's tomato-and-bacon paninis. "What got you into baking?" Kandace asked when she picked Libby up. Libby lived over the bakery, and she smelled like cinnamon. Her assistant could handle the slow afternoon.

"I did it from when I was little. Apple poppyseed muffins. Loved 'em. The lemon ones are good too. Tiny ones. Would bake 'em and put 'em in everyone's lunch boxes." She grinned. "Figured out I could make money at it when my muffins in kids' lunches became traded for things like gum and baseball cards. I baked extra, got a cut."

Kandace laughed. "How enterprising of you."

They rode up and over the mountain, and played Nightwish's "Bye Bye Beautiful." They rocked out while on the curving path up into the hills. They took a series of roads to the edge of the property. The carved wooden sign was clear, *Touchstone Haven. No visitation without consent.*

There was an enormous greenhouse, houses made of stone and wood and a lot of stained glass. There was a foundry and glassmaking shop and firewood piled at the side of each building. "It's beautiful," said Kandace.

"Gorgeous," agreed Libby.

Kandace parked, and they got out. A young man in his twenties, tall, with a shock of black hair and a wide grin, came out of the foundry in a leather apron. "Hello. I am Jacob. You must be Kandace and Libby. I am making knives. Would you like to watch me work?" They followed him in and watched him. The fire ran hot, and they were soon sweating. Jacob wore heavy gloves as he heated the metal to create paring knives. He made two, shaping both, then plunged them into a cylindrical water bath, making them steam. "Questions?"

"This is a poly colony?" Kandace asked, getting right to the chase.

"Actually, we have couples, triads, a few quads, and a line marriage of six," said Jacob. "I have two wives, and my brother has two husbands."

"And the work?" asked Libby.

"There is a list. People like me with specific skills, we do those things. There are also general tasks nearly anyone can do. After this, I will go to the greenhouse and pick tomatoes and cucumbers. We make sure all the work gets done."

"Children?" asked Kandace.

"We have children of all ages. We homeschool. And no, we don't block the Internet. As long as your other tasks get done, like growing food or cutting firewood or teaching the children, you can work online. Several of us do." He put the knives aside to cool. "Back away, you don't want to get metal dust on you." They backed off.

Jacob took out another knife, put on a mask, and began grinding its edge. He finished and polished the knife with a cloth. "We have less chores in winter than in summer, but our greenhouse uses vertical farming and hydroponics techniques. We grow enough food to have a vegetarian diet, but many of us eat fish and eggs. We make our own goat cheese, butter, and milk. We have female goats we have for milk, rent out the boy ones for nibbling on kudzu." The invasive vine was hard to kill and had begun invading Missouri. Goats were good at eating it. "Our goats also clear hillsides in days that would take far longer with equipment and keep properties clear of high grass. We also have honeybees, and grow lavender and other herbs for tinctures. We create and sell all-natural soaps and essential oils. We make enough money to keep going just fine, and we do hire local if we need something done. We use solar, wind, and water power, and are completely off the power grid. In fact, they pay us. I hear you want to build a larger poly house here?"

"Yes," said Kandace. "The outsides of your homes are beautiful. Can we see inside one?"

"My wife, Melody, is inside our house there," said Jacob, pointing across the street lined with leafy trees. "Please, go ask her."

"Thank you," said Kandace.

They walked over to the house with a huge play area on the side. Several children were inside; they could hear the voices. Kandace and Libby went over to the door and knocked.

A woman in her thirties opened the door. She had long brown hair, a lined face, and a ready smile. "Hello, I'm Kandace, and this is Libby. Jacob said we could ask you to see the house?"

"Sure. I'm Melody." Melody gestured them in with a smile.

Kandace looked down. "Amazing hardwood floors."

"Bamboo, and we also use reclaimed wood." Melody shut the door. It was a longhouse with a central area, kitchen in the back corner in cheerful country blues and yellows, the dining area with a long picnic-style table of hewn wood, and padded wooden benches and chairs. There was a classroom with learning stations and soft, comfortable chairs. The kids had their lessons and waved at Kandace and Libby. They ranged in age from three to about seven, and there were four of them. They ran into their playroom with bean bag chairs, books, wooden toys, and puzzles and games.

Each bathroom was long and had two sinks, a toilet, and either a shower or bathtub. They all had beautiful glass tiles in them, in gold and blue. The central area had a staircase and a fireplace and a soft, well-used blue couch and chairs. They went up the stairs, and there were bedrooms on each side and bathrooms in between. "Wow," said Kandace. "Two adult bedrooms and rooms for each kid?"

"Yes," said Melody. They went back down the stairs. "Our husband sleeps in either room and has a loft space on his alone-time nights, which are few."

"This is amazing," said Kandace.

"Let's sit," said Melody. They arranged themselves on the modular couch. "So, you're poly?" asked Melody.

"Kandace is courting my three brothers," said Libby.

"Such a fun, amazing time," said Melody. "We didn't court at once here. Leigh Ann came a year later to the commune. We both looked at her, and that was it."

"We don't want to take up too much of your time," said Kandace. "I just...we want to be safe. We all rent, and that's just stupid."

"Our houses are not cheap, but we save on labor by doing it within the commune as much as we can. We call it a house-raising, and if we do one for you, you must do three in return," said Melody. "We work with local contractors, even had one defect and go to Utah to work with a builder there. Good news, his son came back and works here now as an electrical apprentice." She laughed. "My daughter Seelie has her eye on him."

"I thought..." said Kandace, looking around.

"Previous marriage," said Melody. "The father left us when she was two."

"Terrible," said Kandace.

"It was hard, but now my life is incredible," said Melody. "You said you want to live on the edge, by the stream."

"My future husbands...I can't believe that's plural, that wasn't in my life plan," said Kandace. "Not that I had much of one. Just get through one day to the next. Anyway, my men are private. They love fishing and honey. I'm sure at least one of them would like to help the beekeepers."

Libby burst out laughing. "I'm a baker, and I deliberately make things with honey to make them happy. Our family's land is large enough for the bees. But all three of my brothers have an independent streak and don't want to live right on top of Dad and my mothers."

"You come from a poly family," said Melody. "Unusual."

"Not for us," said Libby. "Anyway, my brothers like privacy. All three are in the medical professions. Doctor, EMT and rescue, and home health."

"Wow," said Melody. "I was a tax attorney and do that once a year here. I have my hands full with the kids and commune tasks."

"I am sorry, I know you're busy," said Kandace.

Just then, the three-year-old came streaking out, and attached himself to his mother's leg. "Keith," said his mother, huge smiles on both their faces. "Attack hug time?"

"Attack hug time," said Keith, giggling.

Kandace and Libby stood. "Thank you. This was wonderful," said Kandace.

"I live directly over my work for now, but if I get a significant other, I may consider this," said Libby. "I lean as poly too."

"Great!" said Melody. "I hope to see you soon!" They saw themselves out and just stood on the wide porch.

"This is..." said Libby.

"No words," agreed Kandace.

They saw the vertical farming greenhouse which rose to the sky. They walked over, went in and found a woman touching a panel. "Hello, I'm Dawn," she said. "You must be Kandace and Libby."

"We are," said Kandace. "I'm Kandace. Do you run this place?" There were trays from floor to vaulted glass ceiling of plants, LED lights overhead. There were strawberries hanging from a rack at head height, ready to be picked by just walking underneath. Rows of lettuce, carrots, potatoes, and herbs. It smelled of water and green, growing things.

"We have a computer overseeing the spraying," said Dawn. "We grow food for ourselves, year-round. We sell all over the valleys here, to restaurants. We have our own vegan restaurant, and as long as you put in the time, you can eat there for free. We also have a fish shack, just order ahead. Libby, I hear you're a baker?"

"I want your herbs," said Libby, eyes aglow. "I have suppliers, but..."

"And grains," said Dawn. "We grind them ourselves and steel-cut the oats. Great oatmeal in winter. We also have an orchard with apples and pears."

Libby grinned. "I'm a baker, and you are speaking my language."

Kandace left them to talk shop and walked outside. She found the library with floor-to-ceiling books, the communal kitchen with both indoor and outdoor seating. She walked back out in a daze. She found Libby again and said, "Did you put in your order?"

"I did. Thanks, Dawn."

"Anytime."

They walked back to the jeep in silence. "Wow. They can get me stuff here for far less than some of my other suppliers. A guy named Sven will run it down in his van three times a week." Libby grinned from ear to ear.

Kandace put on her seatbelt and looked out. "I want all of it. This is amazing."

"How the hell did you find them? I grew up here, and I hadn't heard of it. This operation didn't spring up overnight."

"They have a holding company to protect their name, do business with post office boxes. Many of their people are here because poly was illegal where they were, or they just didn't want the hassle of explaining their lifestyle. They build up businesses that work. I found a whisper of them online and contacted Jacob."

"This is incredible. How do they run themselves?"

"Jacob told me when I swung back around. They elect a committee of three and an alternate for two years, then a new election. No one much wants to do it because it's a pain in the ass, but the scheduling gets done, and everyone eats and has power and water."

They rode down in silence, then Libby said, "Are you going to marry my brothers?"

"We need to..." said Kandace, gesturing with her hand in an obscene way.

"You haven't? You must be popping out of your skin."

"I am." Kandace laughed. "I am."

SKINWALKERS

*J*en said, "Pass it up." Jen and Kandace installed the boxes of underfloor storage, cut the boards, and cut and glued together the lids to the storage. Kandace passed them up by leaning them against the wall and then walking them up two steps on the stairs. They snicked the boards together with glue at the joints. Kandace looked over to where Jen was pointing. She picked up the nail gun, held it upside-down, and passed it up to the loft of the cabin. She saw the two boxes of nails and passed them up as well. Jen put on her ear protectors, put her hard hat back on, checked the gun to see if it had nails, lined it up, and started shooting. Kandace put on her own ear protection because she wasn't stupid and started handing up the boards used for the wall. The lids for the boxes, their hinges, and screws to attach the hinges went up next. The electrical for the dual by-the-bed LED lamps had already been installed and tested. The backboard went up next and the two under-lamp shelves as night-stands took shape under Jen's nail gun and her cordless electric screwdriver.

Jen stopped, smiled, and pointed to the door. They took off the ear and eye protectors and hard hats and put them on the plywood shelf created by a board over two sawhorses. They went out to the pickup truck, and Jen took her water bottle off her utility belt and filled it up with sweet tea. Kandace filled up hers, and the two women put on their sunglasses and stood in the summer sun. "Walk with me," said Jen. Kandace handed Jen a chocolate nut cereal bar, and Jen ate it in two bites. Kandace ate her bar, and they put their trash in the recycling sorter at the edge of the site.

They walked up a small incline and sat down in the grass. "I hear you went up to the Touchstone Haven poly community."

"Libby squealed." Kandace sipped her sweet tea.

"She's considering it too. She's not dating yet, and she loves her little apartment, but that's a post-college place. She's a successful businesswoman."

"She is. I can only visit her once or twice a week, or I would be the size of a house."

Jen laughed. "She is talented." She looked out over the forest surrounding the cabin being refurbished. "I just want you to know, it's a good idea."

"It is? I mean, I'm just getting started in this poly thing. I wanted to see a future life."

Jen smiled. "I can see that. My boys still live like they're in college. Each one, even Davis, had to pay off debt. Davis took on his brothers' debts and paid them off one at a time."

Kandace grinned. "Good. I haven't seen their places yet. They keep picking me up at the cabin."

Jen laughed. "Davis has elegant taste and shares with Vic. He hires a person to clean because Vic is still a frat boy in his head. Len lives over the dojo where he works out. Can't stand living with loud Vic and fussy Davis."

Kandace laughed out loud. "I can see all that."

"Len gets a break on the rent for watching the dojo at night. Why anyone would want to break into a dojo is bizarre. What are you going to steal? Mats? The weaponry is all locked up, and most of it is rubber for the kids."

Kandace laughed again. "Len knows aikido, I know, because he mentioned it."

"T'ai chi as well, and he's now into the Brazilian martial art *capoeira*. He's working his way up to black belts. We got him into it because he vibrated as a kid. Not ADD, just ready to move at any moment. He had his first class at four and hasn't looked back." Jen grinned.

"It gives him his grace."

"He learned that from his father. Huge, but that man can walk like he floats on air." Jen fanned her face. "Fell for him just watching him walk across a room. Met at summer camp. He could swim, and I kicked his ass in archery." She mimed shooting an arrow. Kandace laughed.

Jen's face got serious. "Our tribe, it's gone now. Disease, massacres, a trail of death millennia before the white man even came. We were small to begin with, only about two thousand of us. Skinwalkers, we were called." She shook her head slowly from side to side. "Our language, culture, long gone. And it all started with Ma'maan. Bastard." She spit at the ground off to the left. "Idiot decided, this is nearly two thousand years ago, that the best way to save our tribe was by eliminating those he saw as a threat by killing and eating them, as a mountain lion." She shook with rage. "You must understand, counting coup, touching a warrior while he or she slept, was considered to be the highest honor. Leaving a feather, taking a bead, those things too. But, Ma'maan saw a different path. I don't know if he was evil, crazy, or both, but he convinced one of his wives, Pa'aapata, to join him in this...crusade. Le'aagapi, his other wife, refused, and eventually killed him, years later. Ma'maan and Pa'aapata ran in the forest and caves and hid themselves. We started being slaughtered by the Quapaw, Otoe, Chikasaw, Ioway, even our own children. We turned on Ma'maan and Pa'aapata, desperately trying to stay alive, and scattered. Ma'maan and Pa'aapata turned on the tribe when we turned on them. Le'aagapi killed Ma'maan, and Pa'aapata stole into the forest with their children. Le'aagapi eventually killed Pa'aapata and got their children back, but it was far too late for us by then. There was an extensive runner network, so news of skinwalkers spread far and wide. Some of us managed to infiltrate into other nations before they deliberately decided to massacre us all."

Kandace stared at Jen, wide-eyed. "That sounds horrific."

"We lost all of who we were, our language, history, culture. Became mimics, took on the languages and cultures of where we were relocated. Then, the white man came." They both sat for a while, feeling the warm wind throw about their hair. "We infiltrated more First Nations. Eventually, we intermarried with the whites and found out we had a dominant trait. A lot of marriages ended when a mother or father saw the first change, took the child, and ran off into the woods. Then, we found them, the *loup-garou*, among the French fur traders. People who could turn into wolves. The bears, well, they're old. Thirty thousand years old. We think we were far-north Europeans and Asians that crossed the land bridge during the last ice age, before there was Russia, China, Korea, or Canada. There are some still there too. Those of us that crossed the land bridge never migrated farther south than the Mason-Dixon line, can't stand being without snow. So we found other places to hide."

"With the bears and wolves." Kandace was stunned. "Any other shifters?"

"Some can turn into both bear and mountain lion, bear and wolf, wolf and mountain lion. We think it was intermarriage and a dominant genetic trait. We don't know about many others. There are snakes, jaguars, eagles, horned owls that shift. Large predators. It is kind of stupid to turn yourself into, say, a ferret. The brain must be big enough to hold at least some human thought, and a bird or snake would have to be huge. "

"Tigers, lions?"

"Why not? Other continents, but for all we know this has been with us since we began. We know the Somali have hyena shifters. We haven't personally met them."

"And our babies—if I marry your sons, the babies will be shifters?"

"Dominant trait. It is very rare that a child isn't a shifter, even with a 'normie' parent."

Kandace guffawed. "That's what alcoholics and addicts call people who aren't addicted." She sighed. "I'm afraid that gets thrown into the mix too."

"Heart disease? Diabetes? Anything else we should know about? Just so you know, we haven't had a single diabetic since we found out there was such a disease."

Kandace grinned. "Good for Libby." Jen laughed. "No, low blood pressure in the women. High blood pressure, but my dad was a Type A asshole, so it may not be genetic."

"We are immune to many diseases, but not ones introduced to the New World, like smallpox. We do the whole immunization thing like everybody else. Therefore, we live long lives. We have our families, spread out our children, try to get our numbers up to sustainable levels, while simultaneously not getting caught. Eventually, someone will get caught on video, or go in for some genetic testing when that sort of testing is far enough along that our genetic differences show up. Our goal is to have enough survivors hidden if that happens."

"What about the poly place, Touchstone?"

"We funded it as a haven for poly people, without the whole shapeshifting thing in mind. We helped them set themselves up to remain hidden with a dummy corporation, mail drops. We figured out it would be a good place to retreat if necessary. Be among our own poly kind. We're working with them, buying handmade tools. Libby didn't know they existed, but now she's going to buy their herbs, nut butters, and flours. We wanted to see if it would remain viable before telling our kids about it. It's nearly six years old, and they are just amazing people, all of them." Jen grinned. "You, specifically, would fit in there. You would probably learn to pick tomatoes and turn out knives with the best of them."

Kandace's eyes glowed. "I'd like to learn how to make swords. Ship one out to my friend Tania. She loves renaissance fairs and dragged us all over the region to them." She grinned. "Something to do with my time other than plan projects. My brain bleeds sometimes, you know?" she said, pointing to her head. "And my eyes fall out." She mimed her eyes popping out into her hands.

Jen laughed. "My boys are the cure for that, for now. Get to know the family. Head on up there to Touchstone two or three days a month, learn the skills, get to know the people up there. Bring my sons up there, and let them see it. Make a decision. If you don't want to live there, you can have part of our property and build on the edge. But two of my sons are ex-military, and I don't think they will want to do that. They've very literally been on their own for a very long time."

"Separate houses?"

Jen laughed again. "Some women want their own kitchens, but I don't think that's your thing."

"Meri spilled," said Kandace with a grimace.

Jen laughed so hard she doubled over. "Meri will have you covered," she said when she was able to talk again. "And if you don't want the family to know something, don't tell anyone, not even yourself."

Kandace laughed. "Family tom-tom network that good?"

Jen snorted. "Davis jokes that we know what he's going to do before he does it."

"Do you think we should get married?"

"That's up to you and my sons. If you're asking if I think you're good enough for them, then yes, absolutely. You get hit, you get smashed, and you keep going. You treat my sons differently, a different smile for each one, a different touch. You see them as different men."

"Duh? They...are? Different humans? Um, shifter humans?"

Jen said quietly, "That's a huge stretch for a young woman just out of graduate school to make. First to a man that turns into a bear, and then that all three of my sons wanted to date you, and that they wanted to share a marriage with you, and that they are all very different men. That's a hell of a lot to take in."

Kandace stared out at the cabin, not really seeing it. "I met them as people first. If there had been some sort of poly dating society, I would have thought it was crazy. But I don't think it's crazy after meeting them, meeting you and Lynette." She smiled softly. "I always wanted kids, but having ones that turn into bears, it'll be...something."

"Or mountain lions." Jen gave a quiet smile. "They'll climb everything, get in trouble, human or wild form. You're strong enough to have kids like that."

"I am. I also think I'm plumb crazy to be taking this on. But, I've never heard a word of anything but respect, love, and kindness from you all, and the only bad word from Mabel. The rest of the town, I don't hear any racist or religious shit, don't hear a word about me not being 'from here,' got kids coming all the way up the mountain to sell me freaking candy and cookies and stuff for their school drives. Got my truck washed for a school trip. And it's summer!"

Jen laughed. "We have year-round schools. They get three weeks off in summer, December, a week off in spring, a whole week for Thanksgiving. Most people don't have farms anymore, and those that do, the adults work for the big combines. Kids learn jobs around here, and we...our foundation pays for after-school programs where kids can take a certificate program in any damn thing they want, sixty entire subjects. Anything from animal husbandry to carpentry, coding, art, X-ray tech. The community colleges around here do that online with some busing. Gets high school kids stuff they can do to earn money while they go to college, if they want to go. Graduation rates started going through the roof. Our family home schooled up until middle school. Our kids need socialization, prom, that sort of thing. Most of them graduated early with at least two certificates."

"Wow. I am so glad I picked that little cabin."

"So are we." Jen patted Kandace's leg. "So are we."

~

The gym was no-nonsense, hot and sweaty, fans whirring away, the air conditioner not really keeping up with the heat. Kandace was learning to swing the foam-and-plastic bat Davis had given her. "What did I teach you?" Davis asked.

Kandace grinned then tapped him, starting at the bottom and working up. "Ankle, side of the knee..." She gripped the bat closer to the middle. "Groin."

Davis reflexively moved up his knee and joined it to his elbow to block. "And that's why that shot is often ineffective."

She moved her hand back up the bat a bit. "Kidney shot, wrist, elbow, neck, but that one's hard to hit with a ducking, weaving opponent. Head shot's gotta be a temple shot. Again, hard to hit at the right angle. Len's my height, you and Vic not so much." The men were stair-stepped, each one half a head taller than the other one, Vic the tallest.

"My secret advantage is knowing the human body. All right, let's use the kickboxing stand for this. Use your good hand first, then use the other one slowly. In fact, we can switch to half-pound weights at that point."

"Nothing much wrong with my legs." Kandace danced in place.

"Kickboxing is a good idea for you. But, bat first, since you like swinging that thing so much."

"End goal, batting cage. Don't look at me like that." Kandace glared at his flat stare. "No, I can't handle the shock going up my bad arm now. But, it is the end goal."

Davis sighed. "Let's do this." Kandace hefted the bat, ready to swing.

∿

*D*avis headed off to refill both their water bottles. Kandace wiped herself down with her small towel and eyed the machines. She could do the leg machines, but both Davis and Len had cautioned her about using a machine before she was ready. She walked over, eyed the hand weights. A woman with her springy hair in clips sporting a full six-pack was lifting an enormous amount of weight on a pulldown machine, grunting. She was making a circuit, her cobalt skin glistening with sweat. The blue-black tattoos on her shoulders stood out. Kandace looked away, wondering how many months it would take for her to get in that condition. She stepped towards the hand weights, and a woman in a purple leotard with red leggings, a cascade of brown hair with bangs falling into her eyes, and big blue eyes stepped in front of Kandace. Kandace looked her up and down, then stepped aside. The woman stepped in front of her again, eyes snapping. "Stay away from Davis. He's mine."

Kandace raised her eyebrows. "Did you just claim to own someone? Because I thought that went out four hundred years ago. Wait, that was still happening into the middle of the last century, with women. You might want to be careful what words you use, when, and why."

The woman on the pulldown machine wiped the machine off, and looked over at the brown-haired woman. "Becca, she's right. You want to say that again about owning someone?"

Becca looked around, trying to find a defender. "Davis has been in love with me since the fifth grade."

Davis came up behind Becca and said, "No, the other way around. Becca, I can't be more plain. I'm not interested in you, I don't want you, and I'm certainly not your anything."

Becca looked like she had been punched in the stomach. "Don't say that." Her eyes watered. "We can be…"

Davis walked around her and kissed Kandace gently. Then he said, "Let's work on those hand weights. Very light ones."

Kandace turned towards the springy-haired woman who was stepping forward from the pulldown machine. "Hi, I'm Kandace." She walked over, and held out her hand.

"Tamara." The woman shook Kandace's hand with a firm grip, careful not to squeeze too hard. "Not trying to diss Davis, the man put my little sister, Jaia, back together after a BMX biking trick gone wrong, but he's going about this wrong. I'm a certified trainer, good with kickboxing, and down with that bat thing you're doing."

Davis said, "I can tell you her injuries, give you two time to cook something up."

"You not in this just to get handsy with your lady?" Tamara asked Davis.

Davis snorted. "A nice side effect but no. This is a date, and I promised to show her something. I wanted to do it in a controlled environment. And I kind of hoped you would be here."

Tamara raised her eyes to his. "Oh ho. And your brothers Len and Vic? Don't want them to get handsy with her?"

Kandace snorted. "Not the problem. Both of them are crazy busy, especially this one." Kandace pointed at Davis. "I want to turn my body into one like your body. Over time, maybe a year, but I want it without re-injuring myself."

Behind them, Becca stamped her foot. "You can't just ignore me!"

Kandace turned and faced Becca. "We were ignoring your pain to give you time to get your shit together. But I see now that you don't want to do that. You want to spend your time chasing unavailable men rather than make yourself into someone that is fantastically happy with or without someone to date."

Becca looked as if she had been slapped. "Shit just got real," Tamara said. "Girl, you're the one who got smashed into a cliff—I read about that one, Vic, the EMT guy, rescued her. Becca, this female just told you some truths you won't want to hear. If you feel like listening to her rather than the cotton candy you've got in your head, let me know. I'll help you transform."

Becca breathed out through her nose. She sounded like a horse chuffing. "Y'all ain't got one lick of kindness in you."

"Kindness isn't what you need right now," Kandace said. "Reality is a stone bitch who doesn't care what you like and don't like, want and don't want. I just spent two months on my ass because of the reality of a rock and a cliff face. I'm lucky I wasn't hurt worse. Reality sucks." Kandace shrugged her shoulders. She turned her back on Becca. "Debts are nearly paid off. I probably can't afford you, Tamara, but I need you to get where I want to go."

Davis grinned. "That's our girl." He turned to Becca. "Listen carefully to what these women just told you. Quit looking for anyone in this valley to make you happy. It's an inside job."

"What's she got that I don't?" Becca asked, her voice rising into a near-scream at the end.

Davis and Kandace just looked at each other, grinning. "My cat likes him." Kandace shrugged. "Girl leaves my side for him every time."

Tamara sucked in a breath, let it out. "Becca, that there," she said, waving a finger at Davis and Kandace, "that's love. Take your blinders off, girl, and find someone who looks at you like that." Becca glared at all three of them and stomped off.

Kandace said, "Time, day, and place?"

"Here, tomorrow, ten o'clock," Tamara said. "And you better be able to afford me." She turned to Davis. "Tell me what that cliff did to her, and we'll make a plan." Kandace grinned, grabbed her water bottle and sucked some icy water down her throat, grabbed her towel, and headed towards the showers.

COURTING

$\mathcal{L}$en was at the house, and Kandace let him choose the movie. They put together a puzzle while re-watching *Twilight* and arguing about how the plot would be different if it were about different shifter groups. "I have something to tell you. You know how we're courting you?"

"You forgot to rub my feet. You're off the list." Kandace found a corner piece and snapped it in.

Len grunted. "Too bad. I also know how to work on your neck. No me, no getting out the gnome-kinks you get from dictation and typing all day, and working out three times a week with Tamara."

Kandace snorted. "That woman spots me, and she can lift the weights I'm lifting with her little finger." Len snorted very delicately, in a Zen sort of way. "You forgot to do work on my neck too. Double off the list."

"Maybe that's a post-puzzle plan. Anyway, both Lynette and Jen are done with the kid thing. Each of them lost cubs—pregnancies, not babies that made it full term. It is difficult to stay pregnant with some of our pregnancies. None of us know why. We have two shifter fertility specialists, one here, one in France, helping us get and stay pregnant. Anyway, there is a shifter woman that they—my parents—have been dating, I guess you can say, for a while now."

"Okay. And this is any of my business because...?"

"As of now, you're part of our family." He pretended to ignore the sudden rush of tears to Kandace's eyes. "My parents are courting a new wife. Things are getting really bad for her where she is." Len reached under the table and massaged Kandace's right foot. "Her husband has been censured by us, the community, for failure to support his offspring. The law does that too, but he refuses to pay. He also harasses her, and we've got him on video, repeatedly, audio from his phone rants, and so on. She divorced him, as she was legally married to him. She was his second wife. The first wife had enough and moved deep within our community, and he can't find her because she divorced him and married again. She is married to a grizzly shifter who lives near Yellowstone."

"So, screwing with a grizzly shifter would be bad for this black bear asshole twerp."

"Exactly." Len laughed. He let go of her feet when he found an edge piece and snicked it in. At her glare, he reached down and started rubbing again. "So, we're dug in here. We're friends with cops, Davis is a doctor, Vic works with the rescue squad, and both are military trained. Also, would you care to make either Jen or Lynette angry?"

Kandace shuddered. "No. I'm really glad they like me. It would be not good if they didn't."

"Not good is a massive understatement. We are all delighted they love you, especially Mama Jen. She's very loving, but protective to the point of having hidden weaponry."

Kandace grinned. "I'm a country girl. We're good with weaponry, hidden or otherwise."

Len smiled. "We all grew up learning how to defend ourselves, as bears and people. Anyway, this woman is sweet, and was apparently raised as if what we believe is a secretive cult someplace way north, close to the Canadian border. We suspect some form of abuse, which is bizarre because that'll get you punished."

"This guy was punished for lack of support. How?" Kandace found three edge pieces, strung them together, and grinned triumphantly.

"You know we put money in the pot, and that money funds things we do that help the community?"

"I do. Do all shapeshifter communities do it?"

"As far as I know. That money is a tool. It protects us. We can use it to move away if things become dangerous. We can pay off someone who catches us changing on a cell phone. Our children get above-average educations, even though most of us live in small towns, and often on the edges of federal parks and other protected lands. We also buy lands we protect. We don't live next to other people, usually on farms. We also give back to the community, and that makes people happy. Both my brothers joined the military because they wanted to serve and to prevent large college expenses from wiping out large chunks of group money and plans."

"Okay," said Kandace. "Do you loan each other money?"

"Generally not. We do projects. Lynette had a family meeting and told us about the adults having put money—a lot of it, it turns out—into the poly colony. It became self-supporting in less than a year."

"I'm impressed. I like the poly colony." Kandace worked on the wing of the flying sparkly purple horse in the picture they were putting together.

"We've all been up there, helping out a little, just talking to people, since Libby told us about it. Lynette and Jen have teased us for years about having weird plans. I have some ideas about a house there." He pulled out his cell phone and handed it over. "I call it the in-out house. There's a deck, and the entire back opens with these sliding glass panels." He used his stylus to open up the design app.

Kandace stared at it, wide-eyed. "That's an outdoor kitchen?"

"For Vic. He loves barbecuing."

"I get that. And the home theater setup in the living room? For me?"

Len grinned. "Yes. That little building in the back is a little dojo for me, and it can be used or rented out as a yoga studio, that sort of thing. I'd love to teach the kids there."

"Great!" Kandace used her fingers to widen the plan.

"Davis gets the basement. He can make it as elegant as he wants. Vic gets the middle, and I get the top. You get a loft way up top but with superior insulation. All of us get suites with full baths. Adults on the left side, and kids on the right. You still want kids?"

"Lots of them."

Len grinned. "Okay, so playroom on the bottom and two bedrooms, two up higher, and we can do two up near your suite. We can also add on whenever we want. I didn't want to go all grandiose. We're not even married, still courting."

Kandace shook her head. "You're not a grandiose kind of guy. So the yoga studio can be rented out, and you can teach martial arts to kids and adults. My work is online. What else can we do to bring in money? This house isn't cheap. And we have no idea how many kids will come out."

"I didn't think of that. Physical therapy? I can do that on property. Have machines."

"Maybe a wellness center. Nothing too big. You may have people there that would love it, even want to work there."

"Wow. I knew you would have good ideas, but this is amazing!"

Kandace laughed. "Can I have my foot rub now?" She put a touch of sadness into her voice at his ignoring her feet. She didn't whine; she hated that, especially from herself.

He laughed. "Of course." He put aside the puzzle tray, got out the mint scrub and a basin, washed her feet in hot water, and scrubbed them before getting out the mint-almond oil. Sam the cat made a grumpy sound and stalked off, hating the smell of mint, but mostly pissed about being ignored. Kandace groaned with pleasure.

The movie ended. "Can you tell me more about this woman your parents are dating?"

"Jetta."

"It must be really weird for you." Kandace sipped her soda.

"No, not really. From the outside looking in, yes. But they've dated before, but unfortunately it hasn't worked out yet. My dad and moms have always said they want more kids and that the family is unfinished."

"It's great that they all know what they want and can get it. So, is there some secret place they go to find a date?"

Len laughed. "Social media. It's a hidden page; you have to know it is there to log in. We never use words like 'shapeshifter' on it. We do mention the words "poly" and "lifestyle". There are some old words in ancient languages we use, kind of catchphrases. One is Old Norse and is a proverb about knowing yourself. There are French and German ones, Thai, and a few more. My parents were chatting with an African lady on the website chat program, a hyena shifter, but she chose to stay local."

"Did you three join the site?"

"We did, and we dated, but that all went pretty disastrously. We found controlling, manipulative, violent, crazy, gold digger women in four states."

Kandace grinned. "Don't hold back. Let me know how you really feel!"

Len laughed. "Oh, the stories we have. One was an adrenaline junkie and loved jumping out of planes and base jumping. Vic dated her until she nearly killed him on a jump. One wanted to sleep with people inside and outside the marriage without discussing it with anyone first. One insisted we pay her up front for all the costs of dating, as she put it. One wanted to not work, be waited on, kind of function as a breeder and drop children at our feet for a set amount of time, then she wanted to leave the kids and be set up someplace."

Kandace grimaced. "Wait, that heifer wanted to have kids, and, what, leave them on your doorstep?"

"Kind of. She didn't want to breast-feed, either. Said it would ruin her figure."

Kandace snorted. "She'd be good as a surrogate, get paid for it. If your numbers are low, you may have to."

Len continued with their dating woes. "One crashed Vic's Camaro, when he had one. Another burned all of Davis' clothes because she was mad at him, and he's a bit of a clothes horse. Has to be, as a doctor, can't just show up in scruffy jeans and tennis shoes."

"So, I'm not crazy," said Kandace. She rolled her eyes back in her head when Len dug into the arch of her foot. "At least, not batshit crazy."

"And you're beautiful, smart, sexy, funny, and tough." Len dug into her heel, and she moaned again.

"Can I...can we...I am really sick of making out. I'm not some teenager in a Pinto. I want to explore you." She ran her hands down his arms, and Len shuddered.

"All right. We have a couch, and I bought condoms and hid them here," he said. The midsection of the couch had drinks and a little wooden drawer. He pulled out a handful. "We have super-sensitive, studded, blue, green, and mint."

Kandace laughed. "Mint? Really?"

"So, all our tests came back negative." All four of them had gotten full medical workups when they started dating. "We'll stay safe. Now, in order to start..."

"Yes, I agree to have sex with all three of you. That's part of the point."

Len took out his phone and sent a text. He started on her other foot, and she leaned back and groaned. Len got one ding on his phone, then a second one right after the first. He pocketed the phone. "Davis must not be in surgery. Len dug into the arch of her other foot. She lay back and let her eyes roll up in her head.

Len took his time. Kandace was wearing shorts, and he worked his way up. He dug into her calves, stroked her thighs. He pulled off the shorts, and she grinned at him as her cutoffs flew across the room. He kissed her from the toes on up and slid his hands up to her buttocks. He separated her legs with gentle strokes. He kissed her inside her knees on up, slowly, and kissed back down on the other side. Kandace slid her hands down in between her legs and stroked his hands. He kissed her, closer and closer, and touched her in between her legs. Kandace was shaking by this point. "Omigod, hurry this up."

Len laughed and blew on the little nub. It trembled and rose for him. He kissed it, gently, and Kandace groaned. He took his time, flicked his tongue, then used his finger to push on her clit and shook his finger on her until she came, rising up from the couch. Len slid two fingers inside, and found the spot inside her that made her scream. Kandace came again, and he kissed her way up her stomach. Kandace took control, grabbed him by the hair, stuffed a condom in his mouth, and said, "Fuck. Me. Now."

Len laughed, tore open the condom with his teeth, rolled it on himself, and slid in. She arched her back, moaned from deep inside. He went all the way in and back out, over and over, finally finding a deep rhythm that made her wrap her legs around him and grab his ass. He came, and she rode with him, threw her head back and screamed.

He led them to the shower and washed them both up. He dried her hair, they both put on underwear and T-shirts. Len folded himself around her on the couch. He stroked her hair and held her close. They slid into sleep.

When sunlight hit her eyes, Kandace nearly fell off the couch. Len clenched her close. She reached up and back, tapped him on the nose, then craned her neck, kissed him. "Bathroom. Then food."

"Mmm," said Len. He let her go, and she stumbled to the bathroom and washed herself up. She then went to the kitchen, took out the orange juice, then zapped the bacon first, then two each of the tiny strawberry, blueberry, and lemon-poppy muffins. She put two pats of butter and four pieces of super-crispy bacon on each plate with the muffins, and walked them over to the breakfast table. Len glided in. "I could have done that."

"If you marry me, you will. This is a one-time-only thing. Five minutes and a microwave is as far as I'm willing to go, cooking-wise." Len snorted, sat down at the tiny table, and devoured the food.

"This is cool. I was afraid, since you were all Zen, that you wouldn't eat bacon."

Len snorted. "I'm a bear, I eat fish. Yes, as a human, I eat bacon."

Kandace laughed. "Meri must have fun with fish recipes."

Len laughed. "We do eat sushi, in both forms."

Kandace looked down at her phone. Vic sent her a huge smiley-face and a checklist of things she may want. She doubled over laughing when she realized some of the things on the list were "edible underwear" and "Taco Bell delivery". She checked things on his check-list, sent them back to him, showered, and came back out to find the dishwasher running and Len long gone. Len left a sticky note with a drawing of a heart with a house inside on her monitor, and Kandace grinned. Sadly, she had work to do, so she got a carafe of cherry lemonade and a snack bar, then sat down on her recliner. The cat leaped up, sat on the back of the chair, and rumbled. "You sound like I feel," she informed Sam. Then Kandace went to work.

CLAW MARKS

$\mathcal{V}$ ic and Kandace went out for a hike to the lake. It was the trail to the right. "This property has a lake?" asked Kandace. There was a stony shore, a dock, and a boathouse with a blue roof, the sides weathered to gray.

"We've got kayaks, canoes, and a flat fishing boat. And lots of fishing gear. And life vests. The new blue ones, not the fat orange ones we grew up with."

"They were great padding." Vic laughed. They walked out to the end of the dock, sat down, kicked off their socks and shoes, and put their feet in the water. Kandace chowed down on Taco Bell tacos. Vic had a fat burrito. They had the equivalent of a vat of Mountain Dew.

"I hate to ask this." Vic raised his eyebrows.

"I won't talk about what I did, or do, with your brother."

"The fact that you put that in the present tense is what I needed to know."

"He has a teeny-tiny penis that failed to satisfy me."

Vic whooped out a laugh, and nearly dropped his burrito. "I...can't ...even go there," he said, trying to breathe through the laughter.

"Do you have a teeny-tiny penis that will fail to satisfy me?"

"I'm a bear. I screw my women from behind in the forest."

Kandace nearly dropped the remnants of her taco into the lake as she doubled over laughing. She ate the rest of the taco and licked her fingers. "Right here on the dock too," said Kandace through whoops of laughter.

Vic handed her another chicken taco and her drink. "Seriously, the outside has serious drawbacks. Mosquitoes, the fact that some hiker may come across you on your blanket, the fact that I am so well-hung some women run away from me screaming."

Kandace spat out her Mountain Dew, laughing. She was finally able to breathe again. "I hope you're not that big. I don't think we have any magnum-sized condoms."

Vic laughed. "I'm so sad that you're unable to talk about sex."

"I'm a prude. And a virgin, and I've never even imagined it either."

Vic belly-laughed. They finished eating and rinsed their fingers in the water. Vic leaned in, caught the back of her head, and kissed her. Kandace kissed him back, then leapt on him. Vic laughed, scooted back, and held her close as she kissed him hard enough to rearrange his teeth. Vic was greedy for her, the hard-on from when his brother sent the code—one—to signify they were going ahead with the sexual part of dating. He finally got her to calm down enough so they could both suck in air. "I love the whole attack-sex thing you have going on, Kandace, but we do have to breathe."

"Breathing is for sissies." Kandace glued herself to his lips again. She broke the kiss by pulling off her own shirt. She pulled three condoms out of the pocket of her shorts and dropped them on his chest. "Super-sensitive, studded, and purple."

"What a choice, woman!" Vic choked out more laughter, then pulled off his own shirt and threw it behind him onto the dock. She kissed him again, then made her way to his left ear and pulled on his earlobe with her teeth. Vic groaned. Her nails went over his back, and he felt his rock-hard self get even harder. "Woman, you make my stomach drop, my jaw clench. You're like jumping out of a plane."

Kandace quit nibbling on his ear and stared right into his eyes. "Jump into me." She kissed him and left him unable to breathe in. He fascinated her, the man who could rappel up and down cliff faces, jump out of a plane, restart a heart. She stopped his heart with her kisses and fingernails running all over his body, started it again, made it stutter. She nibbled his other ear, and he stroked her face with the tips of his fingers. His hands were rough, which excited her. He reached down, stroked her breasts, and made her come under his hands, screaming into his mouth.

She stood, pulled off her shorts, and then pulled his off. She rolled on the super-sensitive condom. She raised herself up and slid onto him. "Oh, woman, you are so tight."

Kandace nibbled the side of his neck and clenched. He moaned. "Let's go slow." She raised and lowered herself, her hands on his hips. He slid his hands under her buttocks, and moved her very slightly faster. She tightened every time he went in all the way, and Vic was terrified he'd come in a moment. He went through his climbing kit checklist to keep himself from exploding. She rammed herself onto him, up and down, and he found his thoughts slipping away. He slid an arm across her back, held her close, looked into her gorgeous green eyes. He stroked her long auburn hair, dark with sweat, looked into her eyes, and found himself falling forever. He let go, came, and held her close as they fell into each other, gasping.

Kandace kissed his chest, and their breathing slowed. Vic lifted her off, and she let him go. He slid off the condom and threw it into the waste bag. He leaped into the water, gasped. She ran to the end of the dock and leaped in. They swam, floated, kissed, held each other, separated, swam some more. They laughed, cracked jokes, and swam up to the side of the dock to sip their drinks. She was beautiful, hair glistening with water droplets. She teased, kissed, slid her hands down his back. Clenched his cock in her fist, then let go and swam away, grinning. Vic found himself laughing so hard he'd thought he'd drown.

They pulled themselves up onto the dock. Vic cursed himself for not bringing a towel, but the sun was hot. The wind held a burn, ruffling their hair. They dried off in the sun and wind. She laughed, and they finally finished their Mountain Dew. "Are you disappointed in my tiny dick?" Vic asked as she put the last two condoms in her shorts pocket.

She laughed. "Terribly disappointed." She stroked his back where she'd scratched him. "You're the first man I could claw and didn't make me stop."

Vic kissed her. "I'll never make you stop."

They swam a bit more, dressed and walked back to the cabin. They threw away the trash, and Vic said, "Let's go somewhere."

Kandace shrugged. "Can I bring Sam?"

"Sure," said Vic. Kandace opened the door and said, "Sam, you want to go for a ride?" Sam chirruped and ran to the door, so Kandace put the harness on the cat, then grabbed a bottle of sunblock and one of mosquito repellent. Kandace and Vic applied both lotions, then got in Vic's truck and went down the bumpy mountain roads. The cat purred in the back window, clawing a bit when Vic took a hairpin turn a touch too fast. They drove past farms, and Vic pointed out the places the family owned. They passed a roadside stand selling jellies, jams, and honey, and Vic stopped. They all hopped out. "Marina, what do you have today?"

The woman with the blade face and sharp eyes smiled. "I have clover and lavender honey, maple syrup, peanut and almond butters in the cooler, and strawberry, apricot, and pear jams. I also have pear-honey tea. Great for winter or when you have a scratchy throat."

"Give me two of everything," said Vic. He put two hundred-dollar bills down on the table. Marina grinned, and he went to the back seat to get his own cooler while Sam chirruped and sniffed the outside of the stand. Marina put two blue freezer packs in the bottom and filled it up. Vic's muscles bunched as he lifted the now-heavy cooler and put it in the back of the truck.

"You found a good man." Marina pointed at Vic. "You keep him, hear?"

"If I eat like this when I'm with him, why not?"

Marina held out her hand, and Sam leapt up onto the top of the counter. She sniffed Marina's hand and accepted head-scratching as her due. "Maine coon cat. Excellent. I can see why Vic likes you."

Kandace grinned. "Cat loves me, too." Marina laughed, the lines of her face rearranging themselves into joy.

They swung back to drop off the food, then went out again. They went the other way, past herds of fat cows munching grass, their babies standing next to their mothers. There were goats eradicating kudzu on the hillsides. There were split-rail fences everywhere, and seas of wheat, corn, and sorghum in the fields. There were trails criss-crossing the hills. Hikers with fat packs on their backs wound their way up the hillside paths.

They stopped at a place with a kiln. They hopped out, cat included, and Vic led them into a barn. There were fat pots in every color of the rainbow, Tuscan blue, sunny yellow, corals and crimsons, and greens in the thousand shades of the trees and grasses. There were mugs, cups, plates, bowls, saucers. Kandace took photos and sent them to Davis and Len. There was some texted discussion about the proper colors, and Kandace and Vic discussed their choices.

They decided on Tuscan blue stoneware plates, yellow cups, crimson bowls, and mugs and cups in crimson, yellow, blue, and a deep forest green. They got a set of eight, and Kandace paid for it. They walked the grounds, staying away from the hot kiln. A thin, bony-faced woman in a yellow dress packed the box and wrapped each item in newspapers while her husband, who looked like five matchsticks attached to each other, threw a pot on a wheel.

Vic's muscles strained as he put the dishes in the back of the truck. Kandace admired the view from behind.

They went to a full-on backwoods barbecue and shrimp place. They sat outside on picnic tables and ate ribs, shrimp skewers, potato salad, and cornbread muffins. The cat got a small bowl of water and one of diced chicken and shrimp. Sam sat, licking her lips, while the two humans finished their food. They took turns using the restroom, and then the lovers and the cat got back in the truck.

They ended up at the top of a mountain, watching the sun go down, the cat in between them. They lay back on the hood of the truck and watched the stars come out. They kissed, forgetting to breathe, as the cat fell asleep. They talked about the constellations, held hands, and watched the stars go by.

~

The mosquitoes forced them to close the windows, cutting off the summer night breeze. They drove back down, taking the curves slow, and went back to the cabin. They put on a movie set three hundred years in the future while humans lived on two hundred different planets, each one with an entirely different culture, and sixteen different alien allies. They ate Milk Duds, drank sodas, laughed their heads off at the comedic scenes. They then watched a comedy about people learning to fly with their minds, and they ended up kissing on the couch.

When they made love again, the cat stalked off in a huff as they lost their breaths, and Kandace tried not to make Vic's back bleed with her claws. He rammed himself into her over and over. They both stumbled into the shower and lost their breaths again kissing, unable to keep their hands off each other. They somehow made it back to the couch. Kandace covered the couch with a sheet, and they lay there, naked, holding hands until they both slid into sleep.

*D*avis had a plan. He knew their woman was a backwoods redneck, so taking her to the Four Seasons in St. Louis was out of the question. Anything five-star would just give her hives. He thought it out, questioning himself, checking to see whether or not he was doing the right thing. Then, he knew what he had to do.

The place was nestled in the Ozark Mountains. It really wasn't that far of a drive. The pictures of the room he'd paid for showed an enormous four-poster bed covered in a hand-stitched quilt that he knew was very expensive. It was folded up to show light blue sheets underneath, cool and inviting. There were light blue walls with maroon trim. The room was air conditioned with central air, so no huge whirring, dripping AC unit. It had a deck all the way around the back, with a gorgeous view of the blue-misted hills. The chef had gone on a cooking contest show, came in third, then opened the B&B in order to showcase his talents. They would dine in the country, and then they would see.

Davis drove Kandace up on his day with her, and they talked about the new members of the Camber family. "What is Jetta like? And her kids?" Kandace asked. Jetta and the kids had come in the middle of the night in a rental with next to nothing, so Davis, Len, and Vic had all helped unload it at two in the morning, then had driven it away so no one knew where Jetta and the kids now lived.

"Jetta is really shaky. River and Bethany are like night and day. River is awake, alive, always ready to get into things. Bethany just looks terrified that she even exists, just like her mom. It breaks Lynette's heart and makes Jen spitting mad. Both Adam and Bobby are quiet boys. That's where the similarities end. I think that quietness is artificial, caused by their asshole father. Adam thinks everything through, speaks slowly, not because he isn't intelligent. He is. He just wants to be sure he does the right thing and the right way. Bobby is nervous, shaky. They're boys, bear boys." Davis gustily blew out his breath. "Absolutely no one is acting the way that they should. Personalities differ, but there is, or should be, a natural curiosity, a rough-and-tumble toughness lying underneath. And, make no mistake, the women are far tougher than the men."

"I noticed."

Davis barked out a laugh. "Well, Jen is the rule, not the exception. Jetta startles at noises, doesn't like anyone's hands up at shoulder height." He actually growled under his breath.

"I take it this is against your law," said Kandace.

"Damn straight, and I'm not allowed to be part of the hunting party, but as the older brother to these four children, I have to be able to be honest with them at all times. Actually, we're calling ourselves uncles and aunts, too much to explain otherwise. I can't be the one with the hand in the punishment, and have to admit to the kids years later what I did. That kind of thing tends to destroy trust, and that's the one thing these kids need. And safety, which we will provide." His voice grew stony at the last sentence.

"Please tell me that he won't ever beat women and children again." Kandace's eyes were bright with rage. She'd been on the receiving end of childhood violence herself. Davis took one hand off the wheel, put a hand over Kandace's for just a minute, squeezed. He didn't say anything. He didn't have to. Kandace sighed. "I think I might know why she stayed far too long. Maybe she knew the penalty, and saw the father of her children, not the monster he had become."

Davis nodded, his jaw tight. He looked out the window with the wildflowers waving their heads in the mountain breezes, and wondered how the hell people brought such ugliness into the world. "People like him don't get to keep acting that way. They had him in treatment, in a program for violent offenders, for a while. The problem was, he had been raised that way. He felt that if it was good enough for him, it was good enough for his kids and his wife. His dad is long gone, and so is his mother, and there were only two cubs. The brother normally protects his brother's wife and children, even from his brother, but this one's brother Keith was killed in a bar fight witnesses say he started nearly a decade ago. And that's strange, too, because bears don't back down from a fight, but they sure as hell don't start them."

"We will surround them, we will protect them, we will play on the floor with the kids, take them for walks and hikes. We will make little garlands of wildflowers and play with sticks, swim in the swimming holes, go fishing, camping. We will grill fish, drown pancakes and biscuits with honey, guard the doors if we have to." Kandace looked fierce, a warrior goddess reborn in the guise of a red-haired, green-eyed backwoods woman. "After this trip, I think it's time I visited the farm for a couple of weeks. Still work outside the house or at the cabin, but spend as much time with those kids as I can. I know their pain, and I know the only way to get rid of it is to dump love on their heads in buckets, so much love that the pain gets worn down to some sort of reasonable level."

Davis looked over at her and clasped her hands in his. "Thank you." He took a deep breath. "I won't be there. Unfortunately, this is a broken-bone season. People go hiking, fall down mountains, break their ankles, have car accidents, drive drunk and cause even more accidents, shoot each other drunk or sober. I hate to tell you this, but the reason why I booked two days is because this is the last time we're going to see each other for quite some time." He grimaced. "I've got Shady McCowell covering my shift. Woman's real name, and she's also good at throwing shade."

Kandace snorted. "Sounds like my kind of woman."

Davis grinned. "She is. Shade's going to be busier than a frog during fly season combined with mating season. I can only leave her in there for two days, then her lack of sleep will cause her to start killing patients."

Kandace nodded. "You'll get more days with me than the others back-to-back to make up for lost days."

"Lost days and makeup days. A good system." Davis grinned at her. "Kind of like snow days, but in reverse." Kandace grinned back. "It's kind of the opposite way in winter, actually. People here are used to bad weather, have the grace and intelligence to stay indoors. They might suffer a fall, but they only get hurt indoors, because snow is a really good thing to fall on." He grimaced. "Icy concrete, not so much."

Kandace laughed. "Did you know that we didn't have a single damn snow day on campus, not in the whole five years I was there? I could stand on one corner of the quad and damn near ice-skate to the other corner. Most people lived on campus, and we girls were so poor that we lived on-campus even in graduate school. Got a triple dorm, slept in freaking bunk beds for years. The couch in the cabin is the first one since I lived in the holler."

Davis made an ah-ha sound. "That's why you love the cabin, at least you did before you got in your accident. The loft bed. And that's why Len gave you some sort of king-sized gel loft bed on a platform with drawers underneath for the linens in his drawing. Ingenious, but I wouldn't have pegged it for your style."

Kandace smiled. "I'm like the girl that lived down the hall. Girl put her mattress on the floor and made them remove her bed frame from the room. Aliyah grew up in California, said she didn't want her alarm clock throwing her out of bed at six in the morning."

Davis laughed, then grew serious. "It will cost a fortune to get every single house around here after earthquake standards. We've had them, you know. At some point the Bootheel's going to go," he said, referring to the little part of Missouri that poked into Arkansas, called the Bootheel because of its shape.

"The New Madrid fault. Really stupid name for a fault line over here, I might add. And, you're right. At some point that thing is going to slip, making pancakes out of houses, barns, silos topping over, even going boom." Grain outgassed and could blow up if not properly ventilated.

"Every new building my parents make will either stand up to an earthquake, or skitter around as opposed to falling down." Davis filled his words with pride.

"Excellent."

"We're here," said Davis. The bed-and-breakfast was nestled into the hilltop, all glass and wood and glowing light with a wraparound deck. They hopped out, Sam included, and the delicious smells drew them to the grill on the side. There were ribs and chicken cooking on the outside grill. Corn, potatoes, and yams were wrapped in foil on the top grill. The chef was a short guy, stocky, in chef's whites and blue jeans, brown bushy hair standing nearly straight up under his chef's cap. The chef nodded, and tossed his head at the inn's front door. The inn's entrance was around the side. Davis took his duffel and Kandace took her rolling bag and a backpack full of cat supplies out of the truck and up the wooden stairs. Kandace followed Davis more slowly, taking in the smell of wood smoke, grilling meat, and the slightly cooler air up in the mountains. It felt good after the sweltering heat of the valley.

A woman with a blade face and blue-black hair checked them in. She had a huge smile and moved with grace and strength. "Davis, nice to see you again. I'm Lydia Hatchett. You must be Kandace."

"Nice to meet you," said Kandace. The woman could have been any age from thirty to fifty, her face lined from wind and rain, with crinkles at the corners of her eyes and mouth from her ready smile. She was wearing black jeans and a blue shirt with the name of the inn, HoneyBear, on the pocket with a stylized bear in black poking in a jar of honey with a paw underneath the inn's name.

Lydia Hatchett handed each of them the key on a chain for them to put around their necks. "You have the suite, end of the hall, second floor."

"Thank you kindly," said Davis. He led the way up. He opened the door, and they put their bags to the side. There was a little sitting room, the couch pointing toward the fireplace, the two wingback chairs arranged in front of the bay window with a lovely inset cushion for reading or napping. Books line the walls, floor-to-ceiling, on both sides of the bay window. The bedroom had a fat four-poster bed with an ancient quilt on top, pulled back to show pale blue sheets. From what she could see of the bathroom, it was done in pale wood with a glass tile backsplash. There was a cat box with flushable soy litter in the bathroom next to the toilet. There was a little table in the suite and a breakfast bar. Two French doors let out to a patio with a wrought-iron table and two cushioned wrought-iron chairs.

Davis pushed the bags in, stepped back, shut the door, and locked it again. "Dinner will be served in about ten minutes. I figure we should wash up in the bathroom in the lobby because I'm so hungry I could eat everything on that grill, and the grill besides."

Kandace laughed, ran down the stairs with the cat at her heels, and washed up in the female bathroom downstairs. It had a huge vanity with a chair so she could freshen up before dinner. Kandace knew she was beautiful since her black eyes had faded, so she caught a quick glimpse only and went back out to the deck, Sam trotting after her.

"Richard Hatchett," said the chef. "Took my first wife's name when we married. You must be Kandace." He began plating, putting ribs and grilled chicken on each plate. The potatoes were fingerlings in an herb butter sauce. There were carrots cooked in brown sugar, and fat cheddar-herb biscuits drowning in butter and honey. Richard and Lydia filled their own plates and put them at the same table, and they all stood and did the same sing-songy thing in a language that sounded ancient. They all sat and attacked the food. The cat got her own dish of chicken under the table.

When they came up for air, Davis said, "Lydia, Rich, this is Kandace. She knows who and what we are, but I think she's in love with that bay window in the suite."

"I'll read and pet the cat and watch you play while you go out and change," said Kandace.

Rich grinned, and Lydia laughed outright. "Blunt and to the point," said Lydia. "You'll fit in with our kind just fine."

They talked about the weather, where the fish were. Rich pointed to a river below, fat with summer rains, turning red and orange as the sun went down. "Good fishing there, and what we catch extra will be lunch tomorrow."

"My love is all about the food," said Lydia. "You'll have your two days of quiet, and then we have a family of eight coming in, two husbands and two wives, can you believe it? And cubs, one set a year old, one brand new."

Davis grinned. "Sorry I'm going to miss that."

"Hear your mothers have added a wife," said Lydia. "You have our support."

"You need food, sheets, anything at three in the morning, you call," said Rich.

"We will," said Davis, ducking his head. "But, you taught Libby and Meri, and both are making money, no matter the economy," said Davis.

"No one likes dipping in Clan funds," agreed Rich. "But to be fair, both of them actually went to school. I certainly wasn't their only teacher."

Lydia punched him in the arm. "Ow!" he said.

Lydia glared at him. "What did we say about you putting yourself down? Is that any way to win?"

Rich said, "I was being fair, woman. Meri learned how to cook vegetarian from Brownlee, and Libby learned from Derby, who makes the best sugary things this side of the Mason-Dixon line."

"Doesn't the Mason-Dixon Line run through the state?" asked Kandace, spearing a potato.

"West of the Mississippi then," said Rich. "At any rate, both of them are actually gifted, and both of them watched every damn YouTube video they could on whatever they wanted to cook."

Kandace tilted her head. "All three of us did that. Got ourselves cell phones and learned from the best. Tania, Corinne, me. My college friends—sisters, really. We didn't step back, always forward."

Davis leaned over and kissed her. "You see why I love this woman?" he asked.

Lydia poked a fork at Davis. "You screw this up, I will personally come after you with one of Rich's knives."

"Not my carbon steel," said Rich. "Cost a fortune to replace any of those." They all laughed.

"How is Jaclyn doing?" Davis asked. "She's their wife," he explained.

"Took the kids to summer camp," said Rich. "They're into coding now, and they love the combined day coding-night camping camp."

"Wish I had camp when I was a kid," said Kandace. She sipped from her water glass.

They watched the sun go down on the deck. Then Kandace took Davis' hand and led him up the stairs. The cat entered the room first and ran towards the bathroom then rested on the couch. They kicked off their running shoes just inside the door. There were candelabra on both sides of the bed, and Kandace lit the candles, which smelled of jasmine and roses. Kandace stripped down, making his eyes nearly pop out of his head. Davis stood there in the middle of the room, spellbound, watching her undress.

Kandace walked over to him like a cat, stalking him. She undid the cufflinks, put them on a side table, careful to keep the backs intact. She slid off his blue, lightweight, long-sleeved summer shirt. She hung it up on the back of the chair, then pulled off his blue underwear shirt. His abs were rock-hard, his fingers long and gentle. Precise. She took off his belt, then reached down and unbuttoned his black jeans. She pulled them off, along with his navy blue socks. She took off his underwear and laid them on the back of the chair.

She stood there a moment just looking at him. She touched his scar, the one on the right-hand side, a slice at an angle. "Knife." She touched the puckered bullet scar on the left side, then walked around to the entry wound on the other side. "Bullet." She walked back around and fingered the scars around his right hip bone. "Shrapnel."

"I was a military doctor. Can't always avoid incoming when you're operating."

She reached out, took his hand, and put it on her lower back. He felt the smaller indentation, the square indentation around it. "Belt buckle." She pulled back her hair, showing the scar just at her hairline.

"The reason I don't cut my hair short." She covered it back up again. She showed a cut on her arm. "Kitchen knife. There are more, but they're inside. Certain places I really can't talk about." She stalked around him again, four fingers sliding all the way around him, from his jawline, to his shoulders, stomach, hips, and all the way up, back around to his back, to his stomach again. He drew in a hissing breath. "We both have shrapnel. Mine is just better hidden." She put her hands around his waist, put her head on his back.

Davis stood there, holding her arms, finding his breath hitching, over and over. He turned, held her close, his head on hers. He stroked her hair, ran a hand down her spine to her buttocks. He found another scar there, and hissed. He'd operated on her, but only saw the left side, the arm. He stroked the arm he'd put back together, felt where he'd put the pins, the screws. He'd never made love to a patient before.

An ex-patient. She was healed. Imperfectly, but they all were. He kissed her head, held her face in his hands. He kissed her forehead, both eyes, her nose, both cheeks, then gently, gently on her lips. She fell into him, as if falling from a great height, and he caught her and held on.

She drew him to the bed, after taking something out of her pocket. She put the condom on the table under the candelabra, and smiled when a tear of silver wax hit the foil packet. She stroked her hands through his hair, and kissed him the way that he had kissed her forehead, eyes, nose, mouth. She lingered there, taking her time, so very gentle. After what seemed like an hour of kissing her he stroked her breasts, used those nimble fingers of his, his lips, his tongue, to make her come, make her writhe. She grabbed the condom, ripped it open, and rolled it on. It was blue, but they didn't care. She mounted him, then flipped him over on top of her.

He held her face in his hands while he moved, stared into her eyes, kissed her lips. She came once, twice. Finally, he felt himself let it go, threw back his head, thrust all the way in, felt his sweat mingling with hers. He lay there, gasping, holding her in his arms, his hands on the back of her neck, holding her to him.

Davis rolled off, threw the condom in the trash, padded to the bathroom, and drew a bath for her. He carried her in, making her laugh, and put her in a bath built for two, a clawfoot thing big enough for a bear and his woman. They soaked, washed themselves off slowly. She shampooed, rinsed, ducked her whole body under the water and came up gasping. She rolled over, lay on him, and he held her close, her breasts bobbing in the water. "I love you." Davis' voice was low, husky.

She turned her head to the side, kissed him. "I love you mostest. Don't tell the others."

"I won't," he said, and felt himself falling into something he hadn't thought he'd ever find. A love, a love for them all.

TREED

Kandace was in the kitchen filling up the dishwasher with Jetta. The woman's black hair was dull and brittle. She walked with a limp. Her pale green eyes were hooded and bleak. She often stared into nothingness. Her skin, which should be a reddish gold, was sallow. Her bones were just under her skin. But the woman applied herself to the chore chart as if the chores were going to run away, leaving her behind. Lunch was shrimp and crab-stuffed fish, fries, hush puppies, and salad. The boys ate as if the food would be taken away at any moment, and ran off after the meal to play in the other room. The little ones ate with wide eyes, looking like monkeys instead of bears. They clung like monkeys as well, never letting their mother out of their sight. It was disturbing.

Kandace had one baby strapped to her stomach and Jetta the other one. Both babies slept soundly. They were in charge of the dishes.

"You can quit giving me the side-eye," said Jetta. "I ate, didn't I? Do you think I'm suddenly going to flip out and run screaming out the door?"

"No," said Kandace. "I think you need food, sleep, quiet, and time to relax."

Jetta shook her head. "The last thing I need to do is sit around doing nothing. Gives me time to think, and I don't need that. I need to move around, slowly maybe, but moving around is good for me right now."

"Good that you know what you need." Kandace reached for a glass.

"You think I'm going to break, don't you?" asked Jetta.

"No. If that were going to happen, it would have already happened. No, you just need a ton of time to heal."

"You think I was stupid to stay. Weak. Couldn't defend my own self, my own children."

"Since I have no idea what you've actually been through, be real stupid of me to make guesses like that." Kandace rinsed another glass, handed it to Jetta.

Jetta put the last glass in the dishwasher, found the soap in the cabinet, put some in the dishwasher, closed it, and turned it on. "You're not one of us, so you don't know our ways."

"Not many of them, no," agreed Kandace mildly. "Which one made you stay?"

"Our genetics. You know black bears are killed for their gall bladders? Supposed to have magical properties. Well, the problem is, they had no idea who they were killing. Had no idea we were shapeshifters. I don't think it really matters which kind of us you killed, because there aren't any magical properties in gall bladders. But that's one way we got decimated, killed, over some stupid Asian males who thought that they could screw better because of medicines made from bear gall bladders. Those nasty, evil men paid backwards people to kill off the bears, kill us off, one by one. It was ugly, messy, and pointless, and it's still happening. So, we've got much lower numbers than we should. Far lower than in any other point past our initial decimation."

Jetta's hands were shaking. Kandace touched her hand, then reached for a sponge, started scrubbing pots. "I knew Ronnie was an asshole, knew he drank too much. I also knew he had a wife where he got some babies, and that's what I wanted. Purebreds. I wanted to be absolutely sure that the gene is carried on. His first wife, Bobbi, did what I did. She got her babies and moved on. I did the same thing. I knew what I could do. I knew what was right for me. I knew that I wanted those damn babies, and no one was going to stop me. Had me another man, had miscarriages. Lost the babies twice. Divorced him, got Ronnie."

Kandace gave Jetta a pot to rinse and dry and started on a skillet. "Hard choice."

"Right. I had some stupid notion it wouldn't be that bad, and I knew damn well it would also damage our kids. But I didn't think it would take three damn years before I got knocked up again. That's about three years longer than I planned on staying. Planned on getting knocked up a second time and disappearing into the woods. I couldn't rely on my kin, not a one of them will talk to me. Figured I was stupid. But I'm not. I'm so tired of people thinking that about me. Then I was really weak after the last birth and had to stay to get strong enough to escape with them. Found this family on a dating website, told them the truth about my situation. And no, there's none of that shit about my thinking the father of my children should live. Man did what he needed to do, passed on enough shifter babies. I don't know if my body has it in me to have more, but I will if I can. Now I've got a shit ton of damage to undo, damage I inflicted on my kids because I got sick. Stayed too damn long."

Kandace passed over the skillet, and Jetta rinsed and dried it. "I'm really sorry you got sick."

"Sorry for me or the kids?"

"Both."

Jetta huffed out a breath. "I deserve your censure, the side-eye. People aren't usually dumb enough to do what I did. But I did, and now I have to live with it. The price was far too high and the consequences were not cheap. My beautiful babies are the best thing that's ever happened to me." Jetta gently stroked Bethany's sleeping head. "Worth the price, for me, to me. But not to them. I worry if my boys will ever learn to trust, to love completely and wholeheartedly. I did that to them. I damaged them. And I deserve whatever hell is coming to me for being that stupid."

"I think you already paid the price. For you. The kids. You're going to have to get yourself healthy as hell. These kids need to see a loving, strong, healthy, beautiful mama, or this shit just isn't going to work." Kandace sighed, focused on wiping out the last pot. "The kind of fear, it gets into your bones. Makes you question your every damn decision. I've got a voice in my head that criticizes every single thing I've ever done, counts nearly all the things I do as mistakes, even obviously right things, just because my mama or gran wouldn't have done it that way."

"You ever talk to her?" Kandace handed Jetta the last pot to rinse and dry, and Kandace drained and scrubbed the sink.

"Nope. That woman has one set of principles. Mine are completely different from hers. When I'm around her, I want to strangle her, 'cause her principles damaged me, my body, my sense of trust. Left scars where no scars should be. So, I shouldn't be around her, shouldn't talk to her. Shouldn't be anywhere near her for any reason. Whatever family that I had held together by clouds and Scotch tape is long over, and that's the price she should pay for that. She won't hear from me, not my joys, not my struggles. Never see my babies, hold them in her lap. I wouldn't trust her with my children far enough to throw her."

Jetta flinched, carefully dried the pot and hung it up on its rack. "She never got out, did she?"

"Never paid a single price, either. At least none that I could see. She fell, and was injured, came back from a brain injury, but she never lifted a finger to defend me before, during, or after that. She was the perpetual victim. I could only play the game for as long as I could, and getting sober made it clear that I couldn't lie to myself or others. I couldn't lie and talk to Mama or Gran, either one of them. It would be compromising myself, who I really am."

Jetta's face crumpled, and tears leaked out of her eyes. Kandace rinsed the sink, dried her hands, handed the woman a paper towel, and rubbed her back. Jetta said, "I think things happen in life that you have no intention to have happen. One mistake leads to another, to another. You find yourself in a deep dark hole you can't get out of. The worst thing is, people judge you for being in that damn hole, 'cause they know only a fool would jump in. I did, with both feet.

Now, if that monster isn't dead now, he will be. I leapt straight out of the hole, got me some damn help."

"I fell into another hole, but a hole is a hole. Especially the self-inflicted ones." Kandace smiled a half-smile through the tears in her own eyes. "Alcoholics Anonymous and its sister Narcotics Anonymous are on TV shows, movies, news articles. Hell, half the celebrities in the damn world seem to have gotten sober. Entire bands did. Still didn't have a clue that I needed help." She rubbed her own eyes, wiped the angry tears away. "Women like me put ourselves in hideously dangerous situations where we're too impaired to fight back." She took in a deep, shuddering breath. "My friends don't know this, thought it was the possibility of getting in trouble at school from a prank. I went out after that, got shitfaced. Didn't have the ability to protect myself. It was the second sexual assault that did it. I got sober, didn't look back."

Jetta hissed out a breath. Kandace took Jetta's face in her hands, looked her in the eyes. "Get out of that situation in your head. Gotta be a bear counselor somewhere." Jetta huffed out a laugh. "Get clean and sober in your head. Attend some program. Think there's one for survivors of domestic abuse out there. That's not a sign of weakness. It's a sign of strength. I joined Adult Children of Alcoholics two years ago, and worked through my trauma mountain. My gran's not a drunk, just mean. My mama has the personality of a torn blanket. You get rid of your trauma mountain one teaspoon at a time. You have to for those babies of yours."

The women hugged, side to side, so as not to disturb the babies. They dried their tears, wiped down the table and chairs, and consulted the chore chart for more chores. Kandace put the sleeping River in a bassinet and pulled it close to her as she dusted the living room, while Jetta went upstairs to work on the bathrooms.

Adam came streaking in, tears on his face. Literally streaking; he was buck naked. Jetta was nowhere to be seen, so he hurled his little sweaty body into Kandace's legs. "He turned. Himself. Into a bear. Can't. Get down."

"Show me." Kandace raced after the gasping little boy, and saw a big oak tree. The baby bear was halfway up, howling. "I'm coming! Hold on!" Kandace reached up, grabbed a branch, and hauled herself up. She saw the boys' clothes on the ground. She turned, looked at Bobby. "Lynette is in the garden." She pointed. "Go get her, tell her what you told me. I'm going to get him down." The boy streaked off again, and Kandace made her way up.

The baby bear howled piteously. "I'm coming. Hold on a damn minute." Kandace hauled herself up, up. She kicked off her shoes and socks, and used her toes to get higher and higher. "Just a climb," she said, singing to herself and the bear. "One little bear, stuck in a tree."

"Ladder!" boomed Lynette's voice across the yard. Kandace got one hand loose, waved at her, then kept climbing. She got to the baby bear and said, "I am going to climb around behind you. I will hold you tight when the magic happens so you can't fall. If you fall, I will catch you. You have to turn yourself into a boy. Then you can climb on my back like a monkey, and we'll be down on the ground in no time. We'll have honey with crackers, and pretend this never happened."

The bear shook its head. Lynette climbed around under him, shielded him with her body. "Change, Bobby. I'm right here." The black bear head shook "no" again.

Kandace's previously-broken arm started to shake. She was running out of time. She smacked the bear on the nose, and said, "Change! Now!" There was a glimmer, and the boy fell into her knees. She grabbed him around the waist with her free hand and held him close. He turned around, climbed onto her back, squished the air out of her lungs with his arms around her, burrowed into her neck.

Kandace swung her good arm back up and went back down, as if it were a particularly woody cliff face. She took her time, although time was not something she had, because she just needed to get low enough to drop him into someone's arms. Jetta was below her, baby Bethany still strapped to her. She held her hands out.

A huge blue truck screeched to a stop, and a man came running across the lawn, tearing off his clothes, kicking off his shoes. He passed Lynette rushing forward with the ladder, and flashed into a bear. He hit the tree and began to climb as Kandace made her way back down. The boy on her back turned into a bear again, claws digging into Kandace's skin. She screamed, and her knees buckled under the increased weight. The claws let go as the tree shook with the bigger bear climbing up. Kandace screamed again, and the bigger bear had the little bear in a giant paw, and the little bear climbed onto the male's back.

They all climbed back down, Kandace more slowly as blood trickled down her sides and back. Lynette got the ladder positioned when the tree stopped shaking, and Kandace used it to get back down, her arms quivering. Her previously broken arm was screaming at her, and so was the wetness on her back.

Everyone got down on the ground. The big bear turned into a man again, and the cub turned into a boy and grabbed him, a stranglehold around his new father's neck.

Lynette held Kandace against her. "It's Charlie. Ronnie is dead."

Kandace leaned against Lynette. "I need gauze, cleaning pads, hydrogen peroxide, bandages, and a new heart. Boy gave me a heart attack."

Jetta made a speechless stumble towards man and boy. Each parent stood on each side of the boy, sandwiched him in the middle. Charlie was huge, with deep blue eyes and black hair, his skin darker than the bark of the tree they had just climbed. Lynette found and handed him his jeans.

"Baby," said Kandace, pointing at the house. Lynette grabbed Kandace's shoes and socks, and they made their way across the lawn.

Charlie went over to Lynette, boy still wrapped around his neck, and picked up Kandace around the waist with a beefy arm. She put her foot on his giant one, and he half-loped to the house. The mothers behind him took Adam in with them.

Vic came by in an ambulance, came flying in the back door. "Left my partner at the diner. Told her it was a kid in tree situation, have him out in a jiffy." He looked at the mess of Kandace's back. "Puncture wounds. Boy got his claws in, didn't he? You need stitches, and we can't really take you into the hospital because bear attacks are treated very seriously around here."

"Got any good numbing drugs?" asked Kandace.

"My brother will authorize their use." Vic stood, ran back out to the ambulance.

"I am so sorry," said Jetta.

"You should have waited for me," said Lynette. "Damn fool woman, this is the third time you've been messed up in less than three months." She helped Kandace get her shirt off, leaving only the camisole. Lynette dabbed at the wounds with the hydrogen peroxide, making Kandace hiss.

Kandace glared at the floor. "A naked crying boy wanted me to save his brother who was in a damn tree and needed help."

Charlie entered the room fully clothed and knelt, which was difficult with a boy attached to each side of him. "Daughter. You worked to save my boy. That makes you part of the clan, whether you marry my grown-up boys or not."

"I probably will," said Kandace, hissing with the pain as Lynette mopped up the blood. "But I can't get into a wedding dress like this." She looked up. "Do you even wear wedding dresses to your ceremonies?"

Charlie laughed. "That's my daughter." River let out a shrill cry, then Bethany. "That's our cue," he said, standing. The boys giggled at being lifted off the ground. Bobby looked none the worse for wear. "Bobby, you thank Aunt Kandace for getting you down," he said, in a low, sonorous voice.

"Thank you. She promised me honey and cookies."

Charlie laughed again. "Babies first, then snack. Didn't you just eat lunch? And, Bobby, what's the rule about climbing up trees alone?"

"I wasn't alone," he said, in a piping voice, as Charlie trailed his new wife Jetta to pick up their other baby daughter. "I had my brother."

"He ain't heavy, he's my brother," quoted Kandace.

"Bear boys are like that, you know," said Lynette. "Defend each other to the death, even while trying to kill each other."

Vic came in, swung around behind Kandace, and injected her several times, making her hiss even louder. "Baby. You got yourself into this mess, dumb enough to crawl up a tree after a cub. He wouldn't have fallen, just stayed frozen up there, too afraid to go up or down. I did the same thing a couple times," he said, as he stitched up her skin. "I'm afraid all three of us are going to have to keep our hands off of you for a while. And you'll be sleeping on your stomach or your side until these heal. When they do, they're going to itch like a son of a gun."

Kandace raised her eyebrows. "Looks like we'll be saying things like 'fudge' and 'son of a gun'. Soon you'll get me saying something like h-e-double chopsticks for 'hell'."

Vic laughed. "That's our woman. Now, if you'll excuse me, I need to grab a sandwich and get back on my shift. Woman, can you quit getting hurt for five minutes while I eat my lunch?"

Kandace slapped his arm. "Get on with you." He packed up and headed for the kitchen, the mess in a medical waste bag.

Lynette brought her an ancient soft, green Travis Tritt T-shirt and helped her get it on. "Lie down and watch stupid things on TV," she suggested, as Kandace moved to the couch. Kandace lay on her side, and Lynette handed her the remote. "Good thing your chores are all done, or you would have to make them up later." Kandace made sure no little ones were watching, and flipped her off. Lynette laughed. "You moved quickly to help our boy. We won't forget it." She smiled. "Welcome to the family." She stared out the window. "The ladder." Lynette made a beeline for the door.

Kandace turned on the TV, skipping over the soap operas and talk shows. "I need a bear documentary," she groaned.

HOME

It was strange going out to the special steakhouse with all three of them. Their dating and sex life had been muted by the new puncture wounds but not put on hold entirely. Kandace went to the lakeside or the quarry with Vic. Long drives were on hold because of her back. Davis took her out for dinners, and Len rubbed her feet, and put together puzzles and watched movies with Kandace. Picnics and movie nights were kind of strange, with people arriving and leaving all the time. Meri or Libby showed up for some of them, but never both of them. Someone was always at the farm, paying attention to the kids. Even with four adults, four kids was a reach for anyone, even shifters used to kids in multiples.

They sat on the patio, silvery lights strung everywhere, glowing softly as the sun set and set the sky afire in orange and red. The server brought water for Sam, who accepted it with queenly grace under the table. Len was on her right, Vic on her left, and Davis held out her chair then sat across from her. They were all wearing jeans and loose shirts. "You're Bobby's favorite aunt. Boy won't stop talking about the hero lady with the fire hair."

"I'm probably going to be "Aunt 'Ace" for the rest of my life. River wants to be held twenty-four-seven, and Bethany wants her mama, end of story."

"It is hard bonding with Bethany sometimes," Len agreed. "She is the cutest thing, though."

Vic grinned. "Those boys will give you a workout." He flexed a muscle, and everybody laughed. They ordered a meat and seafood platter, and Vic split the steaks, ribs, bacon-wrapped shrimp, shrimp and scallop-stuffed fish, and stuffed baked potatoes onto plates with no cow for Kandace. None of the men ordered beer out of respect for Kandace, sticking to sweet tea. Conversation was light, about the farm, how Jenna was doing with her therapy, how the boys were coming out of their shells. "That house has never been cleaner!" Vic said. "Leave it to our da Charlie to put the boys to work!"

"What about that summer we got caught teaching non-bear kids our BMX stunts?" Davis asked. "I think you could eat off the floor of the garage when Dad got through making us clean it."

Len groaned. "I get why. The other kids could have gotten hurt. But, still. I was so tired I went to bed early for a week." Kandace laughed. She knew Len was a night owl, like her.

The chef brought out a gorgeous dessert platter, chocolate cheesecake, key lime pie, and caramel apple pie in slices they all shared. They served Kandace first, knowing she wouldn't get any if they fell on the food like they usually did. They finished and ordered another dessert round of slices of cherry pie, peach cobbler, and French silk chocolate pie with a chocolate peanut crust and peanut cream on top. "I can't eat like you do. I'll waddle."

"Not with Tamara riding your gorgeous behind," Vic said. "Davis, thank you for introducing those two."

"I didn't." Davis cut his steak. "Becca got all crazy-like when she saw my hands on our girl."

Len and Vic both stared at Davis, then Kandace. "Why am I just hearing about this now?" Len said.

Kandace shrugged, then winced. Her back was healing quickly, but still, it twinged. Hard. "I told her to get some reality, even if it hurts. And Davis told her that happiness is an inside job." She smiled as she licked her fork. "Becca actually said Davis was hers, like she owned him."

"She didn't!" Len said.

"Girl's always been a few bricks shy of a full load. None of us were stupid enough to date her," Davis said. "Not because she's not...um, well, us, but because she's been a gold digger since Day One. Would like to find someone to marry to keep her in the lifestyle to which she would like to become accustomed. My going to medical school made her more determined, not less."

Vic nodded. "She has never heard the word 'no' and accepted it." He took a deep breath, let it out. He was working his way up to something. "We will, and we may be jumping the gun, but, by now, I think you know all three of us love you. The trees are getting hints of gold and crimson, and we're wearing jeans, not shorts."

"What my brother is stumbling around saying is that we are all in love with you," Len said. "We will respect any wishes you have, slow things down if you want."

"It's just that, you're amazing," Davis said. "And we love you. And I think you love us. You know who and what we really are, and you put up with us and our...quirks."

"And our mamas love you. Even skittish Jetta loves you since you got Bobby out of the tree. We don't know what you said to her, but she's going to counseling, learning how to get past her pain," Len said.

"And our daddy thinks you hung the moon," Vic said. "I've never seen Charlie so happy. With his entire family, we included."

"And we don't want you going away or choosing someone else," Davis said.

"Where am I gonna go?" Kandace joked. "I am heavily into self-injury, remember?" The easy grin slipped off her face when Davis pulled a ring box out of his pocket, and Len and Davis put their hands on it. Kandace reached across the table like she was in a dream. She took the box in her hand, opened it while the servers looked goggle-eyed at them. The little blue silk box held a ring in white gold, with four baguette diamond bars. "Omigod, omigod," Kandace said.

"If it's too soon, we can…" Len began to say. Vic clamped down on Len's hand, and Len grunted as Davis kicked him under the table.

"Shut up," Kandace said, choking on the words. "This is plumb crazy. Like, even weirder than jumping out of planes. I like my planes to land without me jumping out." She held her breath, let it out. "But I don't give a flying…anything if it's weird. I'm weird. Y'all don't drink when we're out, because of me. You take me anywhere I want. You feed me, take me on rides, go swimming with me. And my cat loves all of y'all." She slipped the ring on her finger, and a cheer went up from Jack, owner/chef of Teak House, Dannica the server, and all three of her men. They stood, took turns holding her and whirling her around—carefully, because of her back. Jack tried to comp the meal, but Davis would only let him comp the dessert plate. Kandace kissed them all—Jack and Dannica on the cheek, of course. She couldn't stop staring at the ring, not for a minute.

～

*D*avis and his dad, Charlie, surveyed the land. It jutted up against the tree line at the back of the colony property. It had a wide, clear river, with rainbow trout, speckled trout, and catfish hiding in the hollows. A beaver was in the middle of the river, pounding out a rhythm on its dam with slaps of its tail. The trees were large, old-growth oak and maple, mulberry, pine, silver birch. Their leaves were just beginning to turn, hints of gold and scarlet here and there. There was a flat spot big enough for a house far enough away from the river on a plateau, overlooking the river, the trees. They could see smoke from the foundry and glassworks behind them, little glints of sunlight off stained glass, throwing rainbows in the air.

"Grading this thing is going to be a monster and a half," said Charlie. "Getting a backhoe up here is going to be nearly impossible. The house could be in pieces, assembled and dragged in. A pain on these curvy roads. Doable, but slower than a snail race."

Davis looked up at his father's face. "Dad, the basement is going to be carved into this hill. We've checked it out with the ground-penetrating radar. It's not a First Nations burial site or anything. Wall of glass, so it won't be cold and dark, facing south, so maximum sunlight." He pointed to where the house would be. "It's going to be Vic's domain, so he'll want a theater down there for his nights with Kandace, fat king-size bed and ensuite bathroom for every adult room, another full bath on each floor at the end of the hallway for the kids."

"When they come."

"When they come," agreed Davis. "Middle level is mine. There," he said, pointing. "Sitting room, bedroom, a bay window with a reading nook for our wife. I won't be home much, but I want my time at home to be as calm and happy as possible."

"Once you have cubs, that quiet elegance of yours is going to have to go out the window."

"Probably literally." Davis sighed. "At least two kids' rooms downstairs. Then our girl gets the whole top floor, with a baby room for the little ones, sitting room and another bay window, fat bed, lots of storage."

Charlie said, "A house isn't just bedrooms." Davis snorted. "Utility room, mudroom, whatever the hell you want to call it, laundry room with shelves and places to fold and hang up the clothes. Garage, four-car. Maybe five, if you get some sort of van for the kidlets. Probably build some bedrooms on top of that garage, too. Playroom for the kids on the bottom floor that will probably be turned into a bedroom later. Open plan kitchen and huge table. This thing is going to have to be a freaking castle." Charlie pretended to be overwhelmed. "I've seen Len's sketches."

Davis humphed. "They may not be blueprints, but Len has your hand." He pointed at the schematic on his cell phone, much more detailed than Len's initial drawings. "Len's yoga studio and Zen dojo thing can go over there, to get maximum sunlight. And yes, that can be constructed off-site and put together here like some sort of large wooden puzzle."

"Be better over there." Charlie pointed. "Overlooks the river that way. The yoga types will love it like crazy. Why do all the way around with the porch? You could just have a lip jutting out."

"Be good," agreed Davis. "Our girl still has debt. We can afford maybe half this by pooling our funds."

"You'll use the family trust. Pay us back at five percent interest. This house is an investment in a poly community. Even if you guys decide to vamoose somewhere else, and I have no idea why you would, this place is freaking beautiful. If you did, another poly group would snap it up, pay a premium for it." He stared out at the land. "What about the pool?"

"The one we could only use half the year? The one that has to be drained and refilled every damn summer? The one that will have to have a mile-high fence to keep out neighbor kids so they don't drown? That one?" He pointed down at the river. "There's a hole just up a little ways. Be perfect for swimming."

"You're going to make an excellent dad." Charlie rubbed the back of his neck. "I forgot how it was, running around after two sets of twins." He patted Davis' arm. "I still miss Jonah," he said, referring to Len's brother, long dead from falling off a roof.

"Len has never been the same." Davis sighed. "Literally no one could get to him fast enough. That boy was like lightning, and the word 'no' meant 'yes' to him." Lynette and Len carried the scars from that day, especially Len, who had unsuccessfully tried to stop his brother from doing something that stupid. He had screamed for his dad, but he and his bio-dad were just too late.

"I think your girl is helping. Len talks more, and he can't get enough of his little brothers and sisters."

"I think Len would forget to go to work and play on the floor with them all day if he could. The kids make him laugh. Like our girl does."

They turned and began walking back to the truck. "Good to have you back, Dad. Missed you."

Charlie put his arm around Davis, and gave him a quick one-armed hug. "Missed you too, son."

"When can we break ground?" The colony had accepted all of them. Kandace was teaching coding lessons to the tweens, two girls and a boy. She boasted that she was going to learn to make knives and swords next, once her back healed. Both Len and Vic were taking on extra shifts in order to pay for the house.

Charlie stared off into space, pulled out a cell phone, and then started punching things on it. "Two weeks. Tiger is over in the next damn county." Tiger was their digger, and could dig an entire basement or pool in a day. The man turned into a bear, not a tiger. He was married with three wives already, and took every shift he could because he had a set of twins by each wife. Even with two of the adults bringing in military pensions, they needed the cash. "We can get Tiger's people started this weekend if we pay a hell of a premium, but that will eat into the budget. That glass of yours is hideously expensive."

Davis said, "We have only got the end of the summer and the fall to get this thing done. I want us in, locked down, ready for the snow at the end of October. Halloween in the new house would be awesome."

Charlie looked bug-eyed at his son. "One, you're absolutely crazy. Two, you're setting things up so none of you will be able to spend alone time with your girl. Between the extra shifts and putting in time on the house, none of you will have time to sleep. Third, you're the one putting in extra time at the hospital, broken bone season and all. What you're doing is you're getting your brothers and your wife to do it when you're not around."

Davis smiled. "I never said I wasn't stupid. Or crazy." He sent out a text and got into the other side of his father's truck. By the time they were back down the mountain, he had his replies. "They understand that I'm being an asswipe about this, and Vic says that's my new name, but all three of them want to go ahead and get Tiger over here."

"You are plumb loco, boy. Since I've got my hands on you, until you get the inevitable call back in to the hospital on your freaking day off, you're going to go with me and pick out all the hardware. We'll get everything ordered, cabinets on down. We'll take pictures, send them out, get everyone to vote." He grinned. "You haven't lived until you've had your first fight about cabinets." He used a falsetto voice. "It's not about the cabinets, it's because I'm not being listened to."

Davis doubled over laughing. "I don't know if that was supposed to be either Lynette or Jen, but neither one of them sound like that."

Charlie and Davis split up calls all the way to the store—plumbing, electrical, cement, solar panel people. There were new solar panels that also used the mechanical energy of the rain to power them, doubling their efficacy in a snowbound climate. Davis cringed at the cost and had even more sticker shock running around the hardware store. By the time everyone had figured out what cabinets and drawer pulls they wanted, Davis felt his brains melting right out into his hair. Charlie helped him order everything from light fixtures to paint, put it on a timeline. and laughed at Davis' harried look. Charlie paid the truly frightening bill with the clan trust's credit card, then the two men went out for cheese steaks, sodas, and fries.

Davis got a call from the hospital, so Charlie took him back to his truck. "You got off easy, boy," said Charlie. "Be happy that your mamas are planning the wedding. If you had to deal with that, you would be in a fetal position on the floor, crying." Davis nodded and drove off, delighted that he had surgery, not wedding planning, to do.

WEDDING DAY

Kandace felt saddened on her last day in the cabin. She shook it off, got up, fed the cat, did her yoga, followed by kickboxing, followed by more yoga stretching. Sam the cat "helped" her during her final stretches, finally curling up in her lap while she was trying to touch her head to her feet while seated. "You are not helping," Kandace informed the cat. Sam chirruped. Kandace finally had to move the cat out of her lap and off the mat in order to roll the mat up and put it away in a box.

Kandace showered and got the sole remaining breakfast out of the kitchen; a strawberry muffin, a bowl of blackberries, and peach yogurt. She washed the white dishes by hand, putting them away for the next tenant. The pretty stoneware ones were already at the new house. She turned on her computer and all the screens, and went to work. They still have a lot of mapping left to do, and Kandace had to work ahead because she would be spending the next couple of days on a honeymoon, then she had to make the new house the way she wanted it.

Not that it was hard, not really. They had put up the outside as fast as possible, and had all winter to put the inside together. Between the bear clan and the other poly families, the house had been scrubbed right up to the newly-painted baseboards and the furniture moved in. It looked like a decorator had been drinking moonshine, with a homey bedroom, living room, movie theater, and game room on the first floor, a pristine elegance on the middle floor, Zen on the third, and Kandace with her reading nook-office combo that looked like Zen meets fat recliners and screens in the attic.

The bedroom was a weird space, with sloping ceilings, blue paint on the walls, a huge black platform bed, and big fat cobalt reading chairs. The kitchen, located on what was the first floor from the front entrance and the second from the other side because the house was cut into a hill, was a dream. It had a wide butcher-block counter, barstools, and an inlaid mahogany dining table that could seat twelve comfortably. The playroom already had toys, and the babies' room upstairs already had bassinets and the walls were painted yellow with ducks swimming in a lake and bumblebees sipping from flowers.

Kandace pounded out the chart, completed her tasks, and looked for other tasks she could take on to work things ahead a little bit. On time and under budget and she and the entire team were looking forward to a hell of a bonus. That last one should pay off all but about two thousand of her debt, and she could knock off the rest of that in a month. She stood, stretched, then ran to the bathroom. She threw up twice, changed shirts, walked the cat around the house, then came back in to work a little bit more.

She had her last snack, peanut butter oat balls that were incredibly delicious. Libby had a knack. The oats settled her stomach, and she was able to complete enough tasks so she was nearly two days ahead. She sent out the text to the group that she was standing down for a week and that she'd gotten them two days ahead first, then she closed the laptop. Kandace stood, stretched, popped the top on a can of ginger ale, then closed everything down and packed it up. She looked up at the loft that she rarely had been able to use and sighed.

She showered, treated her hair so it fell glossily to her shoulders. Meri and Libby bustled in. Sam chirruped loudly and rumbled like a Mustang motor. "Hello, kitty," said Libby.

"Where the hell are ya?" asked Meri.

"Here," Kandace said from the bathroom, still in her underwear, the bra and panties a beautiful silver lace. Kandace stretched, popping her back.

Meri said, "I've got this computer stuff and a dolly for the recliner."

"I've got the bride," said Libby. She had a lavender plastic toolbox-looking case in her hand. The bottom had rows of nail polishes. The middle and top parts had makeup and brushes. "Colors. Silver? Blue silver?"

"Silver-green," said Kandace, as Libby buffed her nails. The nail polish made Kandace throw up, so she held her hands out while Libby held back her hair. Kandace washed her mouth out and spat in the sink, and Libby tied her hair back while she worked. The makeup was next while the nails got another coat and dried. Libby did something with a silvery-green eye shadow that made her green eyes pop out of her head. Libby's strokes were deft, the same as when she decorated cakes. Libby touched up the nails, and Kandace was pleased when her stomach stayed put. Libby got her into her slip, then the clingy silk green dress was pulled up over her body, thin but for a tiny belly bump. Libby zipped up the dress and smoothed it out. She did finishing touches to the nails, hair, and makeup. Libby then led Kandace out into the cabin.

The recliner, the last of her furniture, was gone. The only things left in the house had been there when Kandace arrived. Kandace sniffed. Libby held up her hands. "Don't cry, woman, I just did that makeup. This was your home for a short time, and now you have a giant house on the hill that is making me jealous as hell."

Kandace laughed. Meri came up and said, "You were such a scrawny, broken thing when I met you. And you keep damaging your-self, you idiot."

Kandace lay her arm across her belly. "Not damaging myself this time."

Meri's eyes softened. "Of course not. Beautiful," she said, taking Kandace's hands in hers. Meri held back Kandace's hair while Libby put on a necklace. "It's topaz with jade," said Libby, dragging Kandace back into the bathroom to look at the necklace on a silver chain.

"That's the blue and the new. From Jen." She slid earrings into each of Kandace's ears, tiny pearls. "Lynette's, so both old and borrowed."

Meri smiled, and Kandace fought not to cry. "I am so happy that I came here, and found a new family." Meri, then Libby, hugged her, and they walked towards the door. Kandace looked back one more time, then shut and locked the door.

The woods were quiet, and so were all three of the women. They played some Indigo Girls to break the silence and relax. They parked where all the other trucks were, at the trailhead to the clearing. A piper began to pipe, and Meri thrust bouquets of spring wildflowers into Libby's hand. Meri got one as well, and Kandace got three red roses around a white rose. Meri and Libby stepped forward, then Kandace followed as the piper slid into a beautiful, haunting melody. The females wore green, and all three of her men wore black jeans and green shirts and stood in a circle. Kandace walked into the circle, and the music stopped. Kandace was delighted that it was really happening. The wedding had been postponed twice because Davis was pulled into emergency surgery, plus no one wanted an outdoor wedding in winter.

Jen spoke in the ancient language of her tribe and sang and spoke to the wind, rain, clouds, snow, and ice to be gracious to the new tribal members, for the river to have fish, for the hives to be bursting with honey. She sang and spoke of caves, of new life in spring, of babies filling the meadows. Bethany and River looked on, wide-eyed. Jetta had one infant and Lynette the other, both in packs on their stomachs. The men joined in with rumbling voices, Charlie standing at Jen's side with ribbons, Adam and Bobby at his feet as the ribbon carriers. All three men's hands were bound to each of Jen's hands with ribbons of green and silver, green for new life, silver for moonlight. The ribbons were cut, then braided, and each one of them got a braid to hang in their bedrooms.

They walked back to the new house for the reception, Vic on the left, Davis on the right, Len behind. The lawn was covered with picnic tables, and their new, giant poly family was there to greet them, both from Charlie, Jen, Lynette, and Jetta's family, and their commune neighbors. The kids ran and played with one another, the tweens shy and bookish. Two teens held hands, girls falling in love.

Meri and Charlie made fresh-caught fish that Charlie had breaded and fried, hush puppies with either plum or jalapeno jam, macaroni and olive salad, and garden salad bursting with tomatoes, cucumbers, red and green bell peppers, and a choice of homemade citrus and Caesar dressings. Everyone ate, learning how to eat bear style, with the plates filled and passed around. Libby made baked apples with honey, pecans, and a drizzle of caramel for dessert, and plum, apple, and cherry pies. They played loud piping and fiddle music and danced, then everyone crowded onto the deck to watch the sunset.

~

At dusk, all the poly adults except the newly married ones cleaned up, packed up, lassoed the kids, and left the woman and her three men alone. Vic, Len, Davis, and their woman Kandace stood on the back deck, leaning on the railing, when the stars came out one by one, and the river was bathed in moonlight.

"This is absolutely not fair. He gets her for two whole nights, starting on our damn wedding night," Vic groused to Len.

Len smiled gently. "Have fun, you two. Be careful getting down the mountain, and text when you get there." Rich and Lydia were already gone, on their way to get the suite ready for the first iteration of the happy group.

"Hurry up. I'm next, so get gone already." Vic kissed Kandace's cheek.

Kandace smiled. "I promise, love, it will be worth the wait."

Davis gently slapped each of his brothers on the back as he walked to the truck. He had to stop as each of his brothers kissed her cheek, her lips, her brow. Davis helped Kandace up into the truck, got in, and rolled down the window. "See you guys soon!"

"Don't answer the phone," advised Vic. "At all. We'll use the code if we need you." The shapeshifters had complicated codes that they used to communicate with each other with only a few letters or numbers in the form of text messages, especially in case of emergency. But there wasn't a single one in sight. Their first emergency, finding out someone's condom seemed to have malfunctioned, went over just fine. Kandace snapped at any of them nearby when she was in the bathroom throwing up, not knowing which one was to blame about the twins, but they were all excited, Kandace even more than her men. Davis was considering vasectomy reversal surgery, but that could wait.

Davis and Kandace got in the truck, waved, and they were gone. "Good," said Vic. "Time for the honey mead." Their father, Charlie, came back over the hill, bottles of honey mead in hand. They sat out on the deck, drank, and talked about their new family until the sun came up in the morning.

~

The next morning, dawn spilled into the room, making Kandace's fiery hair shine. There was a fire in the gas fireplace sending warmth and low light into the room. Kandace looked up at Davis, who was staring at her adoringly. "Again? I can't…"

Davis held up a hand. "I took the liberty of ordering breakfast for us in bed."

Kandace grinned, stretched. Her emerald-green silk nightie's spaghetti strap fell off her shoulder. She stared at it like she'd never seen it before, then slid it back in place. She looked down at Davis' sweatpants and said, "I guess we're dressed enough for that."

Davis barked out a laugh. "We're shifters, lovely. Nudity is not a problem for us."

Kandace snorted. "Fine, it is for me."

There was a knock at the door, and Davis rolled out of bed gracefully, as if he'd actually gotten sleep the night before. He opened the door, and the smells of sausage, scrambled eggs, salsa, crispy bacon, hash browns, and biscuits with lavender honey had Kandace sitting up in bed and stealing Davis' pillow to sit up. Davis laughed, and got another pillow out of the carved cherrywood armoire. "For the lady, upon her honeymoon morning," said the chef.

"Thanks, Rich," said Davis, and hopped back in bed with his legal wife. He was the legal husband because he had excellent health insurance. Rich set up two trays, gave Davis twice as much food, left one carafe of warm mint tea and the other of orange juice and a glass and a cup each, and withdrew. They ate until the plates were clear, then Davis took one tray, piled it with dirty dishes, and set it out in the hallway. He lay back down, the remaining tray between them with the drinks. "I have something to tell you, love."

Kandace looked down at the tray. "And you're keeping us separated because you think I'll kill you?" She laughed.

Davis lay back and stroked her shoulder. "You might. I did something without your permission."

"Okay. As you're an adult, you don't need my permission."

"Actually, I did something I need permission from you to do. I sent a lawyer to give health insurance to your mother."

Kandace's eyes snapped, but then she relaxed. "She probably needs it."

Davis didn't relax. "I sent a country lawyer named Sheldon Symes to speak to her. It was bad, Kandace, really bad. She was underweight, confined to one room. The lawyer was appalled and called the police. She's now across the state. She knows some of what's going on, but not much."

Kandace looked at Davis out of the corner of her eyes. "This gets worse, doesn't it?"

"It does. It turns out your mama was receiving disability checks that your grandmother was cashing and squirreling away the cash. The house was falling down around their ears, but there was four thousand dollars in a mattress."

Kandace stood, stumbled over to the fire, and held out her hands, suddenly chilled. Davis followed, put a robe around her shoulders. "That bitch." She slid on the robe.

"Your grandmother is in jail for elder abuse and theft. They found drugs in the house, and your mom was too dazed to be responsible. It seems that your granny turned to making illegal substances when you stopped sending money."

Kandace whirled around and looked at him, stunned. "This is the same woman who beat the hell out of me when I got into the moonshine at thirteen."

"She's an idiot." Davis held her close.

"And a criminal." Kandace spoke into his furry chest. She pushed him back. "I...I don't want to see my mom."

"Honey, she wouldn't recognize you. Her marbles are gone. I'm sorry."

Kandace nodded. "We're paying for her health insurance?"

"Yes, she will be cared for. She's got...well, it's a syndrome with a long name. She will die in her sleep, without pain. I guarantee it." Davis looked down into his wife's eyes. "I just found out about this two days ago. I didn't want to ruin the wedding. Did I ruin our time together?"

Kandace shook her head, kissed him. "No. You saved her life. I...I want things to stay the way they are. I don't want to go haring off after my bio-mom. She was so weak and helpless my entire life. I took care of her and got abused for my trouble."

"Then don't do anything."

"Besides, Jen and Lynette are enough moms for anyone."

Davis snorted. "That they are." They kissed more deeply.

Kandace held his hand then started dragging him back to the bed. "Sleep, then more loving."

"Yes, ma'am. You're more like Jen every day." Kandace tripped, laughed, and fell onto the bed. Davis held on, held tight, and they slept away the morning together.

MEET

Kandace sat down with Vic and Len. Davis was working, of course. "I have to tell Corinne. At some point she'll visit. Hell, I probably should just have her visit."

"I get that she's your best friend," said Davis on speakerphone. He talked in between sips of soup and crunching of his salad. He had a between-surgeries break. "But, I balk at anyone knowing where, exactly, we are."

"She's poly, too," said Kandace. "She has two husbands. Who I haven't met. Wasn't at the wedding. She wasn't at my wedding, either."

"Dude, she has tears in her eyes," said Vic to Davis. "I can't handle this."

"We can meet in the middle. Opposite sides of the state," said Len.

"A good option," said Davis. "The problem is my getting time away to go much of anyplace."

"There's the shifter bed and breakfast," said Len.

"Kind of trying to hide what we are," said Davis.

"But we can get furry in the woods without getting shot," said Vic. The hotel and some of the surrounding farms were owned by shifters. No hunting in those mountains allowed, except for the occasional deer.

"Okay, fine, but I really can't get time off right now," said Davis. "And you two get sexytimes with our wife. I will get a whole damn week with her, take her to Mexico," said Davis.

"Sitting right here," said Kandace, drying her eyes. "You just lost ten points for talking about me like I'm not here."

"You'll definitely have to take her for a hike, then feed her, to earn her points back," said Vic.

"Talking about me like I'm not here again," said Kandace. "Vic just lost points. I'll make the damn reservations, and Davis, I get that you're trying to keep a secret. But at this point, you're just being an ass. Len, as the only one being respectful, let's go to the dojo."

"Shit," said Vic. "I hate getting in trouble." Davis grunted and hung up.

They settled on a week when summer was just beginning to break. Corinne was so excited that she kept texting nonstop. *Bringing hiking boots. Send trail pics. What if it rains? I'll bring board games.*

Kandace wrapped up her work, finally done with the leg of the hyperloop she'd been working on. She would start another loop the next week. She watched the numbers go up in her bank account—on time, under budget, bonus time. Sam followed her from her "sitting room"—actually an office—into her bedroom. She double-checked her packing, a mix of jeans, short-sleeved shirts, long-sleeved shirts, two light jackets, socks, makeup. The pretty kind of underthings, because it made Vic insane. Len didn't care; he was too Zen.

She packed the box of condoms and thought about leaving it behind. They were nearly there, but Davis was holding out after his vasectomy reversal, wanting a pregnancy that would end in spring or fall when he could spend more time with newborns. They'd missed their window, so January was now their best bet. The first set of babies were with their grandparents and cousins, getting into trouble. Both Dakota and Sierra were redheads with green eyes, just like their mother. She hated leaving them, but she would be revealing a hell of a secret. She trusted Corinne, but everyone else was freaked out about telling the secret. If things worked out, then the rest of the family would come over, babies in tow.

Kandace checked the Sam bag with cat food, treats, and toys. She attached the Sam bag to the rolling bag, and went to the elevator. She'd agreed to it when she realized she'd be hauling twins and laundry up and down that many floors. Sam seemed to be completely at ease with a box that changed floors. The babies were with Lynette so Kandace would actually leave.

Vic met her at the bottom, kissed her, took the cat bag, and took the human bags to the king cab truck. Kandace went to the kitchen where Len was putting the finishing touches on grilled mahi mahi with chimichurri sauce, a salad, and herbed wheat rolls with cherry water. They sat down to dinner, and the cat had her own bowl of fish. They cleaned up, and Len turned on the dishwasher. They packed the little cooler with drinks, and Len took it out while Kandace got Sam's harness and put it on the cat. Sam chirruped, excited to be traveling.

They walked out and got in the vehicle. Kandace sat in front, Vic drove, and Len sat in the back with the cat in her bed with her harness attached to the seat belt. Vic put on some kick-ass country, and they sang along as they drove along the back roads in the dark. They sipped flavored waters, cracked jokes, and laughed when the cat commented with chirrups.

They didn't have to check in; their electronic keys had been mailed to them. They got into the suite, put down their bags, and the cat immediately found the lavender-scented kitty litter on the balcony, accessible by a kitty door.

Len kissed Kandace first, then Vic. Kandace said, "We've got to wait for Corinne," she said, when Vic snaked his arms around her.

It sounded as if someone was throwing herself against the door. Kandace sighed, disentangled herself from Vic, and opened the door. Corinne attack-hugged her, and both of them cried. "I'm sorry about the not-invited-to-the-wedding thing," said Corinne.

"So am I," said Kandace.

Vic shut the door while Len passed out the tissues. Len grabbed two cans of beer out of the cooler, took the key, and Vic followed him out the door. "Nice to meet you, Corinne. Be back...later," said Vic over his shoulder. Then they were gone.

"The smaller one's Len," said Kandace.

Corinne laughed. "They were out fast."

"They know we have a lot to talk about. And they hate tears. Let me see you." She stood back. Corinne's black hair cascaded over her shoulders. Her arms still looked skinny, but muscles were beginning to peep out. She wore burgundy skinny jeans, black boots, and a blue silk shirt. "Wow. You look lovely."

Corinne grabbed the end of Kandace's hair. "Red mixed with gold. Gorgeous!" Kandace wore a green sweatshirt and black jeans with zippers on both sides.

Sam came back in and chirruped. Corinne grinned and said, "Sam! Such a pretty girl!" She held her hand down low for Sam to sniff. Sam put her paws up on Corinne's knee and chirruped. Corinne laughed and stroked Sam's head. "Lovely lady, aren't you?" she said to the cat.

Kandace felt the wind go out of her. She walked to the couch and sank into it. Sam went up and jumped up. Corinne came up and sat next to her. The cat stretched over both their laps and gave a huge rumbling roar of a purr when Corinne scratched behind Sam's ear. "Wow. Love the cat." She took a deep breath. "I had to...the wedding..." began Corinne.

Kandace took a deep, shuddering breath. "I had the same problem. We have...how the hell did we both end up poly?" She barked out a laugh. "I did the same shit drunk, but these are brothers."

"Are they as different from each other as Mitch and James are? Mitch won't stop talking unless he gets all angry and broody. James is...classier, a real get-it-done guy. Both rough and smooth."

Kandace laughed. "Davis is my smooth one. Len is very Zen. I'm learning tai chi, yoga, that sort of thing. I go hiking every damn place with Vic, rock climbing. There is very little that man won't do."

"Do you eat a lot of...venison?"

Kandace laughed. "I know how to differentiate between types of honey, and I eat fish for nearly every meal." Corinne wrinkled her nose. "Out with it, sister, or I'll go first."

"Shapeshifter. My boys howl at the moon. Dogs, coyotes, wolves."

Kandace gasped then nodded. "Bears. Black ones. We know some grizzlies though."

They hugged, tears spilling out of their eyes, the cat still with paws on their legs, then they just sat there for a moment. "We've got to tell Tania," said Kandace.

"Let's go visit her later. Right now...how the hell do we tell the boys?"

There was a pounding on the door. Kandace sighed, moved the cat, walked over to the door, and opened it. A tall guy in a biker jacket was on the other side. His hair stuck straight up, and he had a dangerous glint in his dark eyes. "You a bear too?" he asked Kandace.

"Nope, just an alcoholic and a drug addict."

"Thought so," said Mitch. "I figured when I realized we were meeting here. You gonna keep our secret?"

"You gonna keep ours?"

"Welcome to the family," said Mitch. He grabbed Kandace and drew her into a close hug. He then stood back, his hands still on her shoulders. "About time we shifters kind of...bonded. Allied. Whatever."

"Cool," said Kandace. She thought about what to say. "Check with Rich if he has any venison. He may or may not want some."

"Will do. See you later, babe." Mitch crushed Kandace into a hug again, let her go, and was gone. The door snicked shut behind him.

"That was..."

"My Mitch." Corinne grinned, teary-eyed.

"Got a whole bad-biker-thing going on, doesn't he? Cherry water or honey tea?"

"Yeah," said Corinne. Kandace laughed and took one of each out of the cooler. She handed the cherry water to Corinne and sat back down on the couch.

Corinne traded bottles, and Kandace complied. "My boys say my scent is intoxicating."

"So do mine."

"Do yours light up at the Change?"

"Flash. Yeah."

They sipped their drinks. "Wonder how this all got started."

"I can trace it back about two thousand years." Kandace told Corinne the story about the skinwalker who decided to eat other First Nations enemies as a mountain lion, and the subsequent destruction and scattering of the skinwalkers to escape death.

"That's—horrific. Sounds like a serial killer, then the rest of the tribe was punished and hunted because of one guy. Sick shit." Corinne sipped from her bottle.

"It was."

"You think your Jen would become our...I don't know...tribal elder? Willing to tell the story, to bring us into some sort of loose association?" Corinne asked.

"I've been thinking that since you revealed that we have the same secret. Which was just now." Corinne laughed. "I can text her, ask her in a really roundabout way." She stared off into space. "No, we can't afford any electronic signatures. But the fact that we're poly gives us a reason to meet. The shifter spouses club, or something." Corinne grinned, and Kandace grinned back. "We actually live in a poly club up on a mountain. My men's parental units—three women, one man—their family secretly funded it. It's got a smithy and a glassworks. They make beautiful stained glass, and bees for honey, and clover and lavender fields nearby." Kandace sighed. "I wanted to make a sword for Tania, but I got a little distracted."

Corinne stared at her tea. "So the honey is lavender, not the tea?"

"Yes. Many of the poly people work online, do crafting and Renaissance Faire stuff and go to fairs, and most just work together to make the place run. We all get turns with the snowplow, that sort of thing. The tweens and teens clean houses, do child care, tutoring, coaching, and make a ton of money coding too. I'm the coding trainer for them. Most of my community hours are teaching hours. Vic has a pre-paramedic program going on, 'cause that's a good thing to do part-time. Easy to do all your hours, and you don't have to do the same thing from one hour to the next if you don't want to."

"I would move our house and go to where you are, but I think we should scatter, shouldn't we? In case someone comes hunting for us." Corinne looked worried.

"If they do, we'll fight. Len runs a dojo, and the poly community and Meri's farm have...let's just say, electronic countermeasures." She grinned evilly. "Now, tell me, how the hell do you manage your life? Different nights? Different weeks?"

Corinne laughed. "Mitch is home most of the time and James is gone except for random days, so Mitch usually goes on rides when James is home. He's seen most of the state. That's how he recognized the name of this bed and breakfast. He did not tell me that it was shifter-run! We had some sort of smoked chicken nachos for dinner. Like to kill me with the deliciousness."

"Well, wait till breakfast. It'll kill you dead." They laughed, hugged, cried, and crawled into the big bed together with the cat, whispering in the dark as the cat purred so loudly that she sounded like a sports car revving up.

In the morning, the men were lounging around the breakfast table. Len and Vic had smoked fish on cheese bagels. The sage sausage smelled heavenly; Mitch and a grinning James, who looked like an older, wiser version of his brother, were eating egg white, cheese, and elk sausage omelets.

Rich came over, grinning. "Ladies. May I be so bold to give you what I believe you will like?"

"Trust you with my life, Rich," said Kandace.

"Go for it," said Corinne.

He flipped something, then plated it. He added things to the plates and brought them over. "Here we have mushrooms sautéed in butter and herbs, sage sausage, eggs scrambled with cheese, and a little arugula and balsamic."

"Omigod!" squealed Corinne. She started eating almost as soon as Rich placed the plate in front of her.

James poured orange juice in front of both women. Two corgis lay under the table. "Who are these ones?" asked Kandace. She pointed over at Sam, who was cadging sausage from Rich. "That's Sam, the Maine coon cat."

"Sheila and Lucy," said James. "Kandace, it is so very nice to meet you." He had a gentle smile that put Kandace at ease. He kissed her cheek, then sat back down.

Len threw a small ball, and the two dogs went running across the deck. "We should get a dog or six," said Len. "Loving these corgis. So sweet and intelligent!"

"James, Len, Len, James," said Kandace, making the introductions. "Len, this is Corinne, one of my best friends. The other one, Tania, is on the other side of the world."

"We met last night," Len said. "Vic and Mitch went for a run."

"They went for a lumber," said James. Len laughed.

"Where are Vic and Mitch now?" Kandace asked, attacking her food. "Omigod, best food ever," she said. "I hate to tell you this, Len, but I was getting a little sick of fish."

"For a price, you can have a freezer container full of elk sausage," said Rich.

"Sold," said Len. "Anything for our woman."

"I hate getting spoiled all the time," said Kandace. "Not." Corinne and Kandace both laughed.

"This is going to get dicey," said Len. "Our women are going to think of ways to make us do more for them."

"Suck it up," said James. "Our women deserve it. And, to answer your question, Kandace, the other two are hiking and have been since dawn. I think they're in touch with someone named Jen about some sort of Naming Ceremony. I think we're getting named as a tribe?"

Kandace looked at Corinne, who looked off into space. "You set this up!" she said, pointing at her friend. "You agreed to texting silence!"

"I texted Mitch, who spoke to Vic this morning," confessed Corinne. "I want my men to know who they are, where they come from. No one else seems to know."

Rich came over with more juice. "I am from France. We're called loup-garou there. Methinks the ability to change goes much farther back than you all think." He grinned. "I have family in Canada. Our kind of family. Wolves, hunting cats, bears, dogs, even an eagle or two."

"And no one thought to ally themselves before this?" asked James, hurt. "We could have been..."

"What, attracting attention to ourselves?" asked Rich. "We have others in Louisiana. The Acadians were kicked out of Canada. At any rate, I have heard whispers of more hiding among the First Nations." He grinned. "We don't talk much, but it may be time to...send representatives."

His wife, Lydia, came out and smiled. "I have already sent out a call. We will meet when it is warm again." She turned towards her husband. "Remember those expansion plans, love?"

Rich groaned. "It's too late in the year to start!"

"I know people," Lydia said. She turned back to the people shoveling food into themselves at the table. "All shifters are welcome here, as long as no one turns cannibal." Everyone shivered.

Len said, "No way. We're not like that."

"Good," said Lydia. "Let's begin the planning, shall we?" She pulled up a chair and sat down. Rich poured juice for her. Lydia pulled out her tablet computer and grinned. "Who wants to start?" Lydia and Rich's wife, Jaclyn, joined them, a tall dark-eyed woman in designer jeans. Below them, two teenage boys walked along the creek. One had Jaclyn's black hair, and the other Rich's finger-in-a-light-socket brown hair. They wore jeans and T-shirts and kicked a soccer ball back and forth.

"Call your mamas," Kandace said to Vic and Len. "I need my babies. Right now."

"I wondered why....oh," said Corinne. Her eyes filled with tears. "You were afraid you couldn't trust me."

"No," said Len as Kandace flew around the table to Corinne and embraced her. "We didn't know we were...having a summit, I guess. Also, I didn't want to interfere with girl bonding time."

Vic stood. "I'll call Dad. He'll want to meet with the wolves, but we need Jen here if we want to be all summit-y."

"Do that," said Kandace. Charlie and Jen were there in two hours, and Corinne, Mitch, and James ran off with Kandace's girls and refused to give them back.

EPILOGUE: REUNION

*C*orinne met Kandace at the airstrip near Cold Stone. "My stars," Kandace said, hopping out of the truck and running over to Corinne, who was just lowering herself to the ground. "You're huge!"

"And I can't believe Tania had twins too!" said Corinne. "By surrogate, but still." The two women hugged.

"I really wish you lived closer to us," said Kandace to Corinne. "Shapeshifter tradition of spreading out be damned, you shouldn't be on the opposite side of the state." Corinne had wolf cubs in her belly. Kandace had left her baby girls at home with their grandparents, who would arrive the next day, giving the women time to bond.

"You know what pisses me off? This secrecy shit." Kandace handed a can of ginger ale to Corinne, who took it gratefully. "We weren't at each other's weddings, which is hideous, and all three of us ended up marrying shapeshifters anyway! We were so busy protecting the secret, and we could have been improving shifter relationships!"

"They did, just one human woman at a time," joked Corinne. Kandace laughed.

Kandace drank from an insulated bottle of black tea dosed liberally with honey. "What the hell is with us all falling in love with shifters! You with the wolves, me with bears, and Tania! Who the hell marries a python?"

"Tania," said Corinne dryly. They both laughed. "Bathroom?"

Kandace pointed to the manager's office. "That's Sparky. Tell him Vic says hi, and he'll let you use the restroom."

"Got it."

"Oh, hell, might as well go with you." Kandace followed Corinne and waited while she headed to the door along the far wall.

Sparky was a short, gnarled, gray-haired, grizzled pilot with wrinkly hands. He wore aviator sunglasses and a pilot's cap. He kept looking out the window, headset on, listening to the plane coming in. "Your friends are about twenty minutes out. Refueled in San Diego. Sure you don't want any coffee?"

Sparky's coffee could peel the paint off a car. Literally. "No, thank you," said Kandace, smiling at the man. She switched places when Corinne came out. Corinne was bone white, and Sparky gently pushed her into a chair to wait.

The plane came in, smooth as silk. The door opened, and the stairs went down. Tania looked lovely, tall and glowing. Cetan was slung over her hip and her husband Sanur had Aye, who was patting her father's face with her chubby hands. "Where are your babies?" Tania asked.

They hugged, and Kandace kissed the baby's head. "Stupid question. Two infants, one car, long drive."

Two beautiful young women came down, each carrying a toddler. "Nice to meet you again," said Corinne, after hugging Tania, kissing the babies, and receiving a gentle kiss on the cheek from Sanur. "Kannika and Achara, right?" asked Corinne.

The women both laughed, and the toddlers clapped their hands. Kandace waved at Cetan, who waved back. Corinne blew a kiss to Aye, who giggled. A van drove up, and two Thai men jumped out. "Your Excellencies," said the driver. The other one opened up the van door. "Car seats," said the one that opened the door.

"You have done well," said Sanur. "Thom, you will drive one of these ladies' trucks. Her Excellency will wish to converse with her friends."

Another Thai woman came out of the plane, two cases in hand. "I will protect Their Excellencies," she said.

"Supayalat," said Kandace and smiled. "So nice to see you again." They had been speaking online for nearly a month, making arrangements for the visit.

"She actually means it," said Tania. "Let's go." The females picked Kandace's bigger truck, Corinne handed her truck keys to Thom, and they followed the van.

The shifter B&B was full to bursting. Wolves and bears roamed together, chatting, talking about their families, honey mead or dark lager in hand. Their children ran around outside, playing soccer, swinging on the swing set, jumping on the trampoline, showing off, acting like they were going to kill themselves with their acrobatics. Rich had installed a climbing wall, and the bears were chasing each other up and down, madly ringing the bell at the top, then skittering back down. There were hikers all over the hills, many of them wearing as little clothing as possible, partly because of the heat, and partly because they planned on turning themselves furry when they got farther into the woods.

Sanur stood just outside the van in khaki pants and a blue linen shirt. His copper hair was pulled back in a rose gold clip. "This is stunning," he said as his wife went over and kissed him. "We should have done this before."

"Probably." Vic came over to kiss his wife, Kandace. "It's really great being able to play sports with people when you don't have to hold back."

"Since my people tend to play chess, holding back isn't something I need to worry about. And cricket really doesn't lend itself to super strength or speed. Now, rugby, things could go horribly wrong with that one." Sanur grinned.

Vic laughed, and the bear and snake shifters shook hands. "Let me introduce you to Mitch, one of Corinne's husbands. He's a real stand-up guy. He might howl at the moon, but we climb trees, so whatever." He dragged Sanur off.

"Sanur looks like he's been poleaxed," said Kandace.

"That's my man, or one of them," said Corinne, pointing at Mitch. "Tell me, girl. Did you ever get Meri to move in with you to help you cook?"

Kandace grinned. "No, but our family single-handedly keeps her in business. I'm telling you, you should move up there. Really fun place. Always have someone to help watch the kids all the damn time, and there's always someone your kids' ages they can play with."

"Convinced me," said Corinne. "Come on, Tania. Bring your babies, and we'll go see Kandace's cubs."

Tania sighed. "Give me Cetan," she said to Achara. "Thank you." Her toddler snuggled up against her, and she followed her two friends to meet their extended family. Cetan and Aye wriggled, wanting down, and their parents put them down. Kannika and Achara chased after the laughing toddlers.

Something blotted out the sun for a moment. Most of the adults and some of the kids looked up. Supayalat drew a ceremonial dagger out of her sleeve and stood in front of Sanur. Both looked up.

Tania looked up, and her heart fell into her stomach. Her husband had said they once existed, even had a shimmering blue scale he kept in a case near his shed golden python skins. But here? Now?

Corinne and Kandace whirled. Kandace, unencumbered by a baby or pregnancy, ran up the slope to the road, over the gravel and concrete, to the path snaking up on the other side. Vic sighed, put on speed, and ran after his wife. Tania moved quickly to Sanur and Supayalat. The dragon circled, going lower. Scarlet and gold scales winked in the morning light. It threw its wings back, and glided down to the rise where Kandace and Vic were running. Sanur and Tania followed, Supayalat at a near-jog, running ahead. Lydia came streaking out of the house, and ran across the road with Sanur and his family.

The bears climbing the wall climbed down. The kids kicking the soccer ball by the river ran back up to the bed and breakfast at a lope.

The dragon bugled, a sound of fierce joy. The kids, Len, and the non-baby-holding adults found themselves standing with their hands over their heads in triumph. The kids did happy dances, then ran up the hill to meet the dragon.

Kandace reached the spot, her hair buffeted by the air pushed forward by the dragon's huge wings. She came to a running stop, and Vic pulled Kandace onto the ground, afraid of being hit by those pebbly wings. The dragon shook out her wings twice, kicking up dust, and then folded them in against her body. She had huge golden eyes, a very toothy smile, and a snout that came very far forward. Her legs had three claw-tipped toes on each foot. The back legs were long and very powerful, the front legs a little shorter and more muscular. Her underbelly was more scarlet-limned gold, and the back scarlet with gold along the edges. She had a leather bag wound around her neck. She raised her front leg, claws retracted. Kandace elbowed Vic off of her and stood. She held up a hand. Vic stripped off his clothes, put them in a pile, and turned into a black bear. He held up a paw.

Supayalat held out the ceremonial dagger and bowed. Sanur and Tania came up behind her, and Sanur bowed deeply. Tania inclined her head, still gasping from going up the incline.

The boys burst up onto the hill, the ones that looked like Rich and Jaclyn's kids, Lydia right behind them. "Lou, Eric," said Lydia. "Bow, please." They did, and held up their hands.

Len was next, with Sam chirruping beside him. Len held up his hand.

The woman shimmered, and Len, Vic as a bear, Sanur, and Supayalat put their backs to her, facing out, congregating around her snout. "Turn around," Lydia ordered Lou and Eric. The did, grumbling. Kandace went to stand next to Vic, and Tania beside Sanur. The dragon's change was slower than with the bear change. The dragon grunted, and there was some rustling as she opened the bag and put on clothes.

The woman that came out from behind the massed bodies was beautiful. She had red-gold, long, curly hair and skin with a faintly golden cast. She wore a black tank top and black cargo pants with holsters attached to each side. She pulled black fingerless leather gloves out of her pockets and put them on. She unstrapped the weapons holsters from the cargo pants and put them back into her leather backpack. "Your Highnesses," she said, in a voice with a definite rasp. She bowed to Vic. "Sir bear," she said. She turned to Lydia. "Wolf mistress," she said. "Greetings. I bring greetings from the Dragon Kind." She swayed, righted herself. "Sorry about the bugling; I'm afraid that will attract attention."

Lydia said, "Lou, Eric, and you," she said, pointing at Vic. "Turn yourself into a guy and follow them. Set up the widescreen in back, and stick folding chairs out there or blankets or something. Hook it all up, too, including the speakers. Needs to be done yesterday." The boys rushed off, and Vic lumbered over to his clothes, turned his bear back, and turned into a man. Everyone kept their backs to him while he changed.

"I'll help," said Len. He jogged down the hill, his brother, Vic, streaking past him.

"Quick thinking, Lydia," said Kandace.

Lydia grinned. "Your Dragonness. You must be tired, hungry, and thirsty from your trip. We would be pleased to serve you."

"I'm Darya," said the Dragon. "I would be most pleased." She reached forward with both hands, and Lydia grabbed them at the wrists. They held on tight. Supayalat put her ceremonial dagger away and did the same when they let go, as did Kandace and Tania. Lydia led the way, and they all went down the hill and across the street again.

Lydia called out orders when she was within earshot of the house. "We need every damn table we have, every folding chair. The neighbors are going to be mighty curious, and they need to see a party. Kandace, you coordinate the boys. They listen to you. Rich, let's come up with a menu, shall we?"

Lydia led Darya to the side deck where Rich was putting shrimp on skewers while Corinne handed him mushrooms. He put a skewer down and wiped his hands on the towel he kept around his waist. He handed Corinne the towel, and she cleaned up too. "Your Dragoness," said Rich, all smiles. "We have venison, or I can make lamb chops or mutton stew. I was just making shrimp and vegetable skewers. I can also make breakfast..."

Darya put up a hand. "It all sounds lovely," she said. "A carafe of water, a second of orange juice. Those skewers will do nicely in a bit, but now I'd like some breakfast. Bacon extra crispy, two eggs, scrambled. Do you have any croissants or pastries?"

Rich grinned. "It just so happens I have some chocolate croissants. Please, sit. I'll be along with your breakfast soon."

They sat at the patio dining table and looked over the valley. "This is stunning," said Darya.

Kandace stopped texting. "My babies and their wonderful grandparents are leaving now. They filled up the van with babies, baby things, and folding tables and chairs."

"This will get expensive, I'm afraid," said Lydia.

Sanur waved a hand. "How much?"

"A few thousand dollars," said Lydia.

Sanur took out his cell phone. "I'll transfer it to your account. What's the number?"

"Ooh, money," said Kandace. She texted her sister-in-law Libby. "We'll have all the desserts anyone wants here in a few hours. Along with babies and tables."

Len came over. "Lydia, setup is going well. Both speakers are in. Found a monster outdoor power cable used for Christmas lights. We're hooking it up to the satellite feed now and finding a dragon movie. Rich, I don't think your freezers will hold. We bears are really good at fishing, and we happen to have a passel of kids here too."

Rich lay out the bacon in the pan on the outdoor grill's gas burner on the side. "Go for it. We can use whatever."

"Cornmeal," said Kandace, sending another text. "Can't have catfish without hush puppies."

"We have a party," said Corinne. "Darya, I'm Corinne. Mitch over there," she said, pointing down to the boys congregated on the dock, "he's one of my husbands. James is..."

"Here, baby," said James, coming out with a bowl of cut up bell peppers in his hands. He kissed Corinne. "There's more bell peppers. Bumper crop up at the poly place, according to Vic. We can stuff some too. I can get the rice cooking if that's what you want."

"Yes, please," said Rich. "I'll be in with the saffron when the rice cooks down." He raised his head. "Pizzas. We'll need to start the dough now."

"On it," said Kandace. "I'll make Meri talk me through her recipe. She makes an amazing tandoori chicken pizza. I can make cauliflower rice pizzas for the gluten-free eaters too." She stood and turned to Sanur. "Libby will want a few hundred for cleaning out her desserts. She runs a bakery. I'll have her text you her details."

Sanur waved a hand. "No problem."

"I'll help in a bit," said Corinne. "First, girl bonding time."

Tania stood. "First, feed babies, then set up for the feast," she said. She inclined her head at Achara, who bowed her head back.

The first neighbors stopped by as Darya was finishing off her eggs and bacon and croissants with butter. Wade Hollingback drove his pickup truck up, opened the door, and hopped out. Rich and the others waved at him. "Heard a real loud noise," he said, coming around the building.

"Sorry about the television," said Lydia, pointing down. "Brought it out for the kids, and they turned on an action movie and turned it way up."

Deputy Crystal Bakan, tall with mirrored sunglasses, showed up, and followed the sound of Lydia and Wade talking. "Heard a loud...Oh. TV?"

"Action movie," said Wade, pointing to the dragon screeching on the screen. "The boys down there damn near blew out the speakers, from what Lydia said."

"Some shindig you have here," said the deputy. "Food, and lots of...fishing," she said, looking over the edge. Vic was handing out fishing rods to the kids and baiting them with worms from a pail.

"For tonight," said Rich, finishing off another skewer. "Shrimp and veggie skewers for lunch. The rice is cooking, and there will be stuffed bell peppers too."

"Full house," said Lydia. "We're bursting at the seams now. Women and babies sleep inside. Should have room for that. Tent city's going up after dark."

"Can you guys use some strawberries? We've got a bumper crop," said Wade.

"Buy them off you," said Lydia, taking two twenties out of her wallet and handing them to Wade. "Go great with the stuff we're getting in. Pastries and the like."

"I can't..." said Wade, looking at the twenties in his hand as if they would bite him.

"Wade, now go on," said Rich. "Need them strawberries yesterday. Need some baskets? There's two on the front porch, big ones."

"I'll help you get them into your truck," said the deputy. Wade had two jobs, and Crystal was quick to catch on that Lydia was funding him.

"Got any zucchini or tomatoes?" Lydia asked.

"Too many," said Wade.

"We'll take what you've got, that you won't eat," said Rich, calling out after him.

Darya watched the deputy and Wade go, then stood, stretched. "I see some excellent chairs out front. I will rest my eyes while you...prepare. I would help, but I'll probably do better when I'm not falling down."

"Of course," said Lydia. "I'll bring you some lemonade."

"Your Highness," said Sanur. "I will help with the preparations in your stead. We will have a feast!"

"Help with your babies first, Excellency," said Darya.

Sanur grinned. "I deserved that." He walked her out to the porch, then went to find his children.

"You people are awesome," said Kandace. She grinned, and reached out to clasp Tania's hand, then Corinne's. Their first dragon party! She couldn't wait!

<<<The End>>>

ABOUT THE AUTHOR

L. J. Hawke is an author, university professor, and avid reader. She writes what she loves to read—paranormal romance, urban fantasy, and science fiction, as well as some nonfiction titles in her fields of expertise. She can be found petting her cats while writing, or with a backpack on her back, traveling the world—after calling the cat sitter.

One last thing...

If you enjoyed this book or found it useful, I'd be very grateful if you'd post a short review on Amazon. Your support really does make a difference, and I read all the reviews personally so I can get your feedback and make this book even better.

9 781734 594751